**Also available from
Linda Lael Miller
and HQN Books**

LINDA LAEL MILLER

McKETTRICK'S *Heart*

H

HQN™

Recycling programs
for this product may
not exist in your area.

ISBN-13: 978-0-373-77681-8

McKETTRICK'S HEART

Copyright © 2007 by Linda Lael Miller

Dear Readers,

I hope you've enjoyed revisiting the McKettrick men and the women they manage to turn into cowboys' brides. After reading Jesse and Cheyenne's story in *McKettrick's Luck,* then Rance and Echo's happy ending in *McKettrick's Pride,* I'm proud to present the final book in the McKettrick Men trilogy, *McKettrick's Heart.*

When Keegan McKettrick first encounters Molly Shields, he's furious to find her in his hometown of Indian Rock, Arizona. At the same time he's never been so attracted to a woman before. Both Molly and Keegan are deeply wary of love—and need to learn to trust their hearts….

I'm also delighted to announce that a brand-new trilogy of cowboys is coming your way! Be sure to look for the first title, *Big Sky Country,* from HQN Books in June. Set in Parable, Montana, this series will feature half brothers, headstrong women and big dreams under an even bigger sky. You won't want to miss this!

With love,

Linda Lael Miller

To Jerry and Anna Lael, with love

McKETTRICK'S
Heart

CHAPTER  1

Molly Shields forced herself to pause on the sidewalk in front of the huge brick house, draw a deep breath and let it out slowly. If she hadn't, she would have vaulted over the gate and covered the flagstone walk at a dead run.

Lucas.

Lucas was somewhere inside that enormous place.

But so was Psyche. And Psyche Ryan, at least in the eyes of the world, was legally Lucas's mother.

Everything within Molly rebelled against that single fact.

Purposefully Molly adjusted her perspective, along with the canvas backpack she'd carried from the gas station at the far end of Indian Rock, Arizona, after getting off the afternoon bus from Phoenix. Lucas wasn't her child; he was Psyche's.

The little boy was eighteen months old now—eighteen months, two weeks and five days. He'd been a newborn, pink and squalling, when she'd last seen him, held him in her arms—all too briefly—before giving him up. Psyche had sent a few snapshots in the interim—Lucas was solid, handsome and blond, with bright green eyes. Molly's own coloring, though her hair had darkened over time, but despite that, he resembled his late father more than her.

Now, in a very few minutes, maybe even moments, Molly would see the baby she still thought of as her own, at least in weak moments.

Perhaps she'd be allowed to hold Lucas. She ached to do that. To breathe in the scent of his hair and skin…

Careful, her practical side admonished.

It was miracle enough that Psyche, a virtual stranger and, it was to be remembered, a betrayed wife, had summoned Molly to this little town, with its shady streets, given all that had happened. She mustn't move too fast, or make a wrong move—miracles were rare and fragile things, to be handled with infinite care.

Molly worked the latch on the shiny black iron gate. The metal felt hot and smooth to the touch. A discreet little sign, fastened to the ornate fence, proclaimed the place a registered historic site.

Psyche had explained, in one of her emails, that the house on the corner of Maple and Red River Drive, her childhood home, had stood empty for nearly a decade. But today the vast lawn looked manicured, lilacs and roses bloomed in freshly mulched beds and the many mullioned windows shone. The white wooden trim looked freshly painted, and the brick, though time worn, was still damp in places from a recent power wash.

Molly forced herself to walk slowly up the walk, toward the front porch, part of which was screened in. No doubt there were patio chairs there, a little table and maybe even a wooden swing.

Molly pictured herself sitting in that swing, rocking Lucas to sleep on a warm summer evening, and her heart beat a little faster.

Psyche's child, she repeated to herself in a silent mantra. *Psyche's child.*

She had no idea why Psyche had summoned her, or how long she'd be staying. The woman had graciously offered first-class airfare from LAX, with a car and driver to meet her in Phoenix. But Molly, perhaps as a form of penance, had chosen to take the bus instead.

She'd have been wiser not to come at all, of course, but she hadn't been able to resist the chance to see Lucas.

The heavy front door swung open just as Molly reached the bottom step, jolting her out of her travel-weary speculations, and a middle-aged black woman appeared, thin and tall, clad in a crisp white uniform and sensible, crepe-soled shoes.

"You her?" she asked bluntly.

Molly was "her," all right. Lucas's birth mother,

the woman who had slept with Psyche's husband. It
didn't matter that Molly truly hadn't known he was
married until it was too late. That was always the
excuse, wasn't it? She was intelligent, with a college education, her own business. Thayer had been
a facile liar, but she should have seen the signs.

There were always signs.

Molly swallowed. Nodded in glum acknowledg-
ment.

"Well, get yourself on in here," the woman said,
fanning herself with one hand. "I can't stand on this
porch all day with the door hanging open, you know.
Air-conditioning costs money."

Molly hid a rueful smile. Psyche had mentioned
her housekeeper several times over the past several
weeks—said she was cantankerous, but kind, too.
"You must be Florence," Molly said mildly, swallowing an urge to explain that she *wasn't* a home
wrecker.

Florence frowned, spared an unfriendly nod. "Is
that backpack all the luggage you brought?"

Molly shook her head. "I have some more stuff
at the gas station," she replied. "It was too heavy to
carry." Some of her private regrets were like that, too,
but she slogged on, mostly because she didn't know
what else to do.

Florence, practically bristling with disapproval,
gave a sniff and adjusted her glasses. It was no great
wonder that she hadn't put out a welcome mat, fig-
urative or otherwise, given the things Psyche must

have told her. Most of which, unfortunately, were probably true.

After issuing a *harrumph,* Florence stepped aside to let Molly pass. "We'll take the station wagon down there later, and fetch it all," Florence said. "Right now, Miss Psyche's upstairs resting, but I've got to keep an eye on her just the same." Behind her thick glasses Florence's chocolate-brown eyes glazed over for a moment, and she gave a sad huff of a sigh. "My poor baby," she added, addressing the shrubbery more than Molly. "It practically wore her out, getting this house opened and moving us in. If it was up to me, we'd have stayed right in Flagstaff, where we belonged, but there's no reasoning with that girl once she takes a notion."

Molly longed to ask about Lucas, but she had to tread carefully, especially around this longtime family retainer. Florence Washington had been Psyche's nanny until Psyche was old enough to go to school, then the family maid. When Psyche married Thayer Ryan, Mrs. Washington had stayed on to run the new household.

Molly felt a sick little flutter way down in the pit of her stomach.

Thayer was dead—he'd suffered a massive coronary a year before, at the age of thirty-seven—and while Molly wouldn't have wished him into an early grave, even after he'd all but ruined her life, she certainly hadn't mourned him, either.

She hadn't gone to the funeral.

She hadn't sent flowers, or even a card.

After all, how would she have signed it? "With sympathy, your late husband's mistress"?

Florence trudged off through an entryway with a grandfather clock and a curving staircase, and then down a long corridor, massive, drape-darkened rooms lining the passage on either side. Molly followed circumspectly, and they finally emerged into a sunlit kitchen with floor-to-ceiling windows forming the back wall and overlooking another enclosed porch. A flower-bright, sprawling yard lay beyond.

Molly finally shrugged out of her backpack and set it down on one of the chairs at the huge antique table in the center of the room.

"You might as well sit," Florence said.

Might as well, Molly thought. She was tired—she'd ridden more than one bus since leaving L.A. two days before—but her first inclination was still to ransack that mansion room by room, flinging open doors until she found Lucas.

She drew back one of the heavy oak chairs and sagged into it.

"Coffee?" Florence asked. "Tea?"

"Water would be good," Molly said.

"Fizzy stuff or regular?"

"Regular, please."

Florence brought her a glass of ice and a bottle. While Molly poured, Florence took up an obstinate pose over by the sink, leaning against the counter with her arms folded.

"What are you doing here?" Florence demanded, evidently having withheld the question as long as she could.

Molly, about to take a sip of water, set her glass down again. "I don't know," she answered truthfully. Psyche had contacted her by phone a week before and issued an urgent summons, with very little accompanying explanation.

"We have to talk about this in person," she'd said.

"Seems to me you've done enough damage," Florence told her, "without coming here. Especially now."

Molly swallowed. She was thirty years old, and she ran one of the biggest literary agencies in L.A., dealt with egotistical, high-powered authors, editors and movie people practically every day. Now, sitting in Psyche Ryan's kitchen, clad in the jeans, T-shirt and sneakers she'd been wearing for forty-eight hours straight, she felt diminished, as though she'd regressed to her college days, when she hadn't had the proverbial two nickels to rub together.

"Don't give her a hard time, Florence," a gentle voice interceded softly from somewhere behind Molly's chair. "I *asked* her to come, and Molly was kind enough to agree."

Both Molly and Florence turned, Molly rising so quickly that she nearly knocked over her chair.

Psyche stood framed in a doorway, a painfully thin woman clad in a peach silk robe and matching slippers. Two aspects of her appearance leaped out at Molly—one, Psyche was beautiful and, two, she was obviously bald beneath the little crocheted cap she wore.

"Will you look in on Lucas, please?" Psyche said to Florence. "He was still asleep a few minutes ago, but he's not used to the house yet, and I'd rather he didn't wake up alone."

Florence hesitated, gave a terse nod, glowered once at Molly and left the kitchen.

"Sit down," Psyche told Molly, gliding gracefully toward her.

Molly, who was used to giving orders, not taking them, immediately complied.

Psyche drew back the chair next to Molly's and sat down with a little sigh and a gingerly wince. "Thank you for coming," she said, offering a hand. "I'm Psyche Ryan."

Molly shook the hand, found it weightless as a wad of tracing paper. "Molly Shields," she replied. Her gaze drifted to Psyche's cap, back to the pair of enormous violet eyes beneath it.

Psyche smiled slightly. "Yes," she said. "I have cancer."

A chasm opened in the bottom of Molly's heart. "I'm sorry," she said. *About so much more than the cancer.* "Is it…?"

"Terminal," Psyche confirmed with a nod.

Tears of sympathy stung behind Molly's eyes, but she didn't allow herself to shed them. She didn't know Psyche well enough for that.

Inevitably her mind fastened on Lucas.

Dear God, if Psyche was dying, what would happen to him? Having lost her own mother when she was fifteen, Molly knew the emptiness and constant undercurrent of fruitless searching that could result.

Psyche seemed to be tracking Molly's unspoken thoughts—at least, some of them. She smiled again, reached across the tabletop to squeeze Molly's hand. "As you know," she said, "my husband is dead. Neither of us have any family. Since you're Lucas's biological mother, I hope…"

Molly's heart leaped over the logical next conclusion, but she reined it in, back over the jump, afraid to risk the shattering disappointment that would follow if she was wrong.

"I've hoped you'll care for him after I'm gone," Psyche said. "Be his mother, not just on some paper in some file—but for real."

Molly opened her mouth, closed it again, too shaken to trust her voice.

Psyche drew back a little, huddling in her exquisite peach robe, studying Molly with a worried expression. "Maybe I presumed too much, sending for you the way I did," she said, very softly. "If you'd wanted to raise Lucas, you wouldn't have given him up."

Desperation, sorrow and hope swelled within Molly, a tangle of emotions she'd probably never be able to separate. "Of *course* I want him," she blurted, lest Psyche reconsider and withdraw the offer.

Psyche looked relieved—and exhausted. "There are a few strings attached," she warned quietly.

Molly's heart scrambled up into the back of her throat. She waited, still terrified of tipping the balance the wrong way.

"Lucas must be raised in or around Indian Rock," Psyche said. "Preferably in this house. I grew up here, and I want my son to do the same."

Molly blinked. She owned a thriving literary agency in L.A., along with a house in Pacific Palisades. She had friends, an aging father, a life. Could she give all that up to live in a small, remote town in northern Arizona?

"Lucas will inherit a considerable estate," Psyche went on. She took in Molly's clothes and the worn backpack on the floor next to her chair. "I have no idea what your financial situation is, but I'm prepared to provide generously for you, until Lucas is of age, of course. You could turn the house into a bed-and-breakfast, if you wanted."

"That won't be necessary," Molly said. "For you to give me money, I mean." It was strange how quickly a life-changing decision could be made, if the stakes were high enough. Several of her clients, if not all, would balk when she told them she'd be operating out of Indian Rock from now on. Some would want out of their contracts, but it didn't matter. Her bank accounts bulged, despite her lifestyle, and as agent of record she would collect commissions in perpetuity on the many works she'd already sold.

"Good," Psyche said. She sniffled, took a tissue from the pocket of her robe and dabbed at her eyes.

For a few moments the two women sat in silence.

"Why did you give Lucas up?" Psyche asked. "Didn't you want him?"

Didn't you want him? The words blew through the bleak, weathered canyons of Molly's soul like a harsh and bitter wind. She could have kept Lucas— she had the resources and certainly the desire—but she supposed that, like taking the bus from L.A., surrendering her son had been a way of punishing herself. "I thought he'd be better off with two parents," she finally replied. It wasn't the whole answer, but at the moment it was all she had to offer.

"I would have divorced Thayer," Psyche said, "if it hadn't been for Lucas."

"I didn't know—" Molly began, but she strangled on the rest of the sentence, couldn't get it out.

"That Thayer was married?" Psyche prompted, not unkindly.

Molly nodded.

"I believe you," Psyche said, surprising her. "Were you in love with my husband, Molly Shields?"

"I thought I was," Molly replied. She'd met Thayer at a party in L.A., and immediately been swept away by his good looks, his charm and that sharp, albeit devious, mind of his. The pregnancy had been an accident, but she'd been happy about it, overjoyed, in fact—until she'd told Thayer.

After all this time, the memory of that day was still so painful that Molly turned away from it, pushed it to a back corner of her brain.

"My lawyer has already drafted the papers," Psyche said, trying to rise from her chair, finding she was too weak and sinking into it again. "You may want to have them reviewed by counsel of your own before they're finalized."

Molly merely nodded, still absorbing the implications of Psyche's words. Instinctively she got to her feet, helped Psyche to stand.

Almost as though she had radar, Florence reappeared, elbowed Molly aside and wrapped one strong arm around Psyche's waist to support her. "You'd better lie down again," the older woman said. "I'll just get you upstairs."

"Molly," Psyche put in quickly, almost breathlessly, as though she were afraid of being swept away before her son's fate was settled, "you come, too. It's time you got to know Lucas. Florence, you'll show Molly to her room, won't you? Help her get settled?"

Florence passed Molly a poisonous glance. "Whatever you want, Miss Psyche," she said, "that's what I'll do."

Molly trailed after the two women, down a hallway, into an elevator with an old-fashioned grate door. The little box lurched, like Molly's heart, as it sprang upward, shuddered its way past the second floor to the third.

Psyche slept in a suite of rooms boasting a marble fireplace, antique furniture, probably French, and elegantly faded rugs. A bank of windows overlooked the street on one side and the backyard on the other, and stacks of books teetered everywhere.

Distracted, yearning to see Lucas, Molly nonetheless spotted the names of several of her authors on the spines of those books.

"Through that doorway," Psyche said, pointing, as Florence steered her toward the bed.

Once again Molly called upon every bit of selfrestraint she possessed to keep from running in that direction. Running to Lucas, her son, her baby.

The nursery, a sizable room in its own right, adjoined Psyche's. There was a rocking chair over by the windows, shelves jammed with storybooks, an overflowing toy box.

Molly took all that in peripherally, focused on the crib and the chubby toddler standing up in it, gripping the rails and eyeing her with charitable trepidation.

He seemed golden, a fairy child bathed in afternoon sunlight, his light hair gleaming and gossamer.

Molly, who wanted to race across the room and crush him to her, did neither. She stood still, just inside the doorway, letting the boy take her measure with solemn eyes.

"Hi," she said, smiling moistly. "I'm Molly."
And I'm your mother.

KEEGAN McKETTRICK STOOD impatiently beside his black Jaguar, waiting for the tank to fill and appraising the pile of designer luggage resting between the newspaper box and the display of propane tanks near the entrance to the town's only gas station/convenience store. Even from a distance, he could tell the bags weren't knockoffs, and whoever owned them had most likely come in on the four-o'clock bus from Phoenix. He pondered the mystery while his car guzzled liquid money.

He was replacing the hose when a familiar station wagon bounced off the highway and rolled by, with Florence Washington at the wheel.

Keegan wanted to duck into the Jag and drive off, pretend he hadn't seen the other car, but that would have gone against his personal code, so he didn't. He'd known Psyche Ryan, née Lindsay, was back in town, that she'd come home, with her adopted son, to die.

He'd geared himself up to go by and see her several times since her return to Indian Rock, but he'd been reluctant to call or knock on the door, in case he disturbed her. If she was as sick as he'd heard she was, she was practically bedridden.

The station wagon rolled to a stop over by the propane tanks and the Louis Vuitton bags.

As Keegan squared his shoulders, he saw Florence turn in his direction, gazing balefully through the window.

He reminded himself that he was a McKettrick, born and bred, and chose to advance instead of retreat, assembling a smile as he did so.

Meanwhile, the door on the passenger side sprang open, and a slight woman with shoulder-length honey-colored hair got out.

Keegan glanced at her, looked away, registered who she was and looked back. He felt the smile evaporate from his lips, and forgot all about his plan to ask Florence if Psyche was up to receiving visitors.

His jaw clamped as he rounded the back of the wagon to confront Thayer Ryan's mistress.

"What the hell are you doing here?" he growled. He couldn't recall her name, but he remembered running into her at a swanky restaurant up in Flag one night. She'd been sitting with Ryan, that scumball, at a secluded table, clad in a slinky black cocktail dress and dripping diamonds—gifts, no doubt, from her married lover, and almost certainly charged to Psyche, since Ryan had never had a pot to piss in.

The woman flinched, startled. A pink flush glowed on her cheekbones, and her green eyes flickered with affronted guilt. Still, her gaze was steady, and more defiant than ashamed.

"Keegan McKettrick," she said. Then she tried to go around him.

He blocked her way. "You have a good memory for names," he told her. "Yours slips my mind."

Florence, meanwhile, opened the back of the station wagon, presumably to stow the bags. "I'm not doing this all by myself," she said.

Keegan remembered his manners—at least partially—and waved Florence back from the luggage. "There's another bus tonight," he told the woman whose face and body he recalled so well.

"Molly Shields," she said, and raised her chin a notch to let him know she wasn't intimidated. "And I'm not going anywhere. Kindly get out of my way, Mr. McKettrick."

Keegan leaned in a little. Ms. Shields was a head shorter than he was, and he must have outweighed her by fifty pounds, but she didn't shrink back, and he had to accord her a certain grudging respect for that. "Psyche's sick," he said in a grinding undertone. "Just about the last thing she needs is a visit from her dead husband's girlfriend."

The flush deepened, but the spring-green eyes flashed with swift defiance. "Step aside," she said.

Keegan was still getting over the brass-balls audacity of her attitude when Florence interceded, poking at him with a finger.

"Keegan McKettrick," the old woman said, "either make yourself useful and load up those bags, or be on your way. And if you can take time out of your busy schedule, you might stop by the house one of these days soon and say hello to Psyche. She'd like to see you."

Keegan deliberately softened his expression. "How is she?" he asked.

Molly Shields took the opportunity to slip around him, grab one of the suitcases.

"She's bad sick," Florence answered, and tears glistened in her eyes. "She invited Molly here, and I'm not any happier about it than you are, but she must have a good reason. And I'd appreciate some cooperation on your part."

Keegan was both confounded and chagrined. He nodded to Florence, lifted two of the five suitcases by their fancy handles and hurled them unceremoniously into the back of the station wagon, doing his best to ignore Molly Shields, who sidestepped him.

"You tell Psyche," he said to Florence, "that I'll be by as soon as she feels up to company."

"She usually holds up pretty well until around two in the afternoon," Florence replied. "You come over tomorrow, around noon, and I'll set out a nice lunch for the two of you, on the sunporch."

Keegan didn't miss the phrase "for the two of you" and neither, he saw from the corner of his eye, did Molly, who was wrestling with the largest of the bags. "That sounds fine," he said, and jerked the handle from Molly's grasp to throw the suitcase in with the others.

She glared at him.

He went right on ignoring her.

"I'd best pick up some bread and milk while we're here," Florence said, addressing Molly this time. With that, she disappeared into the convenience store.

"Does Psyche know you were boinking her husband?" Keegan asked in a furious whisper the moment he and Molly were alone.

Molly gasped.

"Does she know?" Keegan repeated fiercely.

She bit her lower lip. "Yes," she said very quietly, when he'd just about given up on getting an answer.

"If you're trying to pull some kind of scam—"

Molly's shoulders had been stooped a moment before. Now she rallied and looked as though she might be about to slap him. "You heard Mrs. Washington," she said. "Psyche *asked* me to come."

"Not without a lot of setting up on your part, I'll bet," Keegan retorted. "What the hell are you up to?"

"I'm not 'up to' anything," Molly answered after an obvious struggle to retain her composure, such as it was. "I'm here because Psyche…needs my help."

"Psyche," Keegan rasped, leaning in again until his nose was almost touching Molly's, "needs her *friends.* She needs to be home, in the house where she grew up. What she *does not* need, Ms. Shields, is *you.* Whatever you're trying to pull, you'd better rethink it. Psyche's too weak to fight back, but I assure you, I'm not!"

"Is that a threat?" Molly countered, narrowing her marvelous eyes.

"Yes," Keegan retorted, "and not an idle one."

Florence returned with the bread and milk, went around to the other side of the car and put the groceries in the backseat. "If you two are through arguing," she said, "I'd like to get back to Psyche."

Keegan sighed.

Molly gave him one last viperous look and got in on the passenger side.

Keegan spoke to Florence over the roof of the ancient station wagon. "I'll be there at noon tomorrow," he said. "Should I bring anything?"

He'd be bringing plenty, counting the questions he wanted to ask Psyche.

At last Florence smiled. "Just yourself," she answered. "My girl will be mighty glad to see that handsome mug of yours."

Keegan might have grinned if he hadn't been mad enough to bite the top off one of the propane tanks and spit it to the other side of the road. "See you then," he said.

He stood watching as Florence fired up the wagon, popped it into gear and zoomed out onto the street.

"I'll be goddamned," he muttered.

Five minutes later, well down the road back to the Triple M ranch, where members of the McKettrick clan had lived for a century and a half, he punched a digit on his cell phone.

He got his cousin Rance's voice mail and cursed while he listened to the spiel. He'd undergone a transformation recently, Rance had, since he'd taken up with Emma Wells, who ran the local bookstore. Given up his high-powered job at McKettrickCo, the family conglomeration, and started ranching in earnest.

The beep sounded. "That bitch Thayer Ryan was screwing around with is in town," he snapped, without preamble, "and guess where she's staying? Psyche's place."

With that, he thumbed End and put a call through to Jesse, his other cousin. Jesse, who had a type-Z personality, was even harder to reach than Rance, since he refused to carry a cell phone. This time, Keegan didn't even get voice mail.

He was about to backtrack to town, figuring he'd find Jesse in the poker room behind Lucky's Bar and Grill, fleecing unsuspecting Texas hold 'em devotees of their hard-earned money, when he remembered that Jesse and his new bride, Cheyenne, were still away on their honeymoon.

A lonely feeling swept over Keegan, one he was glad no one was around to see. Jesse was in love with Cheyenne, Rance with Emma.

And he was alone.

His own marriage hadn't worked out, and his daughter, Devon, living in Flagstaff with her mother, visited only occasionally. Going back to the big house on the ranch was the last thing he wanted to do, but he couldn't face returning to the office, either.

A lot of the family members were agitating to take McKettrickCo public, and fight though he did, Keegan was outnumbered. He could already feel the company, the only thing that kept him sane, slipping away.

What would he do when it was gone?

Jesse, never involved beyond cashing his dividend checks, didn't give a damn. Rance, once willing to work eighteen-hour days right alongside Keegan, now preferred to spend his time with his kids, Emma or the two hundred head of cattle grazing on his section of the ranch.

Their cousin Meg, who was a force in the San Antonio branch of the company, might have taken Keegan's side, but she'd been distracted lately. Whenever she came to Indian Rock, she holed up in the house that had originally belonged to Holt and Lorelei McKettrick, way back in the 1800s, keeping a low profile and fretting over whatever was bugging her.

He might have talked to Travis Reid, the closest friend he had except for Jesse and Rance, or even Sierra, another of his cousins and Travis's wife. Sierra and Travis were busy moving into their new place in town, though, and no matter how cordially they might have greeted Keegan, he would have been intruding. They were practically newlyweds, after all, settling in to a life together, and they needed privacy for that.

All of which meant, when it came to trusted confidants, he was shit out of luck.

CHAPTER 2

MOLLY'S ROOM AND BATH were on the other side of Lucas's nursery, opposite Psyche's suite. She and Florence schlepped the bags up in the elevator, a few at a time.

Florence lingered in the hall doorway. "That boy looks a lot like you," she said with a nod toward Lucas's room. "Took me long enough, but I finally put two and two together. You're his mama, aren't you?"

Molly didn't answer. It was Psyche's place to tell Florence whatever she wanted her to know, and Molly wasn't about to overstep those bounds.

"Thayer and Miss Psyche tried to adopt a baby for years," Florence went on. "They got close a couple of times, but something always went wrong. The birth mother backed out, or a relative stepped in to claim the child. I can't tell you how it grieved me, watching Miss Psyche put on a brave face, swallowing her disappointment, keeping her hopes up. Then all of a sudden, here's Lucas. The perfect green-eyed, blond-haired baby boy. I should have guessed he came out of your affair with Thayer."

Molly, in the act of unpacking one of her bags, stiffened, and her gaze sliced to Florence's face. Outside, on the front lawn, the sprinkler system came on, making a chuckety-chuckety sound, and the scent of fresh-cut grass blew in through the open windows on a soft breeze. "None of this," she said, "is Lucas's fault."

Florence spared her a dry smile. "So you *do* have some spirit," she observed. "You're going to need it, if you stay around here long. I'm headed downstairs shortly, to get supper started, but before I go, there's one more thing I want to say. I don't know why you're here, but I'll be watching you. You do anything—anything at all—to make things harder for my girl than they already are, and I'll make the devil himself look like an angel of mercy. You understand what I'm saying to you, Molly Shields?"

Molly kept her spine straight. She'd come to Indian Rock like a whipped dog, but she had Lucas to think about now, and it was time to put on her big-girl panties and take care of business. "I'd rather count you as a friend," she said, "but if you want a fight, I'll give you one."

Respect flickered in Florence's eyes, but it was gone in a moment. "Supper's at six," she said, and then she was gone, closing the door quietly behind her.

Molly knew that was a courtesy to Psyche, not her, but she appreciated it anyway.

She looked around the room that would be home for the foreseeable future—brick fireplace, gleaming brass bed, antique bureau and chest, chaise longue, plenty of bookshelves. All of them old-money shabby.

She smiled ruefully, thinking of her own ultra-modern place in L.A., where everything was new, with no history, no memories, no meaning. What a contrast.

The smile faded as she remembered the encounter with Keegan McKettrick back at the convenience store/gas station where she and Florence had gone to fetch her bags. She'd seen utter contempt in his eyes, and he'd certainly made no bones about wanting her out of Psyche's life and out of Indian Rock.

It had been a jolt, running into him. On some level, she realized, she'd still been smarting from their first encounter, in a Flagstaff restaurant, when Thayer had introduced her as a business associate.

Keegan hadn't believed him, even then.

And looking back, Molly knew she should have been far more suspicious of Thayer's glib reaction that night. In retrospect, it was a classic scenario—the guilty husband runs into a family friend and does a song and dance to explain the mistress away. Why hadn't she seen that?

Because you were a fool, that's why, she thought.

Molly opened a suitcase, found a floral sundress

and fresh lingerie. She'd feel better after a cool shower, she reflected. More like her normal, competent self.

As for Mr. McKettrick's obviously low opinion of her, well, that didn't matter in the vast scheme of things. Lucas mattered. Psyche mattered.

Keegan McKettrick was a footnote.

She felt a pang, and her throat tightened.

If all that was true, why did it sting so much to recall the way he'd looked at her?

RANCE RODE ACROSS the creek on a paint horse Keegan hadn't seen before.

He might have come right out of the 1880s, the way he was dressed—boots, jeans, a Western-cut denim shirt and a beat-up old hat resurrected from his college-rodeo days.

"Got your message," Rance said in his usual taciturn way, reining in and swinging deftly down from the saddle.

Keegan glanced across the creek toward Rance's rustic, rambling ranch house, which faced his own, almost a mirror image. The two places dated back to the nineteenth century, when old Angus McKettrick and his four sons had still ridden the sprawling acres of the Triple M, though of course some modern conveniences had been added over the generations since. "You leave the girls home alone?" he asked, referring to Rance's young daughters, Rianna and Maeve.

"Emma's there," Rance said with a slight and

faintly goofy smile. "She's making supper. You're welcome to join us if you want to."

Keegan felt bereft in that moment. He wanted to say yes, be part of a family, if only for an hour or two, but at the same time he wondered if he could cope with the contrast between his cousin's life and his own. "I might," he said to be polite, but he knew he wouldn't go, and Rance probably did, too.

Rance let the reins drop so the horse could graze on Keegan's lawn, which needed cutting. "What's this about Thayer's girlfriend moving in with Psyche?" he asked. "In the first place, I didn't know Thayer ever *had* a girlfriend."

Keegan shoved a hand through his hair. He'd been all-fired anxious to hash things out with Rance or Jesse or both of them, and had rushed outside when he'd seen his cousin crossing the shallow part of the creek. Now he wasn't sure how to put the whole thing into words. "He cheated on Psyche from day one," Keegan said after unclamping his back teeth. As kids, he and Psyche had made a playground pact to get married when they grew up, and have a big family. If she hadn't been dying, he'd have grinned at the memory.

"I didn't know that," Rance replied quietly. He'd known about the pact, though. He and Jesse had teased Keegan unmercifully back in the day, but they'd been as smitten as he was. "I'd have blacked the bastard's eyes if I had."

Keegan recalled the night he'd run into Thayer and

Molly, caught them sneaking around behind Psyche's back, and felt the same clench in the pit of his stomach as he had then. It had been part rage, that feeling, but part something else, too. Something he'd rather not identify.

"She's up to something," he said flatly.

"Like what?" Rance asked.

"I don't know," Keegan admitted after thrusting out an exasperated sigh. "According to Florence, Psyche invited that little viper for a visit. I figure Molly must have manipulated her into it somehow."

Rance arched an eyebrow. "It does seem like an odd arrangement. Mistresses and wives don't generally mix all that well, especially under the same roof." He paused for a beat. "Molly?"

"Molly Shields," Keegan said.

Rance's mouth quirked up at one corner, and a thoughtful smile rose into his eyes, but he didn't say anything.

"Psyche's a rich woman," Keegan reminded his cousin, getting agitated again. "It's got to be a scam."

Rance considered that. "Could be," he said. "Or maybe this—Molly Shields, was it?—maybe she's just looking for a chance to make amends. Psyche's dying. Ms. Shields did her wrong. Isn't it possible she's trying to set things right before it's too late?"

Keegan gave a snort. "Love," he told his cousin, "has softened your head."

Rance chuckled. "That's about *all* it's softened," he said.

Keegan grinned before he could catch himself. "You're a lucky son of a bitch," he told Rance. "So's Jesse."

"Your turn will come," Rance replied, and he looked dead serious.

"I'm through with marriage," Keegan answered. His ex-wife, Shelley, had cured him of any romantic notions he might have had where love and wedding cake were concerned. He was looking for regular sex of the no-strings-attached variety.

"I thought I was, too," Rance said. He looked back over one shoulder toward his own place, and the pull of Emma's presence was visible, for a fraction of a second, in the way he stood, leaning a little toward home.

"Pure luck," Keegan reiterated.

"Come on over and have supper with us," Rance urged, turning back to face Keegan again.

Keegan shook his head. "Not tonight," he said.

Rance clasped Keegan's shoulder briefly with one newly calloused hand. "I know it's hard on you," he said. "Psyche coming home to die and all. But she's not stupid, Keeg. If she asked that Shields woman here for a visit, she's got something in mind. You been to see her yet? Psyche, I mean?"

Again Keegan shook his head. Swallowed hard and looked away before meeting Rance's steady gaze once more. "I'm going there tomorrow, for lunch."

Rance nodded in solemn approval. "You tell Psyche I'll be by later in the week, when she's had more time to settle in."

"I'll tell her."

Rance started to turn away, whistled for the horse. He caught the reins in one hand, put a foot into the stirrup, turned back before mounting up to go back to his woman and his kids. "Keeg?"

Keegan waited.

"If there's trouble and Psyche needs our help, we'll give it. You, me and Jesse. In the meantime, try not to let this eat another hole in your stomach lining."

Until he'd met Emma—known as Echo when she first came to Indian Rock—driving a bright pink Volkswagon with a white dog riding shotgun, Rance had been as committed to McKettrickCo as Keegan was. He'd worn three-piece suits, traveled all over the world driving the hard bargains he was famous for and put in eighteen-hour days when he was in town.

He'd fallen in love, hard and fast, like Jesse before him, and nothing had been the same since. Now here he was, warning Keegan about ulcers.

Keegan was still getting used to the change, and there were times when he thought he never would.

He managed another grin, nodded again. "Take care," he said.

"Back at you," Rance replied.

And then he was riding away. Watching him go,

Keegan felt about as lonesome as he ever had, and given some of the things he'd been through, that was saying something.

Psyche watched from her bedroom window with a slight, wistful smile as Keegan got out of his car in front of the house, steeled himself in that subtle but unmistakable way she knew so well and opened the front gate.

I should have married him, she thought.

"Keegan's here," she told Florence, who had helped her out of her nightgown and into a royal-blue silk caftan for the occasion. She'd actually considered wearing a wig, but in the end she'd decided on a scarf instead. It seemed less pitiful, somehow.

"I'd better get down there and open the door for him, then," said Florence. "You want me to come back for you?"

Psyche squared her shoulders. Turned to face her old friend. "No," she replied, summoning up a smile that wouldn't fool Florence for a moment. "I want to make an entrance."

Florence smiled back, but tears shimmered in her eyes, too. She nodded once and left.

From the nursery, Psyche could hear Molly's voice, comically high-pitched as she read Lucas a story. Psyche's heart pinched; it was hard, withdrawing from her son so he could bond with Molly, but it had to be done. She'd fought the good fight. Psyche had done everything she could to stay alive, but it was a losing battle, and she knew it. Every day she was weaker than the one before. Every day the world seemed a little less real, a little less solid, as though she were retreating from it somehow, dissolving like a wisp of smoke.

She wasn't even dead yet, she thought, and she already knew what it felt like to be a ghost.

Downstairs the doorbell chimed.

Supporting herself by keeping one hand to the corridor wall, Psyche made her slow way toward the elevator.

When the door opened on the first floor, Keegan was waiting there, quick to offer an arm and a gentle smile. His McKettrick-blue eyes were dark with a sorrow he was trying hard to hide.

Something swelled in Psyche's throat. Made it impossible to speak.

Keegan took in the caftan and the flowing scarf. "You look as beautiful as ever," he said.

Psyche knew he was lying, and she blessed him for it, and for giving her a moment to regain her composure. "Stop it, you flattering scoundrel," she said. Then, with a twinkle, "But not right away."

He laughed hoarsely and bent to kiss her forehead. He was still gripping her arm, firmly but gently, and when she wavered a little, turning to lead the way to the back sunporch, where Florence had set the table for lunch, he swooped her up into his arms and carried her.

Tears stung her eyes. She had forgotten such gallantry existed.

When they reached the rear of the house Florence was there, arranging snow-white peonies, big as salad plates, in a shimmering crystal bowl.

Psyche gasped at the sight of her favorite flower. It was the third of July, and the last of the peonies in her garden in Flagstaff had been gone for two weeks. "Where on earth did you get those?" she asked Florence, putting a hand to her heart.

"Keegan brought them," Florence said, sniffling once before resetting her shoulders to their usual proud lines.

Keegan lowered Psyche carefully into one of the chairs at the table. His neck was a little flushed.

Psyche strained to kiss his cheek and gave voice to an earlier thought. "I should have married you, Keegan McKettrick."

He smiled. "I tried to tell you," he teased.

"Sit down so I can serve this lunch," Florence blustered, uncomfortable with all the emotion. "I been slaving in that kitchen all morning long."

Keegan chuckled, drew back the chair next to Psyche's and sat.

Florence brought in a tureen of chilled avocado soup and a platter of biscuits first, then one of her complicated and patently delicious salads. In the meantime, Keegan popped the top on the bottle of vintage champagne chilling in the center of the table and poured some into Psyche's flute, then his own.

"Ambrosia," Psyche said after taking a sip.

Keegan raised an eyebrow. "Are you supposed to have alcohol with your medication?" he asked.

Psyche laughed and toasted him before raising the glass to her lips again. After swallowing, she retorted cheerfully, "The stuff could *kill* me."

Keegan's smile was gentle, but his eyes were moist. "That's not funny," he said.

Psyche reached out and clasped his hand, but just for a moment. She still had some pride, and it was bad enough letting her childhood sweetheart see her as an invalid without his feeling her bony fingers and tremulous grasp. "Yes, it is," she argued. "And don't you dare feel sorry for me, Keegan McKettrick. I could not bear that."

After that, they ate. It gave them something to do, though Psyche suspected Keegan's appetite was no better than her own, and he, like her, was just going through the motions. Neither of them would have hurt Florence's feelings for the world.

"I have a favor to ask of you," Psyche said when they'd both given up and pushed their plates away.

Keegan waited.

Psyche suppressed an urge to lay a hand to his cheek, to tell him not to look so sad, that everything would be all right. Instead, she stared at the peonies for a long time, until they blurred into a misty mass of feathery white.

"Lucas is going to inherit a great deal of money," she said finally. She sat up very straight and prayed

Keegan wouldn't interrupt, because it would take all she had to say what she had to say, and starting over would probably be impossible. "Except for Florence, there's nobody in the world I trust as much as you. She's getting older, though, and when I—when I die, she's going to Seattle to live with her sister. I made her promise she would. Molly—" Out of the corner of her eye Psyche saw him stiffen at the name, and she rushed to get all the words out. "Molly will raise Lucas, but I'd like you to serve as my executor. See that my son's estate is protected and preserved."

"Psyche—"

She raised a hand. "Don't," she said. "Let me finish, please."

He nodded.

"Teach Lucas to ride horseback, Keegan. Teach him not to be afraid. Teach him to play baseball and to—and to be a boy."

"Let me bring him up, Psyche," Keegan said, and she knew he meant it, bless his heart.

"He needs a mother," Psyche insisted.

"*You're* his mother," Keegan replied. "That isn't going to change."

Psyche began to cry. Grabbed up a linen table napkin and swabbed at her wet face. "Molly's going to adopt him," she said. "As soon as I'm gone. I've already made all the preliminary arrangements."

Keegan frowned. "Why her? Of all people, Psyche, why her?"

Psyche wouldn't, couldn't, look at him again. The

linen napkin wafted to the stone floor of the porch, and she intertwined her fingers in her lap. "So you knew, then? About Molly and Thayer?"

"I knew," Keegan confirmed, biting out the words.

"Something good came out of their affair, Keegan," Psyche said, desperate to make him understand. Lucas would need him in the years to come. Her boy would need a man to help him grow, and Keegan McKettrick was the best one she knew.

She saw the realization dawn in his eyes. They widened, then narrowed.

"She's his biological mother," he rasped.

Psyche nodded. "Thayer came to me only a few hours after Lucas was born and told me everything. He begged me not to divorce him—said we could raise Lucas together, as our son, that Molly was willing to give him up. The simple truth is I wanted a child so badly that I agreed."

"Oh, my God," Keegan said on a long breath.

"I loved Lucas with all my heart from the first moment I saw him," Psyche went on, because she was almost out of strength. "I've never regretted what I did, not for a moment. I want him to have a good life, Keegan, and you and I both know, that takes more than money. *Please*—tell me you'll look after him…."

Keegan slid out of his chair, crouched beside Psyche, took both her hands in his, held them with a gentleness that tore her heart like paper.

"I give you my word, Psyche," he said, looking up at her.

She smiled through her tears. Pulled a hand free to stroke his sleek chestnut hair lightly. "McKettrick-true?" she asked.

"McKettrick-true," he promised.

She sagged with relief and exhaustion, let herself cry against his strong shoulder. "I should have married you," she said again.

He held her. "Let's pretend you did," he replied gruffly. "I'll take care of your boy, Psyche—just as if we'd made him together."

Psyche gave a shuddering sob. *"Thank you,"* she murmured.

As surely as if she'd had the room wired for sound, Florence appeared. "You're all done in, Miss Psyche," she said. "Time you rested for a spell."

Psyche nodded, her head still resting on Keegan's shoulder.

He stood, lifted Psyche into his arms again. Carried her—not to the elevator, but up the winding staircase at the front of the house. The one she'd come down, in a prom dress, so long ago. He'd been waiting shyly at the bottom that night, in a tuxedo, with a white peony corsage in his hand.

He mounted the second staircase, too, without so much as breathing hard. Florence followed at a slower pace.

When they reached the third floor Molly was standing in the corridor, watching with sad, enormous eyes.

Psyche felt Keegan tense.

Molly stepped aside.

"This way," Florence said grimly.

Keegan carried Psyche into her room, laid her gently on the bed. Bent to kiss her forehead.

"Don't forget your promise," Psyche told him.

"McKettrick-true," he reminded her. He curved a little finger, and Psyche hooked it with her own.

Then she smiled, closed her eyes and gave herself up to sleep.

MOLLY WAITED in the hallway outside Psyche's room, longing to disappear but too stubborn to run.

After a few minutes Keegan came out. Stopped when he saw her standing there. Narrowed his gaze.

"Is she—is Psyche all right?" she asked.

He hesitated, took a step toward her, stopped again.

Molly stood her ground.

"Bad news for you," Keegan said in a scathing undertone. "She's still alive."

Fury surged through Molly; trembling violently, she clenched her fists at her sides. If it hadn't been for Lucas, and for poor Psyche, she might have launched herself at him, kicking and slugging.

Psyche's door was closed from inside with an eloquent little snap.

Molly advanced, looked right up into Keegan's outraged face. "Of all the reprehensible things to say!" she whispered.

He grasped her elbow and shuffled her down the hall, well away from Psyche's door—and Lucas's. "You want to hear 'reprehensible,' lady? *Reprehensible* is sleeping with another woman's husband, then having the *gall* to move into her house and take over raising her son!"

He's my *son!* Molly wanted to shout. But of course she didn't. She simply stood there, drawing deep breaths and releasing them slowly until she knew she could address this impossible man without shrieking every word.

Keegan only made matters worse. Jabbing at Molly's collarbone with the tip of one index finger, he growled, "Get ready for the fight of your life, *Ms. Shields*. Psyche believes she's doing the right thing, the *honorable* thing, letting you adopt Lucas, because you're his birth mother. But there's one flaw in her logic—one she's too sick and too weak and too damn desperate to see. If you'd really wanted that baby, you wouldn't have signed off on him the way you did."

Molly couldn't have been more stunned if Keegan had struck her a physical blow. She felt light-headed, swayed and reached out to press a hand to the wall of the corridor, so she wouldn't fall.

Keegan was relentless. "I'll stop you any way I can," he said. "You may pull off this—*adoption*—but *I'm* the executor of Psyche's estate, and you won't get a plugged nickel of that kid's money, so if you've got a boyfriend waiting in some tropical hideaway for your ship to come in, honey, you'd better just write this con game off as a loss and get on the next bus out of town!"

That did it. Molly drew back her hand, and she would have slapped him, except that he caught her wrist in a hold that was just short of painful.

Tears of dizzying anger and frustration rushed to her eyes. "You—don't—understand," she said, and it was as if someone else had spoken the words, from a distance.

"I understand plenty," Keegan snapped, flinging her hand free. "*You're* the one who doesn't get it, sugarplum. You're in way over your head here. Go find another gravy train."

Molly rallied. "You listen to me, you obnoxious bastard!" she choked out in a whisper that scraped at her throat like a wad of steel wool. "I'm not a crook, and I'm not some airheaded little bimbo you can bully onto a bus, either!"

He glared at her.

She glared back.

Both of them took deep breaths.

"This isn't over," he said.

"It sure as hell isn't," she replied.

He turned and stormed down the hall to the top of the stairs.

Molly just stood there, leaning against the wall,

afraid her legs wouldn't support her if she tried to walk.

When she felt able, she made her way back into the nursery.

Lucas slept, curled into a plump little ball in the middle of his crib, one thumb in his mouth. The windows were closed and latched, but a breeze ruffled his fine spun-gold hair just the same.

Wild thoughts rushed through Molly's head, an onslaught, sweeping all logic and reason before them.

She could snatch him up in her arms, make a run for it.

Disappear.

Empty her bank accounts.

Start over somewhere, with a new name. Dye her hair, and Lucas's, too. Call him Tommy or Johnny...

Stop, she thought.

She couldn't do that to Lucas, or to Psyche.

She couldn't do it to herself.

She moved to the windows, looked down at the street just in time to see Keegan standing beside his car, staring upward. She could have sworn their gazes collided—she actually felt the impact—but of course that was impossible. He'd have no way of knowing which room she was in.

She was certain of one thing, though.

He was going to make trouble.

Molly folded her arms and dug in her heels.

"Bring it on, Mr. McKettrick," she said softly.

In the next moment, with a decisive, angry grace, he got into the Jag, slammed the door and drove away.

Molly waited a few moments, then slipped out of Lucas's room and into her own. Her cell phone was on the dresser, charging.

She unplugged it, punched in a number.

"It's about time you called," her assistant, Joanie Barnes, said. "Where are you?"

"Indian Rock, Arizona," Molly answered, suddenly weary, sagging onto the side of her bed. She'd told Joanie, and everyone else who inquired, that she was attending a writers' conference in Sedona, trolling for promising new authors. Only one person in L.A. knew the truth, and that was her dad.

"You didn't make plane or hotel reservations," Joanie accused. "I know, because I checked. And Fred Ettington said he drove you to the *bus station.*"

Molly sighed, pushed back her hair. Fred ran a car service, and she kept him on retainer to ferry important clients and editors to and fro when they were in L.A. on business. Desperate to get to Arizona and see Lucas, she'd called Fred out of habit, never thinking that he might blab.

Given a do-over, she'd take a taxi.

"Atmosphere," she said brightly.

"What?" Joanie asked.

"The bus. I rode it for atmosphere."

"You can't beat a bus for that," Joanie remarked

sarcastically. "And what *the hell* are you talking about?"

"I'm writing a book," Molly lied.

"Oh," Joanie said, patently unconvinced and making no effort to disguise the fact. *"Right."*

"How are things going at the office? Any messages?"

"Only about a thousand," Joanie retorted. "Godridge didn't make the bestseller lists, and he's threatening to sign with some New York agent. And then there's Davis. He's called about fifty times, frantic because he keeps getting your voice mail."

Molly closed her eyes. Denby Godridge—"God" for short, at least around the office—was a grizzled old Pulitzer Prize winner with a major attitude and steadily declining book sales. She could handle him, though she didn't relish the prospect. Davis Jerritt was another client—and another matter. His horror-suspense novels were runaway bestsellers, and the work in progress featured a psychotic stalker. A former actor, Dave liked to get into character when he was writing, and Molly had been selected to play the stalkee.

"Tell him I'm dead," she said.

"Davis or God?" Joanie quipped.

Molly sighed again. "Look—I can't explain right now, but there are some things I have to handle, so I'm going to be out of the loop for a while." *Like, for-*

ever. She paused, searching for words, and finally settled on a partial truth, strictly as a last resort. "I think I might need a lawyer."

CHAPTER 3

UNTIL HE DROVE INTO TOWN the next morning and saw the carnival setting up in the vacant lot behind the supermarket, Keegan had forgotten, first, that it was Saturday and, second, that it was the Fourth of July. Later there would be a community picnic and barbecue at the park, and when it got dark enough, the fireworks would begin.

Muttering, he reached for his cell phone and speed-dialed Shelley's number in Flagstaff. He'd promised to call Devon the night before, so they could make plans to spend the weekend together in the Triple M, but because of the situation with Psyche and Molly Shields, he'd neglected to do it.

"Hi, Dad," Devon said eagerly.

"Hi, babe," Keegan replied, pulling over to the side of the road, across from Echo's Books and Gifts and the Curl and Twirl, so he could concentrate on the conversation with his daughter. "Got your bags packed? I can be there in forty-five minutes."

There was short, pulsing silence. Then, "Mom said you forgot me. That's why you didn't call."

Keegan grasped the steering wheel tightly with his free hand. "I blew it big-time, Devon," he replied, "and I'm sorry. But you're my best girl, and I could *never* forget you. I'll explain on the drive down here from Flag, okay?"

"Okay," Devon answered, brightening a little.

"On my way," Keegan said.

"I'll be waiting," Devon promised.

And she was. Long-legged and gangly, with blondish-brown hair reaching to the middle of her back and huge brown eyes, she sat on the steps in the portico at Shelley's, an overnight bag and a giant pink teddy bear beside her.

Seeing Keegan pull up, she leaped to her feet and snatched up the bag and the bear to hustle toward his car.

Behind her the front door opened, and Shelley stepped out. She was a beautiful woman, and someday Devon would look just like her. A one-time flight attendant for an upscale charter jet outfit, as well as a former *Playboy* centerfold, Shelley had a face and body that were categorically perfect. Unfortunately, her personality wasn't.

Shit, Keegan thought. He'd hoped to avoid his ex-wife.

Hell, he'd been trying to do that since about an hour after he married her.

He got out of the car, came around to meet Shelley while Devon stowed her gear in the backseat of the Jag, then jumped in on the passenger side up front to buckle her seat belt.

"She waited all evening for you to call," Shelley said. She was wearing a skimpy tank top and jean shorts with frayed hems—designer stuff, probably, made to look as though it came from a discount store.

Keegan thrust out a sigh. "You could have called *me*, you know."

"It's not my job to monitor your schedule," Shelley retorted.

Conscious of Devon watching them through the windshield, Keegan kept his temper. "I should have called," he said tersely. "I didn't. Shoot me."

Shelley smiled bitterly. "Oh, I'd love to shoot you, Keegan. If only there weren't that troublesome little matter of prison, I probably would."

Keegan unclamped his back molars by an act of will. "Sucks to be you," he said.

"You wish," she retorted. "Thanks to our divorce settlement, and Rory, it's really pretty excellent to be me."

"I'm so happy for you," Keegan told her.

She grinned. "No, you're not," she countered. "You don't miss much, do you?"

"Bite me, Keegan."

"That's Rory's job, thank God."

Shelley's saucy little smirk faded to a pout. "Rory and I want to live in Paris," she said. "I surfed the internet and found a wonderful boarding school for Devon."

It wasn't the first time Shelley had mentioned moving to Paris, but the boarding school was a new element. "You and Rory can go live in Riyadh, for all I care," Keegan told her. "But you're not taking my daughter out of the U.S. Period."

"She's not your daughter," Shelley said.

Keegan felt nothing for Shelley, but the words struck his solar plexus like a ramrod, just the same. He stole a glance in Devon's direction. It would have been impossible for her to overhear, but for all he knew, the kid read lips. Thank God she was smiling blissfully at the prospect of a weekend on the Triple M.

"We were legally married when Devon was born," he said evenly. "Unless you want to go on TV and let Maury Povich announce the results of a DNA test to the nation, you're up shit creek and the paddle's miles downstream."

Shelley glared.

"I guess Rory could adopt her," Keegan went on, having no intention of letting that happen while he still had a pulse, "but it would mean the end of the child support, wouldn't it?"

"I freaking *hate* you, Keegan McKettrick."

He chucked her chin, because he knew it would

piss her off. "Right back at you, kiddo," he said. Another glance at Devon told him the kid was worried. He smiled at her, then gave Shelley a jaunty wave and turned his back on her.

"*Fuck* you, Keegan," Shelley told him.

He faced her again, smiled warmly, for Devon's sake, and kept his voice low. "We might still be married," he said, "if you'd limited yourself to that. Sleeping with me, I mean. But that would have cramped your style, wouldn't it, Shell?"

"Like you were so perfect," Shelley challenged, but she'd pulled in her horns a little.

"Nice talking to you," he said. Then he opened the door on the driver's side and slipped behind the wheel.

Shelley stood watching from the portico as they drove away, her face like a gathering storm.

"I don't want to go to Paris," Devon told him.

Startled, Keegan gave her a sidelong glance. Maybe she'd heard all or part of his conversation with Shelley after all. God, he hoped not.

"Don't worry about it," he said.

They pulled out onto a quiet, tree-lined street, in one of the best neighborhoods in Flagstaff. Despite her coffee-tea-or-me experience with the airline and the centerfold, Shelley probably would have been renting a single-wide in some trailer park if it hadn't been for him. She had the financial instincts of a crack addict.

"I can't speak French," Devon told him.

He reached across to squeeze her shoulder, found it stiff with tension. "You're not going to France," he said.

"Mom says it's romantic. Paris, I mean. She gets all dreamy when she talks about it. She and Rory are going to hold hands in the rain."

Keegan suppressed a sigh. Rory worked as a personal trainer. Shelley didn't work at all. If she and Rory got married, there would be no more alimony, and she'd have to sell the fancy house and split the proceeds with her pesky ex, settlement notwithstanding.

All of which meant he wouldn't be shopping for a wedding gift anytime soon. Damn it.

"I've been thinking, Dev," he said, stepping carefully into a delicate subject. "How would you feel about coming to live with me on the ranch? Permanently, I mean?"

"Mom won't let me," Devon answered, and out of the corner of his eye Keegan saw her shrink in on herself, shoulders stooped, chin lowered to rest in the pink fluff on top of the teddy bear's head. She had a death grip on the stuffed animal, both arms locked around it. "She needs the child support."

Keegan's stomach clenched like a fist. "She told you that?"

"I heard her and Rory talking."

Silently Keegan cursed his ex-wife and her muscle-brained boyfriend. "She loves you, sweetheart. You know that."

Devon shrugged. "Whatever." After a short silence, she added, "They fight a lot."

It was all Keegan could do not to pull a U-turn in the middle of the street, speed back to the house and confront Shelley, back-to-the-wall style. "Is that right?" he asked carefully. Moderately.

Inside, he seethed.

He'd talked to Travis Reid, who was his attorney as well as a friend, about suing Shelley for full custody. Travis figured things would get ugly if he did, and most of the fallout would come down on Devon.

"About money," Devon went on, mercifully oblivious to the turmoil going on inside the man she believed to be her father. "That's mostly what they fight about. Rory wants to get married, but Mom says they'll be broke if they do."

Keegan's sinuses burned, and the backs of his eyes stung. He drew a deep breath. "You like this Rory yahoo?"

Another shrug of shoulders too small to carry the burden of two parents who despised each other, plus a boyfriend. "He's all right," Devon said.

"You aren't going to any boarding school in Paris," Keegan told her. It wasn't much in the way of consolation, but it was all he had to give at the moment.

"You promise?"

"As God is my witness," Keegan said.

Devon quirked a grin. "Scarlett O'Hara said that in *Gone with the Wind*."

"Okay." Honesty time—the kid had enough deception to deal with. "I didn't see the movie."

"There's a book, Dad." She imparted this information gently.

"I know that, shortstop."

"Did you read it?"

He laughed. God, it felt good to laugh. How long had it been?

"Is there a quiz?"

Devon released her grasp on the bear long enough to slug him affectionately on the upper arm. "No, silly," she said. Then, in that confounding way of females, heading full steam in one emotional direction and suddenly hairpinning into a one-eighty, her eyes filled with tears. "How come you don't like Mom?"

For the second time that day Keegan pulled off onto the side of the road. He laid both hands on the wheel, deliberately splayed his fingers to keep from making fists; any reference to Shelley had that effect on him, and it was time he got the hell over it. "We've discussed this before, Dev," he said. "When people get divorced, they tend to be mad about it for a while."

"You and Mom were mad *before* you got divorced," Devon pointed out.

Keegan sighed. It was true. He'd been twenty-four when he married Shelley—stupid and horny, on the outs with Psyche. Out to prove God knew what.

"I'm sorry, Dev," he said. "I'm really sorry for everything we put you through."

"People shouldn't get married if they don't like each other."

For some strange reason, Molly Shields flashed into his mind. "You're right," Keegan replied. "They should like each other first. Be friends."

"Did Uncle Jesse like Cheyenne?"

Keegan considered. "I think he did."

"Even when they first met?"

"They had some rocky times, but, yeah, I think they were friends."

"Before they fell in love?"

"Before they fell in love."

"Uncle Rance and Emma, too?"

A bleak sensation passed through Keegan's spirit, cold and hollow. "Them, too," he said.

Devon beamed. "So you just have to find some woman you like, and be sure you're friends, and then you can get married."

"It's not that simple, Dev."

"Sure it is," she said.

"You'd like that? If I got married again?"

"If she was nice to me, like Emma is to Rianna and Maeve. They like her a lot. She lets them help in the bookstore, just like they were grown-ups. And they get to try on her shoes, too. She has *lots* of shoes."

"So does your mom," Keegan suggested, at a loss.

"She won't let me try them on, though," Devon said.

"There's something to be said for wearing your own," Keegan reasoned, baffled. "Isn't there?"

"It's not as much fun," Devon explained. "How many ten-year-olds do you know with high heels?"

"You're too young for high heels."

Devon rolled her eyes. "Dad, you're such a *guy*."

He grinned. "Yeah," he said. "And you're stuck with me for the duration, kid. Furthermore, I don't own a single pair of high heels."

She laughed, and the sound rang in the confines of that car like the peal of a bell from some country church steeple.

Keegan shifted the Jag back into gear, checked the rearview and pulled out onto the road again. "You hungry?"

"Starved," Devon said, sucking in her cheeks in a comical effort to look emaciated. "Mom's a terrible cook, and Rory won't eat anything but trail mix."

"I guess I saved you from a terrible fate—breakfasting at Casa de Idiot."

Devon giggled again, and Keegan wondered why it made his vision blur for a moment.

They stopped at a pancake house, stuffed themselves with waffles. Keegan would have preferred to keep the conversation light, but he'd promised to explain why he hadn't called Devon the night before, as agreed, and she pressed the issue.

He told her about Psyche. How they'd been friends since they were little kids, and now she was really sick. He'd gone to visit Psyche, he told Devon, and he'd been so upset when he left her, he hadn't been able to think of much else.

Devon's eyes rounded. "Is she going to die?"

Keegan swallowed. "Yes," he said.

Devon slid out of the booth, rounded the end of the table and squeezed in beside Keegan. Laying her head against his arm, she murmured. "I'm sorry, Dad."

Keegan's throat closed. He blinked a couple of times.

"You want to cry, huh?" Devon asked softly.

He didn't dare answer.

"Poor Daddy. It's hard to be a man, isn't it?"

He swallowed. Nodded.

"Do you wish you'd married Psyche?"

The question surprised him so much that he turned and stared down into his daughter's—*his daughter,* by God—upturned and innocent little face. "No," he said. "I don't wish that."

"Why not?"

He managed a smile. "Because I wouldn't have you," he told her. "And that's something I can't imagine."

"Know something, Dad?"

"What?"

"I love you."

He kissed her forehead, held her close against his side. "I love you, too, monkey," he croaked. They just sat there like that, side by side in a restaurant booth, for a while. "You had enough of those waffles?" he asked finally.

She nodded. "Let's hit the trail."

He laughed. "We're out of here."

MOLLY PAUSED outside the bookshop, peering through the display window at the latest bestsellers. Two of her authors were represented—unfortunately, neither of them was Denby Godridge. She dreaded calling the arrogant old tyrant—smoothing his ruffled feathers would take a lot of emotional energy—but she would have to do it. And soon.

Lucas, sitting in his stroller, reached up and laid a hand on the glass, making a little-boy smudge. While Molly was scrambling for a tissue to wipe it clean, the bookshop door opened and a woman peeked out, smiling. She was blond and about Molly's age, and warmth glowed in her eyes.

"Emma Wells," the woman said, putting out a hand and holding the door open with one slender hip.

"Molly Shields," Molly answered, shaking the offered hand.

"Come in," Emma said. "I just made fresh coffee, and I promise, you don't have to buy anything."

Molly smiled. Since her arrival in Indian Rock she'd met exactly three people besides Lucas: Psyche, Florence and Keegan McKettrick. Her relationship with Thayer precluded friendship with all three of them, though Psyche had been kind. Molly was a woman with an active social life, a mover and a shaker, and she missed the buzz, the power lunches, the parties-with-a-purpose.

Since she'd boarded the bus in L.A., though, she'd become a person she didn't know how to be.

"I'd like some coffee," she said. "And I might even buy a book."

Emma laughed and stepped back to admit her.

The shop was small and cozy, brightly lit. Two little dark-haired girls played in the children's section, clomping around in high heels selected from a massive pile.

The sight did something strange to Molly. Filled her with a nameless, bittersweet yearning so strong that she clasped the handle on Lucas's stroller hard to steady herself.

Meanwhile Emma crouched to smile at Lucas. "Hey, there, handsome," she said. "What's your name?"

"It's Lucas," Molly told her.

The little girls clomped over to inspect him.

"I'm Rianna," the smaller one said. "And this is my sister, Maeve. We've got a dog, but he's at the vet, getting neutered. He has to stay there till Tuesday." She looked up into Molly's face, her expression earnest. "Does Lucas like dogs?"

"I don't know," Molly said.

"Our dog's name is Scrappers, and he doesn't bite. Dad got him at the pound when Snowball had to go home with her real owners."

Scrappers. Snowball. There was obviously a story here, but Molly couldn't guess what it was.

She didn't know any children. Was this the kind

of thing they liked to talk about? She glanced hopefully at Emma, who was still on her haunches, admiring Lucas. Her pink skirt fluffed out around her in a spill of soft material. "That's really nice," she said.

Before Molly could figure out *what* was really nice, the conversation hit a snag.

"How come you don't know if your own little boy likes dogs?" Rianna asked, clearly concerned.

"Lucas and I are…just getting to know each other," Molly said awkwardly.

"Enough questions," Emma told the child gently, straightening. Her expression was solemn as she regarded Molly. "How about that coffee I promised?"

Molly nodded gratefully. "Thanks," she said.

"Do you take sugar and cream?"

"Black, please," Molly answered.

Rianna and Maeve went back to their shoe pile.

Lucas fidgeted, wanting out of the stroller.

Emma went up the back stairs.

Molly was just standing there, minding her own business and waiting for Emma to come back with the coffee, when the shop door banged open behind her.

A girl-child dashed in, long butternut hair flowing behind her. "Shoes!" she yelled.

Molly smiled—until she saw the man coming through the doorway in the little girl's wake.

Keegan.

McKettrick.

"I do read, you know," Molly said defensively, to explain her presence.

Keegan's jaw tightened, but he didn't say anything.

Molly flushed, furious with herself. It was free country, for Pete's sake. She didn't need a reason to be in a bookstore.

Keegan crouched in front of the stroller, much as Emma had done a few minutes before. "Hey, buddy," he said.

"Hey, buddy," Lucas echoed.

Keegan smiled at that, and Molly was thunderstruck by the effect of it. The man's whole countenance changed when he wasn't being a judgmental hard-ass. There might even be a human being in there somewhere, behind all that attitude.

As if he felt her gaze on him, Keegan looked up.

The second Ice Age arrived instantly.

"Does Psyche know you're here?" he asked, rising to his full height.

Molly's face heated. "No," she snapped, keeping her voice down because of Lucas and the three little girls parading around in Emma's high-heeled shoes. "I thought we'd make a break for it, Lucas and I. I plan to push his stroller overland. We'll travel by night and sleep in trees during the day."

He chuckled, and the sound was even more disconcerting than the smile had been.

Molly was still getting over it when Emma returned with the coffee.

"Keegan!" she cried, and stood on tiptoe to kiss his cheek.

"Tell me you've come to your senses," Keegan teased. "You're dumping Rance and marrying me."

Molly, standing on the edge of the encounter, wondered what it would be like to know this other Keegan.

Emma handed Molly a ceramic mug filled with fresh coffee, but she was looking at Keegan. Smiling. "You're a shameless flirt," she accused.

The little girl who'd come in with Keegan high-heeled it over to Molly. "Do you like shoes?" she asked.

"I have a closetful," Molly said, confused.

"I'm Devon," the child told her. "Devon McKettrick. This is my dad."

Molly smiled stiffly. "Hello, Devon," she responded, glancing at Keegan. "My name is Molly Shields. Your dad and I have already met."

"She has a lot of shoes," Devon told her father.

"Go play," Keegan answered.

Devon didn't move. She looked down at Lucas, then up at Molly. "Is this your little boy?"

Molly didn't know how to answer.

"Go and play, Devon," Keegan repeated.

"I'm just trying to find out if she's on the market," Devon told him.

Emma laughed.

Keegan's neck reddened.

"Are you married?" Devon persisted, turning back to Molly, keen as a prosecutor pursuing a point of law in a courtroom.

"Devon," Keegan warned.

"No," Molly said nervously. "No, I'm not married."

"But you have a baby?"

Keegan awaited her answer.

Emma shuffled Devon off to join the other kids at the shoe-fest.

"What's with that kid and shoes?" Molly asked, to forestall the sarcastic remark Keegan had surely been planning to make.

"It's a fixation, hopefully temporary," Keegan said. "How's Psyche?"

Molly sighed, saddened. "Weak. She's hoping to attend the Fourth of July picnic and stay for the fireworks, though."

Pain flashed in Keegan's eyes. He started to say something, then stopped.

Molly felt compelled to speak, even though she knew it would have been better to hold her tongue. "Florence and I both thought she should rest," she said, "but Psyche's got her heart set on joining the celebration. So we're bringing her."

Keegan considered the plan in silence, probably disapproving.

Molly pushed the stroller over to the counter and set the coffee mug down. "I guess Lucas and I had better be getting back," she said. She smiled at Emma. "Thank you."

"Come back soon," Emma said, looking puzzled.

Keegan held the door open so Molly could push the stroller out onto the sidewalk. Was he being courteous, or did he just want to get rid of her as quickly as possible?

He followed her outside. "Molly?"

She turned, frowning.

"I could give you and the boy a ride back to Psyche's," he said.

"Do you have a car seat?" Molly heard herself ask. As *if* she'd get in a car with Keegan McKettrick, after the way he'd treated her.

He shook his head.

"We'll walk, then," Molly said righteously.

It gave her some satisfaction to march off down the street without once looking back.

But not much.

SEATED ON THE FRONT PORCH swing, Psyche watched through the screen as Molly pushed Lucas up the walk. He'd fallen asleep in the stroller, hunkered down, with his head lolling to one side.

"They're bonding," she said to Florence, who was setting out a light lunch on the small wrought-iron patio table.

Florence grumbled as she poured lemonade into chilled glasses, one for Psyche, one for Molly and one for herself.

"Give her a chance, Florence," Psyche pleaded softly.

"She's probably some kind of crook," Florence whispered. "Keegan thinks so, and so do I."

"Well, you're both full of sheep-dip," Psyche said. "I had Molly's background checked. Do you think I'd hand my baby over to some stranger?"

"No telling *what* you'd do," Florence groused.

"Hush," Psyche said, but gently. She'd been younger than Lucas when Florence had joined the family, pushed up her sleeves and put Psyche's topsy-turvy world to rights. Her parents, both alcoholics, had been content to donate money from a distance and leave their only child's upbringing to a person they referred to, on the rare occasions they referred to Florence at all, as "the domestic."

Molly stopped at the bottom of the porch steps, crouched to unbuckle Lucas's safety strap, hoisted him into her arms. He rested his head on her shoulder and snoozed on.

Molly carried Lucas up the steps with an ease Psyche envied.

There were so many simple things she couldn't do anymore.

"Here," Florence said, reaching out for Lucas. "I'll put the little guy down for his nap. He can have lunch later."

"Let Molly do it, Florence," Psyche said.

Molly gripped Lucas a little more tightly and made for the door.

Florence stepped out of the way, but only at the last possible moment.

"She's a *stranger*," the older woman insisted, once Molly was well inside and she'd closed the heavy door. "Whether you paid a bunch of fancy detectives to investigate her or not!"

"Nonsense," Psyche replied, sitting down at the table and reaching for her lemonade with an unsteady hand. "She's Lucas's mother."

"*You're* Lucas's mother," Florence said staunchly.

Psyche shook her head. "I'm a ghost," she said pensively. The lemonade was ice-cold and struck just the right balance between sour and sweet. She relished the taste, though she knew it would probably make her violently ill later on. Almost everything she ate or drank did. Calling a halt to the chemotherapy hadn't relieved her of the nausea.

"Don't you talk that way!" Florence scolded, shaking a finger under Psyche's nose the way she had when she was a little girl, tracking in mud from the backyard or fidgeting in church.

"Why not?" Psyche asked, nibbling at a corner of a little sandwich with smoked salmon and cream cheese inside. "It's the truth."

"I've never heard such silliness!" Florence ranted on. "You're as alive as I am. As alive as *anybody*."

"No, I'm not. It's strange, Florence, but the grass seems greener than I've ever seen it, and the sky is bluer. I hear every bird, every bug rubbing its wings together in the flower beds. And yet there's something—remote about it all. As though I'm… receding into another place."

Florence, reaching for a sandwich of her own, suddenly bent her head, curved her always-straight shoulders inward and began to sob.

"I can't bear it," she cried. "Why isn't it *me* that's dying? I've lived my life—"

"Shh," Psyche told her, rising to stand beside Florence, put an arm around her and kissed the top of her head. "It's all right."

"It *isn't* all right!" Florence fumed. "It's a damn *shame,* is what it is! It isn't fair!"

"You were the one who told me life isn't fair, so we oughtn't to expect it to be," Psyche soothed. "Remember?"

Florence looked up, her beloved face ravaged by grief. "You're like my own child, my own baby girl…."

Psyche's heart turned over. "I know," she said. "I know."

"Look at me, carrying on!" Florence boomed, straightening her shoulders, picking up a table napkin and swabbing at her tears. "You need me to be strong, and I'm falling apart like an old potato sack with its seams bursting."

"It's all right," Psyche repeated.

The door opened again, and Molly stood on the threshold, looking as though she didn't know whether to join Psyche and Florence or dash back into the house.

"Come and sit down, Molly," Psyche said. "I want to hear all about your walk with Lucas."

CHAPTER
4

INDEPENDENCE DAY.

Ironic, Molly thought as she joined Psyche at the table on the front porch. She was about to give up her personal freedom, her life in L.A. and, essentially, her career, for the sake of one little boy. Once the various documents were signed, she would be a captive, an emotional hostage, for all practical intents and purposes—to a child.

Lucas's fate would be interwoven with her own—forever.

If his heart was broken, hers would be, too.

Was it worth it?

Molly had absolutely no doubt that it was, but neither did she suffer any illusions that the process would be easy and pain free. Joy, in her experience, was a Siamese twin to sorrow, conjoined at the heart.

She drew back a wicker chair with a bright floral

cushion. "I saw Keegan while I was out," she said. "He asked about you."

Psyche smiled. "Keegan," she repeated somewhat wistfully, as though by saying his name she'd conjured him and could see him clearly in the near distance.

Florence, her face wet, immediately fled into the house, muttering to herself and scrubbing at her eyes with a cotton handkerchief as she went.

"Are you in love with him?" Molly asked, and then was horrified, because she hadn't consciously planned to ask the question. She didn't pry. She was not, after all, a nosy person, nor was she impulsive. Indeed, she prided herself on her practicality, abhorred denial, went into things with her eyes wide open—her affair with Thayer being the one notable exception.

Now she awaited Psyche's reply with a strange sense of urgency, braced, at one and the same time, for a stinging rebuke.

Psyche was silent for an interval, her expression still softly distant, almost diffused. Finally she shook her head. "No," she said, and Molly marveled at the depth and swiftness of her own relief. "Keegan and I were childhood sweethearts...." She paused to sigh. "Such an old-fashioned term, 'childhood sweethearts'—don't you think?"

Molly wanted to avert her gaze, but she didn't allow herself to do so, because it would have been cowardly. "I think Keegan loves you," she said, helpless against this strange and unwise part of herself suddenly rising up to say things she had no right or intention to utter. And she chafed at the stab of helpless sorrow her own words wrought in her.

Keegan hated her, and the feeling was mutual.

Why, then, did she care whether or not he loved Psyche?

More to the point, how could she *stop* caring?

"He does love me," Psyche agreed. "He's fiercely protective of anyone he cares about—all the McKettricks are."

A lump rose in Molly's throat and swelled there. She swallowed, determined not to break down.

Something moved in Psyche's eyes—compassion, perhaps. She reached out, touched Molly's hand.

"Keegan and I are *friends,*" Psyche went on gently. "Nothing more."

"I'm not so sure he would agree," Molly said. "Psyche, I—"

"What?"

"I'm so sorry—about what happened between Thayer and me, I mean."

"Water under the bridge," Psyche said. "When Thayer died I was—in some ways—relieved. It's horrible to admit that, and maybe I'm being punished for it now. Maybe that's why I have to let go, leave Lucas—"

"No," Molly protested weakly. As much as she wanted to raise Lucas, the cost was simply too great.

Psyche smiled, but her eyes were misty, and her

chin trembled ever so slightly. "Isn't it remarkable, Molly? Your being here, I mean? I actually think we would have been friends if we'd met under other circumstances."

Molly gulped. "I would do anything to go back and change things."

"Would you?" Psyche asked. "Where would that leave Lucas?"

Molly couldn't speak.

"You slept with my husband. You bore his child. And while convention would dictate that I ought to hate you for that, I can't. You brought Lucas into the world, Molly. Try as I might, I can't feel anything but gratitude."

Tears burned in Molly's eyes. "You are the most amazing person, Psyche Ryan," she managed, fairly strangling on the words. "Worth ten of me, and a *hundred* of Thayer. He didn't deserve you."

Psyche gave a hoarse chuckle. "Well, I agree with you about Thayer. The man wasn't fit to lick my shoes. But you, Molly Shields, are an entirely different matter. You are a far finer person than you think."

Molly shook her head. "I was such a blind fool—"

"Stop," Psyche said abruptly.

Molly blinked, surprised.

"Yes, you made a mistake," Psyche allowed. "But something very, very good came of it. And now I'm dying." She stopped, regrouping. Perhaps absorbing, yet again, the fate she couldn't escape. "I have no time for hand-wringing or for regrets, yours *or* mine, so buck up and get over it. The first moment I held Lucas in my arms I forgave you for everything. I *blessed* you. Now you need to forgive yourself, if only for Lucas's sake. Can you do that?"

Molly pondered the question, then nodded. "Yes," she said. "But it won't be easy."

"Nobody said anything about easy," Psyche responded. "Lucas will have fevers, and skinned knees, and all manner of required boy-experiences. Dealing with Keegan won't be any stroll through the lilies either, but then, I suppose you've deduced that already."

Ruefully Molly nodded again.

"I've asked Keegan to be the executor of my estate," Psyche confirmed. "He wanted to adopt Lucas himself, you know. Leave you completely out of the picture. I refused, because I believe a child needs a mother."

"How— " Molly choked, cleared her throat, started over. "How can you trust me, after all that happened?"

Psyche smiled. "This wasn't a spur-of-the-moment decision, Molly. I'm not giving Lucas to you just because you happen to be his birth mother. You've been checked out by the best private investigators in Los Angeles."

"But you said something about not knowing my financial situation."

"I lied," Psyche said sweetly.

Molly laughed. Suddenly, unexpectedly, a raw, soblike guffaw escaped her, and she put a hand over her mouth, too late.

Psyche's pain-weary eyes twinkled. "Perhaps we *can* be friends, even this late in the game," she said. "What do you think?"

"I think I'd be honored to be your friend," Molly answered.

"Know what?" Psyche asked.

"What?"

"Thayer wasn't good enough to lick *your* shoes, either."

Once again Molly laughed. She laughed so hard that she finally had to lay her head down on her folded arms and cry as though her very soul were bruised.

Which, of course, it was.

At sunset, Keegan stood looking up at the Ferris wheel looming in the middle of Indian Rock's small park, trying to work up a celebratory mood. Try as he might, he couldn't.

Psyche was dying.

McKettrickCo was being torn apart from the inside.

Shelley wanted to take Devon thousands of miles away and install her in some institution so she and the boyfriend could walk the streets of Paris and hold hands in the rain.

What a load.

Keegan, meanwhile, was on tilt, like a pinball machine with a phone book under one leg.

"Dad?"

He looked down, saw Devon standing beside him, flanked by Rianna and Maeve. Rance and Emma would be along later. In the interim, all three of the kids were munching on big pink fluffs of cotton candy, and would most likely be puking up their socks any second now.

"Can we go on the pony ride, Uncle Keegan?" Rianna asked.

"It's a donkey ride, ding-dong," Maeve said importantly.

"There's only one donkey," Devon pointed out sagely, "so we'll have to stand in line."

Keegan sighed. "Sure," he said.

The girls raced away across the lush grass of the park, past the barbecue being set up under a canvas canopy, and he ambled after them, feeling foolish in his white shirt, dress slacks and gray silk vest. The rest of the men were wearing jeans or chinos.

The donkey was small, and its hide was mangy. It lumbered doggedly around and around a metal center-pole, chained to the mechanism. The creature's ribs showed, its hooves needed trimming and it kept its head down, as though slogging into the face of a heavy wind. The child on its back kicked it steadily with the heels of his sneakers.

As the animal passed Keegan, making its endless rounds, it turned its head, gazing at him with dull brown eyes. It stumbled, and a wiry little man standing to one side whacked it on the flank with a stick and growled, "Wake up!"

Keegan, in the act of taking out his wallet to give Devon and his nieces money to buy tickets, stopped cold.

The donkey keeper's gaze sliced to the wallet, as if magnetized, then slithered, snakelike, up to Keegan's face. Passing him a second time, the donkey stumbled again.

The man raised the switch.

Keegan, without realizing he'd moved at all, was there to jerk it out of the keeper's hand. He might have flung the stick halfway across the park if there hadn't been so many kids standing around. Instead, he let it drop to the ground, opening his fingers slowly.

"You got a problem, mister?" the man asked. He wore grease-stained jeans and a grubby white undershirt, and his upper arms were tattooed with intertwined serpents, apparently consuming each other. A plastic name pin pinned to his shirt identified him as "Happy."

Keegan made a mental note to appreciate the irony later.

"No," he replied flatly, keeping his voice down. "I don't have a problem. But you will if you pick up that stick again."

Happy ruminated, spat. "Old Spud belongs to

me," he said. "I reckon I can do as I please with him."

"Do you, now?" Keegan inquired, still holding his wallet in his free hand. "You traveling with this carnival? It's been coming here twice a year for as long as I can remember, but I've never seen you before."

A stream of tobacco juice shot out of the man's mouth, narrowly missing Keegan's shoe. "I'm an independent contractor" came the answer. "Not that it's any never-mind of yours."

"You have any other donkeys?"

"Just old Spud here. Truth is, he's about worthless. Gotta pop him one every once in a while, just to keep him going."

"Dad?" Devon asked at Keegan's elbow. "Are we going to buy tickets? The line's getting *really* long."

Keegan took in the queue of impatient kids.

"I'd sell him for the right price," Happy volunteered cagily.

"I imagine you would," Keegan drawled.

"Dad?" Devon prompted.

Keegan handed his daughter a bill without looking away from Happy's beady little eyes. "Forget the donkey," he told her. "Ride the Ferris wheel."

"But, Dad, we want—"

"The Ferris wheel, Devon."

Devon heaved a dramatic sigh, but she obeyed. She and Rianna and Maeve immediately headed for the ticket booth.

"How much?" Keegan asked.

Happy named his price, which was, as expected, astronomical.

Keegan counted out the money, flourished it, but didn't hand it over. "I'll need a bill of sale," he said. Then he crossed to the donkey, hoisted the overzealous rider off its back and turned to face the straggling line of kids. "Spud," he told them, "has just retired."

There were a few groans of disappointment, but in general the crowd took the news well.

Keegan removed the donkey's harness, stroked his rough, nubby hide with one hand while the keeper wrote out a receipt on a scrap of paper pulled from his pocket. Spud, barely reaching Keegan's middle, looked up at him, then nuzzled his arm.

"You didn't waste much of your profits on feed, did you, Happy?" he asked, looking at Spud's ladder of ribs while swapping the money for the bill of sale.

"You just made a fool's bargain," Happy said, ignoring Keegan's remark, folding the fat wad of bills and tucking them into a battered wallet attached to one of his belt loops by a tarnished chain. "That critter is stupid, and he's lazy. Good for nothin'. Now he's your problem, not mine."

Keegan took off Spud's saddle and the worn blanket beneath it, tossed them both aside. That left the bridle. Taking a loose hold on the reins, he turned to walk away, and the donkey followed willingly.

Rance had just arrived with Emma, and he spotted Keegan and his four-legged purchase right away. Grinning, Rance approached.

"If you're short on horses," he said, looking Spud over, "I could lend you one of ours."

"You know, Rance," Keegan replied tersely, "sometimes you're just so freakin' hilarious, I can't stand it."

Rance's grin broadened. "What the hell do you want with a jackass?"

"Damned if I know," Keegan said. "But I've got one now."

"How are you planning to get him out to the ranch?"

Now it was Keegan's turn to grin. "Well, I figured since you own a horse trailer, you'd haul him out there for me."

Rance chuckled. Then he took a closer look at Spud and frowned. "He's half-starved," he said. "And it's a wonder he can walk, with his hooves grown out like that."

"My thoughts exactly," Keegan said.

Expertly Rance lifted one of Spud's feet and inspected it. Did the same with the other three. "I'll go back to the Triple M and hitch the trailer to the back of my truck," he said when he was finished. Dusting his hands together, he looked Keegan in the eye and grinned again. "If you're going into the ranching business, Keeg, you're off to a pretty pitiful start."

Keegan made a this-is-me-amused face. "Want me to ride out with you? Help with the trailer?"

"In those dandy duds?" Rance joked, shaking his head at Keegan's clothes. "Do you *own* any jeans or a decent pair of boots?"

"Never mind my wardrobe," Keegan said. Until he'd taken up with Emma just a few weeks before, Rance had lived in custom-tailored suits himself.

Rance looked over toward the barbecue area, where the picnic was starting up in earnest. Folks were loading up their plates, and the bar and the cold-drink stand were already doing a brisk business. "There had better be some beer left when I get back," he warned.

Keegan laughed. He'd added a mangy donkey to all his other problems, but his spirits had risen a little, just the same.

Go figure, he thought.

Rance crossed to Emma, said something to her and headed back to his truck.

Emma wobbled toward Keegan on a pair of pink high-heeled shoes, which matched her cotton-candy dress, sticking in the grass every few steps. Cautiously she reached out to pat Spud on the nose. Then she smiled, and Keegan figured the fireworks would suffer by comparison.

"Molly's here," she said. "And the new people."

Keegan looked around and, sure enough, there was Molly Shields over by the picnic tables, looking delectable in a floaty blue dress and a straw hat with a bent-back brim. Psyche was there, too, seated in a lawn chair, with a blanket covering her lap. Flor-

ence, intent on lifting Lucas from his stroller, wore
her usual starchy uniform.

As though she felt him watching her, Molly
looked his way.

Smiled, probably because of the donkey.

Keegan hooked a finger under his shirt collar,
trying to loosen it. It was the heat, he figured. The
air seemed charged, and he actually looked up, expecting to see storm clouds.

The first stars winked in a clear, placid sky.

Emma tugged at his sleeve, whispered, "Keegan.
You're staring."

Molly spoke to Psyche, then strolled his way.

"I guess it's never too soon to start practicing for
the Christmas pageant," she said, her eyes warming
as she took in poor, bedraggled Spud. "Are you playing Joseph this year?"

"I'd better go and find the girls, make sure they
don't eat too much cotton candy and spoil their
supper," Emma said before Keegan could respond,
and promptly vanished.

Keegan swallowed.

Molly smiled, clearly enjoying his discomfort.
Then, as Emma had done, she stroked Spud's long
face, threw in an ear-ruffling for good measure.

Spud lifted his head and brayed.

Keegan felt like doing the same thing, and that
made him set his back teeth.

Molly's leaf-colored eyes shone with amusement,
turned tender when she looked at the donkey again.

The blue cloth flower, pinned to the turned-up brim of her hat, bobbed. "We have to be civil to each other, Keegan," she said quietly. "Because of Lucas."

He sighed. Wished she'd look at him the way she was looking at the donkey. "I can be civil," he said without a trace of civility. "And that is a really goofy-looking hat. Does that flower squirt water?"

She laughed, and the sound gave Keegan the same quivery feeling in the pit of his stomach that he used to get when he was rodeoing, back in college, with Rance and Jesse. Just before he climbed the side of a chute and lowered himself onto the back of a pawing, snorting bull, crazy to buck. "I wish it did," she said. "I'd like nothing better than to let you have it right about now."

Against his will Keegan grinned. Loosened his hold on Spud's reins a little so the critter could munch on the well-kept municipal grass. Psyche, sitting up straight in her lawn chair, smiled tentatively and waved.

Keegan's grin faded. "It isn't right," he said.

Molly, still petting the donkey, turned to follow his gaze, looked back at his face. "Don't spoil this night for her by being sad," she told him.

He worked up another smile, waved to Psyche. "Better?" he asked.

"Much better," Molly said.

Lucas came toddling toward them, his face alight. He was barefoot, wearing nothing but a diaper.

Molly probably knew as well as Keegan did that

Spud was the big attraction, not either of them. Still, it did something to Keegan, watching that little boy toddle across the grass.

Keegan handed Molly the reins, went to meet Lucas and swept him up in his arms. Over the child's head he saw Psyche watching with a faint smile.

"Ride!" Lucas crowed, straining for the donkey. "Ride!"

"Not tonight, buddy," Keegan said, shifting Lucas onto his hip so he could reach out and pat Spud's neck.

Spud twitched his spindly tail a couple of times.

"Ride!" Lucas yelled.

"Another time," Keegan told the child quietly, looking into Molly's eyes again. Feeling as though he'd just tumbled headfirst down some storybook rabbit hole.

"Why not?" Molly asked, reaching for Lucas, soothing him.

"Spud's been abused," Keegan said, indicating the donkey with a motion of his head. "He'd probably mind his manners, but until I know that for sure, I'm not putting Psyche's child on his back."

Molly's mouth tightened, probably because he'd said *Psyche's child.* The flower on her hat jostled around some more as she bounced Lucas on her hip, whispered to him. The boy whimpered, rested his head on Molly's shoulder, gave a little shudder as he settled in.

Keegan realized he'd taken back Spud's reins at

some point, and it bothered him that he didn't remember when it had happened.

"You may have given birth to Lucas," he told
Molly in an undertone, returning the greetings of
old friends and passersby with a rigid smile and a
nod, "but *Psyche's* his mother. She's the one who
protected him, provided for him, *loved* him."

"Do you think I need you to tell me that, you
pompous ass?" Molly shot back, doing the smile-
and-nod thing herself.

So much for the two of them being civil to each
other, Keegan reflected, shoving a hand through his
hair.

Molly turned on her heel and marched away, lug-
ging Lucas with her. The boy struggled and reached
back, not for Keegan, who was after all a stranger to
him, but for the donkey.

Devon appeared, balancing a plate of barbecued
chicken, potato salad and coleslaw in one hand.
"What do donkeys eat?" she asked, looking as
though she might be about to offer Spud her picnic
supper.

"The same things horses do," Keegan answered,
still way too aware of Molly. He was practically
spinning in her wake. "Grass. Hay. Alfalfa. Grain."

"How come he's not giving rides?"

"His carnival career is over. He's going home with
us."

Devon brightened. "Really? We get to keep him?"

"Yes," Keegan said, just as a familiar roar filled

the air. A sleek jet passed overhead, bearing the McKettrickCo logo, an updated version of Angus's original brand, on the undersides of the wings.

"They're back!" Devon cried. "Jesse and Cheyenne are back from their honeymoon!"

"Maybe," Keegan agreed.

"What do you mean, 'maybe'?" Devon asked. "Who else could it be?"

Keegan could have named several possibilities—from famous country singers to a detachment of Texas McKettricks bent on taking the company public whether he liked it or not. He sure as hell hoped it was Jesse.

"Dad?" Devon pressed, sounding worried.

"Let's find a place to park this donkey," he said, trying to smile. "I'd like a cold beer and some supper."

"Good idea," Devon said, relieved.

He'd have eaten with Psyche, but Molly was there, and he'd had enough of *her* for one night. Make that one lifetime.

In the end they stowed Spud in the churchyard across the street from the park, behind a picket fence. He immediately began dining on the petunias, and Keegan made a mental note to send the pastor a check.

He ate with a flock of women, Emma among them. Cora Tellington, Rance's former mother-in-law, was there, too. Cora ran the Curl and Twirl, a combination beauty shop and baton-twirling school, and Keegan had always liked her. Since Rance's first wife, Julie, had died in a riding accident five years before, Cora had taken up the maternal slack with Rianna and Maeve. Rance hadn't made it easy for her, either.

"You're looking pretty down in the mouth tonight," Cora confided affectionately, sitting beside him on a bench at one of the picnic tables and bumping his upper arm with her shoulder.

"I'm fine," he lied. Fact was, since that last set-to with Molly, he'd been feeling a little sorry for himself, and a hell of a lot sorrier for Devon. Maeve and Rianna had a devoted grandmother in Cora, and Rance's parents, divorced years before and dating again since they'd hooked up after Jesse and Cheyenne's wedding, both adored the kids.

Keegan's own folks had died in a plane crash when he was in high school, and even though the rest of the family had looked out for him straight through college, it was as if a part of him had gone down in flames right along with his mom and dad. He'd been working at McKettrickCo for a few years when he met Shelley and thought he'd found a way to fill that hollow spot at the back of his heart. Shelley was already pregnant with Devon when they eloped, and he might never have known he'd been conned if the baby hadn't needed a transfusion after emergency surgery.

He'd gone straight to the lab to give blood, only to learn he couldn't because Devon's was of a rare type. The doctor hadn't exactly said Devon couldn't be Keegan's biological child, but the facts had been there in his eyes. Later, tearfully, Shelley had admitted that she'd been with somebody else while they were engaged. She'd never said who.

He closed his eyes against the memory.

A stir in the crowd made him open them again.

Jesse and Cheyenne were indeed back from wherever they'd gone, both of them smiling, walking hand in hand toward the center of the festivities.

Devon, Rianna and Maeve all shrieked with delight, ran toward them and practically knocked Jesse off his feet. Grinning, he greeted each one in turn.

Jesse had a way with women, all right. Big ones, little ones, old ones, young ones and everything in between. They *all* adored him.

Keegan excused himself from the table, got up and went to kiss Cheyenne's cheek and shake Jesse's hand.

"I heard about Psyche," Jesse said quietly, when Cheyenne was surrounded by chattering girlfriends and spirited away. "I'm sorry, Keeg."

"Who told you?" Keegan asked, frowning. Jesse and Cheyenne hadn't mentioned where they were going on their honeymoon, and as far as he'd known, no one had been in contact with them since the reception.

"Myrna," Jesse replied. Myrna Terp was the office manager at the Indian Rock branch of McKettrickCo, and she prided herself on knowing more about other people's business than the average CIA mole.

About that time, Rance rolled up in his truck, the horse trailer hitched behind. He got out of the pickup, walked around and slapped Jesse on the shoulder. "How was the honeymoon?"

Jesse merely grinned.

It said it all, that grin.

Rance chuckled and whacked Jesse again. Then he turned to Keegan. "Where's that damn donkey?"

"Across the street in the churchyard, eating petunias," Keegan answered.

"You go get some supper and spend a little time with Emma and the kids. I'll load Spud."

"What donkey?" Jesse asked, clearly out of the loop.

Rance's smile widened. "Keegan's starting a herd," he said. "He's going to be very big in the lop-eared jackass trade."

Keegan just shook his head and made for the churchyard.

"I'll help," Jesse said, falling in step with Keegan, while Rance went to join Emma and the others.

"You're just back from your honeymoon," Keegan reminded him, his strides lengthening a little. "Shouldn't you be hanging out with your new bride?"

Jesse kept pace. "How long does it take to load a donkey into a horse trailer?" he reasoned.

Spud, watching them approach, nickered a welcome.

Keegan opened the gate and the donkey came right to him, reins dangling.

Just as Rance had, Jesse checked the animal's feet, ran a hand over his protruding rib cage. There was no trace of the trademark grin when Jesse faced Keegan. "He's been neglected, and abused, too, from the looks of him."

Keegan nodded, and as the three of them crossed the street he explained briefly how he'd acquired Spud.

Jesse threw the bolt on the back of Rance's trailer and lowered the ramp. Keegan led the donkey inside and was glad to see that Rance had thought to put hay in the feeder and make sure there was water.

After removing the bridle and buckling on a halter, adjusted for size, from the selection on the tack wall, Keegan fastened on a lead rope and tied it with a slip knot, so Spud wouldn't rattle around in that trailer like a dry bean in the bottom of a tin bucket.

"There'll be fireworks later," Jesse observed. "Lots of noise. Maybe we ought to take old Seabiscuit here out to the Triple M right now. Get him settled into a stall."

"I don't imagine he's too skittish," Keegan observed. "Not after carrying a lot of screaming, kicking kids around in circles for who knows how many years."

"Keeg," Jesse said.

Keegan didn't look at him. Didn't answer.

"You're taking it pretty hard—Psyche's being so sick, I mean."

Keegan felt his backbone stiffen. "I guess Myrna told you that, too."

"Nobody had to tell me, Keeg."

He and Rance and Jesse had grown up together, like pups from a barn litter. They didn't have many secrets from each other.

"I'll be all right," Keegan said, stepping out of the trailer to join Jesse in the road. He put the ramp up again, closed and fastened the doors. "Once I get over the shock."

He *would* be all right, he knew.

But Psyche wouldn't.

And Lucas might not be, either.

Jesse regarded him silently in the dim glow of a streetlight. Carnival music played, and the Ferris wheel turned, and little kids shrieked with delight on the spinning cars on the spider ride.

"I'll be all right," Keegan repeated.

Jesse rested a hand on his shoulder. "I know," he said. "But the meantime is bound to be hard."

Keegan swallowed, nodded. Again, he didn't trust himself to talk.

"We'll be here, Keeg," Jesse told him. "Rance and me."

Keegan was counting on that, though he couldn't say so.

"McKettrick-tough," Jesse said. It was one of a dozen such phrases, drilled into them from the time they could understand the spoken word.

"McKettrick-tough," Keegan confirmed.

CHAPTER  5

PSYCHE SAT ALONE under a tree, with Lucas snoozing on a blanket nearby. Seeing Keegan returning with Jesse, she beckoned.

Keegan's heart turned over. She was so brave. By comparison, he felt like a sniveling yellow-belly.

Nonetheless, he approached. Jesse immediately bent and kissed Psyche's cheek. "Hey, beautiful," he said. "Welcome home."

She smiled. "I hear congratulations are in order," she replied. "The uncatchable Jesse McKettrick has been caught."

Jesse chuckled, nodded. "Snagged, bagged and tagged," he said.

"I'd like to meet your wife," Psyche told him. "I promise I won't tell her what a rounder you've always been."

Jesse flashed that famous grin. "I think she suspects," he replied. "I'll go find her." With that, he slapped Keegan once on the shoulder and walked away.

"Sit down, Keegan," Psyche said.

He sat cross-legged in the fragrant grass.

"You and Molly look wonderful together," Psyche remarked, probably trying to be subtle.

Keegan had known Psyche all his life, and he knew instantly what she was getting at. "No possible way," he said. "Forget it."

"Forget what?" Psyche asked innocently.

"You know damn well what," Keegan answered.

She grinned. "Okay, so I thought it would be nice if you and Molly fell in love and got married. Lucas would have a real family then—he'd be a McKettrick. I can just picture all of you beaming out of one of those photo Christmas cards—'Happy Holidays from the Four of Us.'"

"Lucas can be a McKettrick," Keegan said. "All you have to do is let me adopt him, instead of Molly."

Psyche sighed. "It would be much simpler if you married Molly, and the two of you adopted him together."

"I had one cheating wife," Keegan retorted, without intending to. "I don't need another."

Psyche held out a hand. After a moment's hesitation, spent feeling like an idiot for spilling his emotional guts the way he had, and to a dying woman, for God's sake, Keegan took the hand.

"I always thought Shelley was a real bitch," she said. "Frankly, I wondered what you saw in her."

Keegan chuckled. He'd expected something different from Psyche, though he didn't know exactly what. "I had similar thoughts about you and Thayer," he said.

She squeezed his hand, then released it—an ordinary gesture, and yet Keegan felt it as a precursor to the permanent parting yawning up ahead like the mouth of a dark cave.

"They dated, you know," Psyche said. "Thayer and Shelley, I mean. While they were in college. I think it was pretty hot and heavy."

Keegan remembered. It was, he had to admit, if only to himself, one of the reasons he'd never liked Psyche's husband. "Yeah," he said. "I know. It would have saved us a lot of grief if they'd married each other, and left you and me out of the equation."

"But they didn't," Psyche reflected. Her gaze fell on Lucas, his little body covered by part of the blanket he was lying on. "I called Travis this afternoon, about the documents—the adoption, and your appointment as my executor—and he said he'll have everything ready by Monday."

Travis and Sierra were away in Scottsdale, with Sierra's seven-year-old son, Liam, shopping for furniture for the new house they'd just built on the other end of town.

"There's still time to change your mind," Keegan said.

"I'm not going to change my mind, Keegan,"

Psyche told him pointedly, "so stop nagging me about it. I've given this a lot of thought, and I want everything in order before I—well—before. I need your cooperation, damn it."

Just then, Jesse reappeared with Cheyenne.

Keegan stood.

Jesse introduced the two women.

Marital bliss looked good on Cheyenne, Keegan thought, but then, just about anything would. She was a beauty—dark-haired and slender, and smart as hell.

After she and Psyche had exchanged pleasantries and Jesse started chatting Psyche up just as if everything were normal, Cheyenne turned to Keegan and pulled him aside. "You're ready for the meeting on Monday morning?" she asked.

"What meeting?" He'd left his cell phone in the car and hadn't been to the office at all that day.

"Eve and Meg are coming in from San Antonio," Cheyenne told him quietly. Eve McKettrick was Meg and Sierra's mother, as well as president and CEO of McKettrickCo. "Along with most of the board of directors. This is it, Keegan. They want a final vote on the decision to go public."

Of course they did. Eve, actually a distant cousin, had been like a mother to him, but when it came to company business, she was a force of nature.

Keegan swore under his breath. "What's going to happen to your job?" he asked, trying to get some kind of foothold.

Cheyenne touched his arm. "I'll be all right," she said. "I might stay on, or go into business for myself. It's you I'm worried about."

He sighed. "Has Jesse said anything about how he plans to vote?"

"You'll have to talk to him about that," Cheyenne said reasonably.

Alarm coursed through Keegan, like a shock from a live wire. He glanced Jesse's way, and in that moment he knew. "Damn," he rasped.

Cheyenne's voice went soft. "He's tired of all the fighting," she said.

Keegan took a step toward Jesse, who was looking at him now, and stopped. This was no time for a confrontation, but Keegan felt betrayed just the same. Jesse had had plenty of time to tell him what he'd decided while they were loading Spud into Rance's trailer. Instead he'd promised that he and Rance would be there, help him through the imminent loss of one of his closest friends.

"Damn," Keegan repeated, more fiercely this time.

"Is something wrong?" Psyche asked.

"Nothing at all," Keegan said, glaring at Jesse.

"You'll be by Monday afternoon to sign the papers?"

"Monday afternoon," Keegan promised. Then he turned, without another word, and walked away.

MOLLY STOOD with her back to a tree and a finger in one ear, talking into her cell phone. It wasn't easy, given that a carnival and town picnic were going on all around her.

"Denby, listen to me—"

"I want a new agent!" Denby Godridge screamed. He was taking it hard, not making the bestseller lists with his last epic novel. Molly had sold it for big bucks on the strength of a Pulitzer Prize won in the 1970s, and the publishers weren't too pleased, either. "It was bad enough when you worked out of L.A.," Denby ranted. "Now I'm supposed to deal with someone in *Indian Rock, Arizona?*"

"Denby, please—"

"You're fired, Molly!"

Molly closed her eyes.

Denby hung up with a crash.

Tears seeped between Molly's lashes.

"Boyfriend tired of waiting for the loot to start rolling in?" The voice was only too familiar.

She opened her eyes. Sure enough, there stood Keegan, with his hands jammed into the pockets of his grass-stained slacks, hair mussed, as though he'd been running his fingers through it. Behind him, the pink, green and blue lights of the Ferris wheel blended like colorful amoebas.

She shoved the phone back into her purse, marched over to him, wrenched off her favorite straw hat and slapped him in the belly with it. "You know what, Mr. Smart-Ass Keegan Freaking *McKettrick?* I've had just about *enough* of your snide remarks and sleazy insinuations!"

His eyes widened when she popped him with the hat. They were the most extraordinary blue, those eyes. The color of new denim.

Then, remarkably, he laughed.

"Are you drunk?" she demanded.

"No," he said. "But I wish I were." He paused a beat. "Who made you cry, Molly Shields?"

The question took her aback. She looked down, saw that the flower had fallen off her hat, and bent to retrieve it. Unfortunately, so did Keegan at the same moment, and they conked heads.

"Oww," Keegan complained, laying a hand to his crown as he straightened. He looked and sounded so much like a small boy that Molly, contending with a skull fracture of her own, laughed right out loud.

Keegan's eyes softened slightly, and Molly felt a tiny pinch, smack in the center of her heart.

"Who made you cry?" he asked again.

She sighed, fumbling to pin the flower back onto the brim of her hat. "It was nothing," she said. "I've just had a lot of emotional ups and downs lately."

"Haven't we all?" Keegan muttered.

"Nobody more than Psyche," Molly replied, giving up on the flower and shoving it into the twilight zone of her bag, where the phone had already disappeared. A chilly breeze made her hug herself.

"Cold?" Keegan asked.

"I'm fine," Molly said.

"You look like somebody who could appreciate a good joke."

She squinted. "Huh?"

"Psyche thinks you and I ought to get married," Keegan told her, "and adopt Lucas together. How crazy is that?"

"*Real* crazy," Molly was quick to say. Now, why did it hurt so much that he thought the idea of marrying her was ludicrous enough to be funny?

His eyes turned serious now, intent. Molly wondered if she had barbecue sauce on her face, and while she was considering the possibility, he took her by surprise with a kiss.

Electricity coursed through her, like a bolt of lightning.

Keegan's mouth rested lightly on hers, barely more than a breath.

Molly stepped back, blinking and breathless.

"Sorry," Keegan said.

"You really have a gift for saying the wrong thing, you know that?"

He grimaced. "So I've been told."

Molly trembled. If he noticed, she decided, she'd blame it on the coolness of the evening. "We'll just pretend it didn't happen," she said.

"You're pretty good at that, aren't you?"

Five seconds ago the man had kissed her. Sweetly. Tenderly. Made her toes curl. Now he was digging at her again.

"Pretty good at *what?*" she demanded.

"Pretending things didn't happen. Like your affair with Thayer Ryan, for instance."

"I'm not pretending I didn't have an affair with Thayer Ryan!"

"Yes, you are. Either that, or you have no conscience at all. Molly, how can you do it? How can you move into another woman's house—take over raising her child, as if nothing had happened?"

The words *pelted* Molly. Knocked the breath out of her, like a fall onto hard ground.

"Well?" Keegan pressed. They were ruthless now, those impossibly blue eyes, and colder than a January wind.

Molly swallowed, determined not to lose her temper and make a scene at the Fourth of July celebration. Indian Rock was a small town—she had to make a home here for Lucas and she didn't need the kind of notoriety a screaming match with Keegan McKettrick would bring. "Pay close attention, you lamebrained, arrogant son of a bitch," she said, acidly pleasant. "I'm not going to say this again. *I came here because Psyche asked me to. Because—*" *Because Lucas is my son and because there were times when I missed him so much, I curled up in a fetal position on the floor and cried until my eyes swelled shut.*

Keegan didn't answer.

Overhead, the first of the fireworks erupted in a splash of blue fire, swelling into a huge flower against the night sky, then spilling gracefully down like the tears of an angel.

Keegan looked up at the display, and so did

Molly, but out of the corner of her eye she noticed his profile—the strong jawline, the conservative haircut that didn't really suit him, the straight nose. He was probably the most obnoxious man she'd ever met, not counting certain waiters and some of the panhandlers on Sunset, and yet something about him stirred her, way down deep.

Maybe it was just the barbecue sauce.

"I'd better go and find my daughter," he said.

"I'd like to share the experience with my son," she replied in terse agreement, putting only the slightest emphasis on the last two words.

With that, they went their separate ways.

It was after midnight when Molly maneuvered Lucas into his pajamas and laid him in his crib.

"Isn't he beautiful?"

Molly hadn't realized Psyche was in the room, and she started slightly before turning to face the other woman. "He is," she whispered.

Psyche crossed to Lucas's crib, touched his sweat-curled hair with a tremulous hand. Her eyes glistened in the semidarkness. "Dear God," she murmured. "What I'd give to see him grow up."

Had Psyche been anyone but who she was, Molly might have put an arm around her in an effort to lend comfort. But Psyche was the wronged wife, and Molly had played a major part in that betrayal.

"Let's go downstairs," Psyche said very softly,

tucking Lucas's favorite blanket around him. "I could really use a glass of wine."

"Me, too," Molly admitted.

They rode down in the elevator, neither one speaking.

The kitchen was dark and extra-empty without Florence there, peeling potatoes, warming milk for Lucas or muttering while she listened to the commentators she loved to hate on the countertop radio.

Psyche got out a Napa red while directing Molly to the wineglasses.

Enervated by the day, Psyche soon collapsed into a chair at the table.

Molly wielded the corkscrew and poured.

"It's a hard thing, dying," Psyche said.

"I suppose you tried all the treatments," Molly replied after swallowing hard. She'd been doing that a lot since coming to Indian Rock.

Psyche hoisted her glass in a wry salute. "Everything," she said. "Trust me, the 'cure' definitely *is* worse than the disease."

They each sipped their wine.

Then, out of the blue, Psyche said, "Keegan is a good man, Molly."

"He's a—well, never mind what he is."

Psyche smiled, but there was a lot of sadness in her eyes. "I've known him since kindergarten," she mused. "He always fought my battles for me. That's one of Keegan's problems, you know. He's an Old West kind of man, trapped in a modern world."

"I saw his Jag," Molly said moderately. "His clothes are expensive. I don't get the Old West connection."

Psyche sighed. "Wait till you see him on a horse."

The image came to Molly's mind, in living color. Once again she felt an inner shift, painful and sweet.

"You will, you know," Psyche went on. "See Keegan on a horse, I mean. Because I want Lucas to learn to ride, and there's no one better to teach him."

Molly looked into the future, saw it stretching out before her, filled with Lucas growing up through the stages of a typical boyhood. Days, weeks, months and years filled with Keegan McKettrick and his unrelenting contempt for her. She'd tried to establish a truce; he'd thrown it back in her face.

"You could marry him," Psyche said.

Molly almost choked on her wine, and she was still trying to catch her breath when Psyche went on.

"I bet the sex would be apocalyptic," she said.

Sex with Keegan McKettrick.

Don't go there.

"I'm just guessing, mind you," Psyche continued between sips of merlot. "Keegan and I never slept together. More's the pity."

Please, Molly begged silently, uncomfortable with the direction the conversation was taking, *don't ask me how it was between Thayer and me.*

"Frankly," Psyche said, "I didn't think Thayer was all that great in bed."

Molly filled her mouth with wine, practically making her cheeks bulge. In the next instant she had to jump up and dash to the sink to spit it out, because she was laughing.

Laughing.

"What?" Psyche asked.

Molly gripped the edge of the sink, her back to Psyche, her shoulders shaking.

"What?"

Molly turned to face the woman whose husband she'd—as Keegan had so inelegantly put it—*boinked.* Her cheeks were burning, and her eyes hurt.

"Good Lord," Psyche said. "Are you crying?"

"No," Molly managed. "I'm laughing."

"Why?"

"Because this conversation is bizarre, and because you're right."

"About Thayer?"

Molly nodded.

Psyche broke up. She held her sides and giggled until Florence, cinched up in a pink chenille bathrobe, stuck her head out of her room adjoining the kitchen and scowled.

"Do you two know what time it is?" she asked. She had one of those little blue breathing strips stretched across her nose, which only increased the hilarity.

"It's time to laugh," Psyche said, recovering a little.

Florence's face softened.

"And laugh and laugh and laugh," Psyche added. Now there was something frantic in her tone.

And then she began to cry.

Florence went to her, drew a chair up close and took Psyche in her arms. "There, now, baby," Florence said, holding her tightly and rocking her slightly back and forth. "You just let those tears out. God knows, you got the right."

Molly stood stricken, and over Psyche's head her gaze collided with Florence's. And what Molly saw in Florence's eyes made Keegan's disdain seem like unbridled praise.

"I guess I'll go to bed," she said, as if anybody gave a damn whether she turned in for the night or jumped off the roof.

"You do that," Florence said.

"I could help Psyche upstairs—"

"*I'll* take care of Psyche," Florence interrupted.

Molly fled, avoiding the elevator to bound up all three flights of stairs, hoping to exhaust herself.

Nothing doing.

She looked in on Lucas, left the door open between his room and her own. Took a shower. Went to her laptop and checked her email.

Major mistake. At the moment she wasn't any more popular in New York and Los Angeles than she was in Indian Rock.

She paced.

The elevator ground its way up to the top floor.

Molly peeked out into the hall, and was surprised to see Florence there, without Psyche.

"She's in a bad way," Florence said. "Hurting something awful. You've got to take her to the clinic. I done called the doctor, and he'll meet you there."

Molly didn't hesitate. She dashed back into her room, exchanged her shorty pajamas for jeans and a tank top, shoved her feet into a pair of sandals and grabbed her purse.

"You'll look after Lucas?" she asked, in the hallway again.

"Of course I will," Florence retorted. "You can take the station wagon. Psyche'll never be able to get into that big SUV of hers. You call me soon as you know anything. Anything at all."

"I will," Molly promised. She stole one last peek at Lucas and raced to the elevator, nearly shutting the door in Florence's face as the housekeeper joined her.

Still in the kitchen, Psyche was bent double and groaning.

Molly realized she didn't know where the clinic was.

Florence gave her directions, and between the two of them they managed to get Psyche into the garage, then into the car. If Florence hadn't raised the rolling door from a switch, Molly probably would have backed right through it.

"It hurts," Psyche moaned. "Oh, God—it hurts—"

Molly's heart seized. "Hang on," she said, zooming backward along the driveway and shooting out onto the road.

"What if this is it?" Psyche fretted between groans. "I didn't get to say goodbye to Lucas...."

"Don't even think like that," Molly snapped, spinning the steering wheel of the big station wagon. It was like driving a tank. "And isn't there an ambulance in this chickenshit town?"

Psyche laughed, despite what must have been almost incomprehensible pain. "It would have to come from Flagstaff," she said. And then she doubled over again and gave a keening cry that chilled Molly's blood.

When they screeched to a stop in front of the clinic, there were people with stethoscopes hanging around their necks waiting, thank God. And they had a gurney.

Two nurses and a doctor who looked older than dirt.

Molly's panic escalated.

The doctor had gray hair and a Hal Holbrook kind of face, kindly and full of character. Gently, with a strength Molly wouldn't have guessed he had, he lifted Psyche out of the station wagon and single-handedly laid her on the gurney.

"Easy now, sweetheart," he said to Psyche. "Remember when you were thirteen, and your appendix ruptured? I took care of you then, didn't I?"

Molly froze, right there on the pavement outside the entrance to the clinic, suddenly unable to move.

In fact, she was still standing in the same place minutes later when the black Jaguar zipped in, passing so close it nearly crushed her toes.

Keegan got out, wearing hastily buttoned jeans and a white T-shirt, partially tucked in. "What happened?" he demanded, as though he thought Molly might have given Psyche a dash of drain cleaner as a nightcap.

Florence must have called him, Molly thought distractedly.

But she did manage an answer. "She's—Psyche's in a lot of pain. A *lot* of pain."

"And you're standing out here because—?"

A ferocious anger rose up within Molly, along with something else, some emotion she wasn't ready to acknowledge, let alone analyze. "Well, because it's such a nice night!" she yelled, flinging her arms out from her sides.

"Oh, shut up," Keegan said, starting for the clinic's entrance.

Molly had to scramble to keep pace. "What if she dies?" she pleaded.

Keegan stopped just inside the double glass doors and looked down into her face, frowning. "Keep up. Psyche has terminal cancer. There isn't going to be a Hallmark moment."

"Do you have to be such a prick?" Molly whispered, not even trying to keep back her tears.

From somewhere in the rear of the clinic, Psyche screamed.

Keegan bolted in that direction.

Molly paced.

Her phone rang.

She ferreted it out of her purse, flipped it open and barked an anxious hello.

"You're fired," Denby said. Though he'd uttered only two words, it was obvious that he was roaring drunk.

"Denby?" Molly replied. "Screw off."

Having made that professional and dignified remark, she snapped the phone shut.

The woman behind the reception desk gave her a disapproving look.

Molly homed in on her. "Tell me something about Psyche," she said.

"She has terminal cancer," the woman replied. She was about thirty, a little overweight and distinctly homegrown.

"Thanks for the news flash," Molly said. "I just heard her scream. I want to know *what the hell* is going on back there!"

"Are you a member of the family?"

"No. I'm a—friend."

"Then I can't give you any information without Mrs. Ryan's permission."

"Keegan McKettrick is with her. How come *he* didn't need permission?"

"Because he's Keegan McKettrick."

Molly drew a deep breath, huffed it out, sucked in more air. "Look, let's start over here, okay?"

"Okay," the woman said placidly.

"There's a woman back at Psyche's place, waiting to hear what's going on. I need to tell her *something*."

"That would be Florence?"

"That would be Florence."

"I'll see what I can find out."

"That would be fabulous of you."

The woman disappeared into the bowels of the clinic.

Before she returned, a good-looking blond man rushed in, as sleep rumpled as Keegan had been.

The receptionist returned. "Doc's called for an ambulance," she told Molly and the blond man. "They're taking her to Flagstaff."

"Christ," the blond man muttered.

And then *he* disappeared, just as Keegan had.

"I suppose he's a McKettrick, too," Molly said tersely, digging for her phone again.

"You suppose right," said the receptionist.

Molly punched in Psyche's home number. Florence answered on the first ring.

"Tell me what's happening to my baby," she demanded.

"They're taking her to Flagstaff."

"Dear God," Florence said.

Keegan stormed out of the back.

The blond man followed.

Keegan banged out through the front doors, practically springing the hinges.

"Damn it," said the receptionist. "If they're going to fight, we might be here until next week patching them up."

Molly headed for the doors.

Under the outside lights she saw Keegan shove the blond man. The blond man shoved back.

"Molly?" Florence said from the cell phone.

"I'll keep you updated," Molly replied, and hung up.

The receptionist shouldered past her. "Keegan!" she yelled. "Jesse! Behave yourselves, or I swear to God, I'll call Wyatt Terp and have *both* your asses thrown in the clink!"

CHAPTER  6

JESSE, HIS SHOULDERS HEAVING with exertion under his white T-shirt, slanted a grin at Keegan and sagged back against the side of his truck in the clinic parking lot. "She'll do it, you know," he warned, cocking a thumb toward the entrance, where Carrie Johnson, the night receptionist, loomed, glowering obstinately at the pair of them, hands propped on her wide hips.

Keegan knew Jesse was right. Carrie was a woman of her word. Moreover, even though Terp was a family friend, blessed with a high tolerance for McKettrick shenanigans, the lawman would most likely be in a piss-poor mood after pulling a double shift to keep local Independence Day revelers on the straight and narrow.

"You're damn *right* I'll do it," Carrie vowed, stomping over to them. "What's the matter with you two, anyhow? We got a real sick woman in there, and you're out here carrying on like you did back in high school!"

Keegan reddened, painfully aware that Molly Shields had been standing in the background all along, watching him make a fool of himself. He was ashamed to the core—and still spoiling for a fight.

Jesse played the diplomat, lifting both hands, palms out, in a conciliatory gesture. "Look," Jesse said to Carrie, throwing the charm switch. "Keeg's just a little stressed out, that's all. We're cool, I promise."

"Your promise and a quarter will buy me a phone call," replied Carrie, who had dated Jesse while they were all seniors at Indian Rock High and therefore had good cause to doubt his word. Some of the huff went out of her, though—that was the magic of being Jesse McKettrick. When he flipped that internal switch, there was juice behind it.

"You know I was never good enough for you," Jesse told Carrie sweetly, all big eyed and earnest.

Just hang the halo on one of his horns, Keegan thought, fighting a rueful smile. He was still furious with Jesse for siding with the Texas McKettricks and not telling him about it, but at the same time he couldn't help admiring the bastard for his nerve.

"You're so full of bull-crap," Carrie answered, fondly skeptical. "And you make me come out here again, either of you, you'll regret it." With that, she turned and flounced back inside, with no idea she'd just been hoodwinked by the master.

Molly hesitated a moment, in a pool of light near the entrance to Indian Rock's only medical facility, then squared her slight shoulders and marched toward them. Stood at a little distance, looking as though she wanted to say something but couldn't quite work up the gumption to do it.

Keegan was desperate to ignore her. "Who called you?" he asked Jesse.

"Devon," Jesse answered. "After you dropped her off at Rance's tonight and laid rubber down the driveway in a big hurry to get here, she got scared. Figured you might get killed on the way to town."

Keegan remained aware of Molly, though he didn't let on, wishing she'd take the hint and make herself scarce, hoping she'd stay right where she was. "You can go home anytime now," he told Jesse.

"I'm not going anyplace until I know how Psyche is," Jesse said, leaning back against the side of his truck now, his arms folded.

"She's dying," Keegan said flatly. "Now you know."

Jesse set his jaw, McKettrick-style. Waited.

"I was just wondering—" Molly began. The sentence fell apart in the middle, though, and she just stood there under the cold stare Keegan turned on her, looking miserably determined to hold her ground.

"*What* were you 'just wondering,' Ms. Shields?" he asked.

Jesse stiffened a little, no doubt in gentlemanly objection, but he had the good sense to keep his mouth shut.

Temporarily, anyway.

Molly stiffened her spine, raised her chin a notch. "I was—I was wondering if you're planning on going to the hospital with Psyche," she said bravely. "She shouldn't be alone, and Lucas and Florence are at home, so I ought to get back…."

Jesse thrust himself away from the side of the truck and approached. After skewering Keegan with a glance, he told Molly, "You go on back to the house. Florence and the boy might need you. Keegan and I will follow the ambulance up to Flag and make sure Psyche gets settled in okay. If anything happens, I'll let you know right away."

To Keegan's private shame, Molly's eyes brimmed with tears. "Thanks," she told Jesse.

Her gratitude made Keegan want to shove Jesse again. Hard.

She gave Keegan one unreadable look, then got into Florence's old station wagon, fired up all eight cylinders and drove off.

"You're a piece of work, you know that?" Jesse rasped, watching her go.

Keegan was half-again too proud to do the same, but he wanted to. Lord, he wanted to. He wanted to fill his eyes with Molly Shields, fill his heart, fill the lonely, barren places in his soul.

Fat chance.

Keegan merely scowled. He'd have trusted Jesse with his life—right up to tonight, in the park, when Cheyenne had told him Jesse was throwing in with the Texas bunch. Voting to let McKettrickCo pass into the hands of strangers.

Jesse just couldn't let it alone. "What the hell's the matter with you, Keeg? You know better than to treat a woman the way you did Molly— It's a wonder old Angus didn't rise up out of his grave, get you by the scruff and douse you in a horse trough."

"Now you're an expert on chivalry?" Keegan snorted. "Maybe you ought to write a book." He needed to distance himself from what was happening to Psyche, if only for a few more minutes. He'd have fought Jesse in a bare-knuckle brawl, not giving a damn whether he won or got his ass kicked, just for the brief distraction, for time enough to get his emotional bearings.

An ambulance pulled into the lot, lights whirling, no siren.

"Christ," Keegan rasped.

Jesse laid a hand on his shoulder. "You've got to stay on this bull till the buzzer goes off, Keeg," he said, grave and quiet. "McKettrick-tough."

The backs of Keegan's eyes burned like acid. "McKettrick-tough," he replied gruffly.

"MARRY HER."

Keegan, who'd spent the night in a Flagstaff hospital room in a chair next to Psyche's bed, sat up straight, blinking himself awake.

Psyche was watching him, looking as white as the pillows behind her head. The oxygen machine made a rhythmic *puff-puff* sound, and various monitors beeped out their dismal chorus.

For her sake, he worked up a grin. "You know," he said, "I'd swear I heard you say—"

"Marry her," Psyche repeated.

"No," Keegan said after scrounging around for a politer word and coming up dry.

"Not even if it's my last wish?"

"Come on, Psyche. Play fair."

"Why should I? I'm dying." She reached out, caught his hand, squeezed it with surprising strength, considering her condition. Smiled. "I'm going for broke, Keeg," she went on, barely whispering. "My son's future is at stake. Lucas needs a mother as well as a father."

"I don't love her," Keegan said, figuring that ought to matter.

He should have known better. After all, he was dealing with another species: female.

"I've never seen you so stirred up." Psyche paused, gave a small, slightly wistful smile. "When it comes to Molly, you don't know whether to turn tail and run or slam her up against the wall and kiss her senseless."

Just then, Jesse reentered that dismal atmosphere, with the tumbling, end-over-end energy of a space capsule. He carried a cup of coffee in one hand, and he looked about as bad as Keegan felt—as if he'd been dragged backward through a knothole, as the old-timers used to say. "Much as I hate to interrupt such a fascinating conversation," he said easily, moving languidly to Keegan's side, "Florence and Molly are here for a visit. They brought Lucas along."

Psyche's face lit up, but the look she tossed Keegan before focusing her gaze on the doorway held a silent plea.

Molly came in first, holding Lucas in both arms. Florence followed.

"My baby," Psyche whispered, reaching for her child.

Keegan had to look away.

"Let's get you some coffee," Jesse told him, and steered him out into the corridor. Herded him along it, toward the elevators.

"I don't want any goddamned coffee," Keegan rasped.

Jesse's grin was wan. "Well," he said, "I checked, but they don't serve whiskey in this place, so you're going to have to settle."

They got into one of the elevators, rode down to the first floor in silence.

There was a franchise coffee place next to the pharmacy, and Keegan bought a cup. Jesse led the way out into a sunny courtyard, walled in stucco, with benches and trees and a fountain in the center.

Keegan gulped in the fresh air, but the peace of the place eluded him.

Jesse stood at a little distance, with one booted foot resting on the seat of a metal bench. Except for a wizened old man in a wheelchair, clutching a folded newspaper and muttering to an unseen companion, Jesse and Keegan had the space to themselves.

"Talk to me, Keeg," Jesse said after a long time.

"Okay," Keegan answered. "Cheyenne told me how you plan to vote tomorrow, at the big meeting. You're selling McKettrickCo right down the river. Thanks a heap."

"So that's what's gotten under your hide," Jesse mused, sipping his coffee.

"You might have mentioned it."

"I didn't figure the Independence Day picnic was the place for a conversation like that." Jesse took a few more sips of coffee, looking thoughtful. "At least I understand now why you tried to goad me into a fight in the clinic parking lot last night."

"What did you *think* it was about?"

Jesse raised one shoulder in a brief, idle shrug, but the look in his eyes was sharp and direct. "Psyche," he said.

Keegan sagged a little, at least inwardly. "Psyche," he repeated.

Finishing his coffee, Jesse crumpled the cup and tossed it into a trash bin. "I'm heading back to the ranch," he told Keegan. "You coming along? I can take you back to your car, but I'm sure you could hitch a ride with Molly and Florence if you want to stay a while."

"Right," Keegan scoffed quietly. "I'm sure as hell

going to do that." Devon was still at Rance's, watching the road for his car. He had to get back.

"Why do you hate her so much?" Jesse asked. "Molly, I mean."

"I told you," Keegan said.

The newspaper slid off the old man's lap, and Jesse bent to pick it up and give it back.

"You told Rance," Jesse argued. "And he told me."

"Well, then, you just answered your own question. And I *don't* hate her. I just don't trust her."

Jesse folded his arms, rocked once on the worn heels of his cowboy boots. "Hmm," he said. "Could be you've got a sore spot because of Shelley."

"Oh, good—more cowboy psychology."

"Yeah. And here's my diagnosis—you're acting like a self-righteous, judgmental asshole, Keeg. Psyche's right—you don't know whether to make love to Molly or head for the hills." He paused, grinned again. "I know the feeling," he said.

Keegan instantly bristled. Threw the rest of his coffee, along with the cup, into the trash. "This isn't like it was with you and Cheyenne," he asserted.

"I wouldn't be too sure of that if I were you," Jesse said. The old man's newspaper slipped to the ground again, and Jesse retrieved it. "Nobody *ever* pissed me off the way Cheyenne did. Imagine my surprise when what I was feeling turned out to be passion."

"Imagine," Keegan said dryly.

A nurse came out of the hospital, wheeled the old man inside.

"I'll go get the truck," Jesse said. "If you want to ride with me, you'd better go tell Psyche you're leaving."

Keegan nodded. He didn't like leaving Psyche, and he wasn't too wild about the prospect of running into Molly, either. Unfortunately, he didn't have much of a choice either way.

"No," MOLLY TOLD PSYCHE flatly, whispering so Florence, who was in the bathroom, wouldn't overhear. Lucas, snuggling against Psyche's side, was half-asleep and sucking his thumb. It made Molly's heart ache the way he clung to his adoptive mother, as though he knew she was slipping away. "I will *not* marry Keegan McKettrick."

Psyche looked down at Lucas, stroked his hair lightly with a veined hand. "I could make it a condition of the adoption," she said, instantly freezing Molly's blood.

"Even if I *wanted* the irascible Mr. McKettrick for a husband," Molly replied hastily, hearing a flush from the bathroom followed by the opening of the taps in the sink and some subsequent splashing, "which I DO NOT, in case there's any mistake, he would probably rather be electrocuted!"

"Close," Keegan said from the doorway.

Molly stared at him, suddenly speechless.

Florence emerged from the bathroom.

Keegan crossed to Psyche's bed. Leaned down to kiss her forehead, then stroked Lucas's cheek briefly with the backs of his fingers. He ignored Molly, having already delivered the salvo of the hour, and she was surprised at how much it hurt.

"I've got to head back to the Triple M," Keegan said. "Devon's there, waiting." He looked up, his gaze sweeping past Molly to connect with Florence's. "You'll call me if there's any change?"

"You go," Psyche told him, frowning a little. Apparently she hadn't liked being left on the fringes of the question any more than Molly had. "I'm not dying yet. You heard what the doctor said this morning, Keegan—I only needed a change in my medications. I'll probably be home by tomorrow."

Molly saw the flicker of pain in Keegan's strong face and registered it somewhere down deep inside her. She had a crazy need to lay a hand on his cheek, or touch his shoulder.

Anything to comfort him.

Anything to assuage the impending loss of the woman he clearly loved.

Molly sighed and turned away from the scene to stand looking out the window, unseeing and shaken.

She'd come to Arizona at Psyche's request, not to make amends for her affair with Thayer—nothing so noble as that. No, she'd made the trip simply because she'd hoped so desperately for even a glimpse of Lucas. She'd had no idea the woman was gravely ill, or that she would be willing to give back the precious little boy she'd adopted just eighteen short months before.

Molly wanted Lucas, wanted to raise him as her son.

But why did Psyche have to die? Why?

She rested her head against the glass pane of that hospital window and grieved a deep and grinding, painful grief for a woman she barely knew.

A hand came to rest on her shoulder, and Molly stiffened, thinking it was Keegan's. She turned, ready to pin his ears back, at least verbally, and was paradoxically disappointed to find Florence standing there instead.

"Will you take Lucas downstairs?" she asked quietly, kinder in her weariness and her resignation. "Psyche's worn to a frazzle. She needs to rest."

Molly looked around, realized that Keegan had gone. She should have been relieved; instead, she felt as though he'd taken something vital from the room, something that might have sustained three sad women and a little boy about to lose his mother.

She nodded.

Took Lucas gently from Psyche's arms.

He fussed a little, then settled against Molly with a sigh that twisted her heart. He was so young. Could he be aware, somehow, that a hole was about to open in the very fabric of his life?

"Mama," he said.

Molly nodded to Psyche, turned and hurried out of the room, everything within her collapsing.

Somehow she kept going—stepped into the elevator,

pressed the button for the first floor. She'd glimpsed a courtyard earlier, when she and Florence entered the hospital with Lucas, a place with flowers and a fountain. An oasis, a sanctuary.

She would wait there, she decided, until Florence returned.

Find a way to pull herself together.

She'd barely taken a seat on a shady bench and rocked Lucas to sleep when Keegan intruded. He had clearly not expected to find her there—his expression told her that—and his obvious discomfort was some compensation for the fresh shock he'd given her by showing up unexpectedly.

"I was looking for Jesse," he said.

"Well," Molly said pointedly, "he's not here."

If he'd had any decency at all, Keegan would have left her alone then. Been satisfied that he'd given her a start, rattled her a little.

But, no. He wanted blood.

"I'll be signing the papers tomorrow," he said, watching her for a reaction. Maybe he thought she was going to jump up and tear her hair because some dastardly plot had been foiled.

What had happened to this man to make him so suspicious? It was more than just seeing her with Thayer that one time—it had to be.

"If I had a handlebar mustache," she replied tartly, "I'd twirl one tip, like a villain in a cartoon."

He gave her another jolt, worse than any that had gone before.

He actually smiled.

Plates shifted beneath the surface of the earth. Fissures opened up, spewing steam and a disturbing kind of fire.

"Psyche's still on that marriage kick," he said.

Now it was Molly's turn to smile. "Maybe it's the drugs," she replied.

He chuckled, and the sound was wickedly pleasant— sexy and rumbling. Suddenly Molly could imagine herself naked in bed with this man, skin sleek and sweaty with passion, her back arched to welcome him into her body.

Yikes, she thought. What was going on with her libido? This was the second time it had kicked into overdrive just because Keegan was in close proximity.

She was so busy dealing with the back-flash of *that* invisible bomb that she missed what he said next. Just in case it had been something requiring immediate and stinging retaliation, she said, "Sorry. I didn't catch that."

"I said he looks like you." He nodded to indicate Lucas.

Molly was oddly stricken by the remark; it lodged in her heart like a dart with the tip blunted, and she held her son a little closer. "Thanks. I think. Don't you have somewhere you have to be?"

"I'm waiting for Jesse. I figure he either left without me or parked the truck on the other side of town when he went to pick up breakfast-in-a-bag early this morning."

"You were here all night." Molly couldn't figure out exactly *how* she felt about that. Relieved, certainly, for Psyche's sake. Moved by the uncommon gallantry of such an act. And maybe a little envious, too, because she didn't think there was one person in her life who would do that for her. Sleep upright in a hospital chair just to make sure she was all right.

Once, perhaps, her dad would have. Now that he was almost certainly drinking again, probably not.

Keegan nodded. "All night," he confirmed.

"Jesse stayed, too?"

"Jesse, too," Keegan said.

A horn honked somewhere nearby. It made an ah-uggah sound, and normally she would have been amused by the unabashed red-neckism of that.

"Jesse?" Molly asked.

"Jesse," Keegan said.

He turned to go, then turned back.

"Molly?"

"What?"

"Maybe you were right before. About us having to learn to get along—because of Lucas."

She got that now-familiar prickly feeling behind her eyes, and her throat cinched itself up tight. "Okay," she croaked.

The horn sounded again, more insistently this time. *Ah-uuuuuugah!*

"You'd better go," Molly said.

Keegan nodded, and left the courtyard. A truck door slammed.

Molly's cell phone rang from sixteen fathoms down in her purse. The sound woke Lucas from his doze, and he struggled to get off her lap so he could toddle over and pull the heads off several petunias nodding in a big stone planter.

By the time she'd corralled him the phone had stopped ringing, but she got it out anyway to check the caller ID panel. If it was Denby Godridge, or some other maniac from her old life of endless glamour and excitement, they'd have to wait.

But the number was her dad's.

Molly hesitated. It was early, so maybe he wasn't drunk yet.

He could also be in the backseat of a police car or on his way to a hospital, though. She gave him time to leave a message on her voice mail, then listened.

"Hey, sweetheart," he said. "It's Dad." He sounded sober, which was encouraging. "Call me back, okay? I've been waiting to hear how things are going in Arizona."

I've been waiting to hear how things are going in Arizona.

She'd called him twice since she'd arrived. Told him about Lucas and about Psyche. Said she'd be back in L.A. to get some of her stuff soon, but she was planning to stay in Indian Rock indefinitely.

As in, until Lucas went to college.

Obviously her father not only didn't remember

what she'd said, but didn't remember that she'd called at all.

She was used to it, but it still struck her in the stomach like a punch.

She hit the digit to speed-dial his landline. He'd lost their little house in Los Feliz long ago—now he lived in a condo in Santa Monica. Molly had bought it for him with her first big commission, and her name was still on the deed.

"Molly?" he said, instead of "hello." She could just see him squinting at her number on his phone before he answered. He needed glasses, but he was too vain to wear them.

"Hi, Dad. You been going to your AA meetings?"

He took instant offense. "Do I sound drunk to you?"

"No," she replied, keeping an eye on Lucas as he sat on the stone floor of the courtyard at her feet, playing with the keys to her classic Thunderbird convertible. She missed that car suddenly. Missed her dad, troublesome as he was.

So she decided not to mention her previous calls.

"Where have you been?" he asked. "I was worried when I didn't hear from you."

Molly bit her lower lip. "Just busy," she said.

"Did you do anything for the Fourth?"

"I went to a picnic," Molly said. "There were fireworks." She flashed back, for an instant, to the night before, when she and Keegan had stood watching color splash the sky.

"When are you coming home?"

"I'm not, Dad. Not to stay, anyway." Quickly, keeping her voice low, she told him—again—about Psyche's illness, about Lucas, about her promise to stay in Indian Rock for the duration.

"That's stupid," he said abruptly. "You have a business here in California. You have a house. You have a—"

"Father," Molly finished for him when he suddenly got tongue-tied.

"I know all that, Dad, believe me. But I've read the draft of the agreement Psyche wants, and it's ironclad. If I don't promise to stay here and raise Lucas in the family home, I don't get to adopt him."

"The woman is going to die," Luke Shields said. "She won't know the difference once she's gone. You and the kid can hop a plane then, and come home."

Molly closed her eyes for a moment. Who was this man who took over her father's body during his cyclical lapses from sobriety? The *real* Luke Shields was honest, a straight shooter. He cared about other people, not just himself. "I can't do that, Dad. Make a promise and then break it. I've been given a second chance with Lucas—your *grandson*—and I'm not about to blow it."

"What about me? Do you expect me to move to Indigo Rock, or whatever it is?"

A shiver went through Molly. She loved her dad, but she didn't want him around Lucas if he was going to drink. "Indian Rock," she said carefully, injecting a bright note into her voice. "You wouldn't like it. It's small and it's a long way from everything." *Like your favorite watering holes.* "But not to worry. Lucas and I can visit, once he's had some time to adjust—"

"What am I supposed to do in the meantime?"

"Dad, this isn't about you. It's about Lucas."

"No, it isn't," her dad argued. "It's about you. You mess around with a married man, you get pregnant, you *finally* do the sensible thing and give the kid up. Then, just because the wronged wife holds up a hoop, you jump through it!"

"Dad," Molly said, struggling to keep what little patience Keegan McKettrick hadn't already drained out of her. "Psyche is *dying.*"

"Is that your problem?"

A tear slipped down Molly's cheek, and she dashed it away with the back of one hand. Lucas got to his feet and jingled the car keys under her nose, giggling.

"Ride," he said. "Ride!"

It was one of the few words she'd heard him say. She smiled at her baby. "Ride," she repeated.

"What?" her dad snapped.

"I was talking to Lucas," Molly explained gently.

Luke cleared his throat. It was both a good sign and a bad one. He was going to let the other subject go, but he had another one ready to spring on her. "Listen, honey, I'm a little short of cash—you know how it is…."

She knew how it was, all right. Only too well. A retired homicide cop, Luke drew a decent, if unspectacular, pension. He had no mortgage, his living expenses were minimal and he was always strapped.

"We talked about this," she said. "You, me and your AA sponsor—remember? When I give you money, it's called enabling."

"Look, Molly, don't give me that twelve-step bullshit right now, all right? My car broke down and—"

She sighed. "You're drinking again."

"No," he replied vehemently. "You know what it's like to live in L.A. without a car. It's impossible."

It *was* impossible. And suppose he was telling the truth?

"Fax the repair bills to Joanie, at my office," Molly said, defeated. "If your story checks out, she'll cut you a check."

"Sweetheart, this jitney is way past the repair stage. I've got my eye on a truck—"

"Okay, fax a copy of your driver's license," Molly said. "Joanie will call the DMV. If it hasn't been suspended—" she bit her lip to keep from adding "again," "—we'll get you back on wheels."

"What are you, some kind of cop or something?" Luke snapped.

"No, Dad," Molly said gently. "*You're* a cop."

He slammed the receiver down so hard that she winced.

She closed the phone, dropped it into her purse

and, sensing something, turned around. Florence was standing at the entrance to the courtyard, looking at her in curious concern.

Molly managed an uncertain smile. "Is Psyche ready to see Lucas again?" she asked.

Florence shook her head, still pensive. "She's asleep. And I'll be darned if she wasn't right about coming home tomorrow—the doctor stood right there and said there wasn't much they could do for her here. I've got a number right here, to call one of those rental places and get a hospital bed delivered to the house."

"They're discharging her?" Molly couldn't believe it.

Suddenly Florence's eyes glistened, awash in tears. "She wants to die at home," she said. "I'm to ask the delivery people to put the bed on that glassed-in porch, back of the kitchen, so she can see the garden."

"Oh, Florence," Molly said, standing.

Florence sank onto another bench nearby and put her arms out for Lucas. He bustled to her, chortling and jingling Molly's keys. "I'll stay with the baby," the older woman said wearily. "It would be a favor to me if you'd go get the car."

Molly nodded, lingering because she sensed that Florence wanted to say something more. Something important.

"Are you all right?" she asked.

Florence wouldn't look at her. "I'll be just fine

unless you try to break your promise to Psyche and take that boy away to California. I heard what you said on the phone, about going for a visit after she's gone."

Molly took a moment to absorb the fact that Florence had heard all or part of her conversation with her dad. Sifted back through it for anything else the woman might have misconstrued.

"I'll raise Lucas in Indian Rock, Florence," she finally said.

"See that you do," Florence replied. "I'll be gone to my sister's place in Seattle once poor Psyche is dead and buried, but Keegan McKettrick will be around. You can bet on that. You try to pull a fast one, go back on your word, and he'll nail you before you get to the city limits."

A new sadness settled over Molly like a damp fog and sank into the marrow of her bones. For a little while she'd actually hoped she and Florence might establish some kind of working truce, even if they couldn't be friends.

Now she knew she was still the outsider.

And that wasn't going to change.

"Wait here," she said quietly. "I'll go get the car."

CHAPTER 7

THE DONKEY STOOD contentedly in a barn stall built for an animal three times his size, happily munching alfalfa pellets. Spud appeared to like the Triple M, at least so far.

Devon, perched on a cross board of the stall door with Keegan standing beside her, sighed.

"He sure poops a lot," she said.

Keegan, who'd showered, shaved and donned chinos and a blue sport shirt after picking up his daughter at Rance's, chuckled at the observation.

"Yeah," he agreed. "Better get the pitchfork and the wheelbarrow."

"You look real tired, Dad," Devon told him solemnly, studying his face. "I wouldn't mind if you went inside and crashed for a while."

Keegan was, if anything, too tired to sleep. And maybe too cowardly. Once, dozing in his chair beside Psyche's hospital bed the night before, he'd been flung upward, soaked in a cold, clammy sweat and breathless with alarm, from the dregs of a dream he hadn't had for years.

In it, he'd seen a plane spiraling toward the ground, nose-first. Known his parents were aboard. He'd heard the roar of the explosion, seen the fireball bulge against an otherwise placid blue sky, felt the scorching heat blistering his skin. He'd tried to get through, even though he knew it was hopeless—he couldn't save his mom and dad—but the blaze had turned solid as a wall.

"Dad?" Devon said.

He smiled. "Your mom will be here to pick you up in a few hours," he said. "I can sleep later."

Devon's shoulders slumped a little under her yellow T-shirt. "I wish I could stay," she told him. "Live here all the time. I could do chores, like Rianna and Maeve. It would be my job to feed Spud and shovel out his stall."

Keegan laid a hand on Devon's nape, squeezed slightly. Sunday afternoons were bittersweet when she spent the weekend. He enjoyed every minute with her, and yet he was conscious all the while that their time together was slipping away. It bothered him, too, that she apparently thought she had to earn her keep.

"Sorry about being gone so much this time," he said. There was a lot more he wanted, needed, to say, but he couldn't seem to find the right words.

She jumped down off the stall door and stood

close, resting her head against his side. "You couldn't help it," she told him. "Your friend is sick."

Before Keegan could answer, he heard a car drive up outside, then the slamming of a door.

He frowned, checked his watch.

Devon stiffened, clung a little more tightly. "It's too early for Mom to be here," she protested.

"It could be somebody else," Keegan reasoned, but he knew, as Devon clearly did, that when they stepped out the barn door Shelley's Lexus would be parked in the driveway. The purr of the engine was distinctive.

"Let's pretend we're not here," Devon whispered. "Maybe she'll go away."

Keegan ruffled his daughter's hair, gently disengaged from her. "No such luck, kid," he said. And he went outside.

For a moment the sunlight dazzled him, but Shelley came into focus quickly enough, picking her way across the barnyard in pointy heels. Her hair was pinned up, and she wore a tailored gray pantsuit—not her usual uniform for a visit to the Triple M, brief though her stays always were.

Seeing him, she smiled winningly.

He wondered, as he invariably did during these encounters, what he'd ever seen in her. How had he overlooked the callousness, the calculation, the cold, relentlessly self-serving dynamics that powered her? Sex would have been an easy excuse—but the truth was, that didn't wash, either.

The sex hadn't been that good with Shelley.

"You're early," Keegan accused, aware of Devon standing just behind him.

Shelley beamed apologetically. Spread her hands. What the hell was she up to?

Keegan waited.

Shelley tilted to one side, tracking Devon, who was trying to hide, like a heat-seeking missile. "Go say hello to Rory, sweetheart," Shelley said. "I need to talk to your dad for a few minutes."

"I don't want to talk to Rory," Devon said.

"It's okay," Keegan told her. Rory was at the wheel of the Lexus, a slouching shadow, no doubt hoping to go unnoticed.

Reluctantly Devon crossed the grassy expanse between the barn and the Lexus. The window on the driver's side whirred down.

Shelley looked back, watching the exchange for a moment, then turned to Keegan again. The high-beam smile went on like a floodlight.

Keegan folded his arms.

Shelley blushed prettily. "Rory surprised me with tickets to Paris," she said. "For my birthday."

"I bet that *was* a surprise," Keegan drawled.

Shelley let the gibe pass. "First class," she said. "His sister works for one of those online travel agencies."

"And there's always my American Express card for pesky little incidentals like food and hotel rooms," Keegan said evenly, but his heart, jolted by a sudden rush of adrenaline, beat a little faster, thrumming in his ears.

"Well, it *is* my birthday," Shelley said. "Not that I would have expected you to remember."

"We've already discussed this, Shelley," he reminded her. "You're not taking Devon out of the country."

Shelley lowered her voice to an earnest, almost desperate whisper after glancing back at Devon again. "That's sort of what I wanted to talk to you about. Rory could only get two tickets...."

There it was, the reason for the adrenaline rush.

She was going to ask if Devon could stay with him. Keegan was exultant, but he didn't let it show, and he didn't let Shelley off the hook, either.

"I was hoping Devon could stay here until we get back," Shelley said. "With you."

"Which will be when?" Keegan asked.

"I—I'm not sure," Shelley said. He knew she wanted to take his head off, but she couldn't afford to be snippy. He loved that.

"You're not sure."

"The tickets are open-ended. Rory and I were going to look at apartments while we're over there, and Devon is out of school for the summer, so—"

"Okay," Keegan said.

"Okay?" The stadium-light smile faltered a little, and he saw her temper, forcibly restrained, roiling in her eyes. About to bust loose. "What does that mean, exactly?"

"Devon can stay."

The real Shelley came through. She narrowed her eyes to slits and set her hands on her hips. "You enjoyed that, didn't you? Making me squirm?"

"Immensely," Keegan replied.

"Bastard," Shelley said.

He smiled. "Now, there's an opinion I can value."

"You still have to pay child support."

"No problem," Keegan said.

"And you'd better not cancel my credit cards as soon as I drive out of here, either."

"I wouldn't do a thing like that."

"Like hell you wouldn't. I'm doing you a *favor,* Keegan, by letting Devon stay here. I could have taken her to my mother's, you know."

"Your mother lives in Boise. My guess is the plane to Paris leaves Phoenix around eight o'clock tonight. You don't have *time* to dump Devon on your mom's doorstep."

Shelley's face reddened with frustration. "Why can't you just let this be easy?" she demanded in a furious whisper.

Keegan let his glance slide to Rory, then back to Shelley again. "You're easy enough for both of us," he said. "The word ought to be tattooed on your ass."

"I don't have to stand here and listen to this, Keegan!"

"No," he said. "You don't. You can get in the car, head for Phoenix and jet off to the City of Light with lover boy."

"And I'm *not* easy," Shelley sputtered, a beat or two behind, just like always. "Rory and I are *in love*—not that you'd ever understand such a concept."

Keegan laid a hand to his heart. "It's a beautiful thing to see," he said.

"*Screw* you, Keegan!"

"Oh, you already did that—with a lot of help from your lawyers."

Rory must have mentioned the trip to Paris to Devon, and broken the news that she wasn't invited, because she started jumping up and down. Muscleman got out of the car, taking care not to look in Keegan's direction, and opened the trunk. Hauled out a couple of small suitcases and plunked them on the ground.

Shelley, meanwhile, glared at Keegan once more, then turned and minced her way back toward Devon.

Keegan watched as mother and daughter embraced.

Rory was already back in the car, with the engine running.

Keegan enjoyed a brief fantasy in which he walked over, dragged Rory from behind the wheel and beat the crap out of him on the spot. He wouldn't actually do it, of course, because Devon was there, because it wasn't the McKettrick way and because deep down he was grateful to the meathead for carrying his job as a personal trainer to a whole new level.

The day he'd walked in on Rory and Shelley, caught them enjoying a nooner in the exercise studio at the back of the house in Flag, he'd expected to feel rage.

Instead, he'd been jubilant. Dizzy with relief.

Shelley gave Devon one last distracted hug, then got into the Lexus. She and Rory sped away, leaving the child gazing happily after them in a spinning plume of dust.

Keegan walked toward her, grinning. Took a suitcase handle in each hand and started for the house.

Devon scampered after him, fairly dancing with glee. "Can I go across the creek and tell Rianna and Maeve I get to stay?" she prattled. "Can we have hot dogs for supper? If I feed Spud and clean out his stall every day, will you raise my allowance?"

Keegan laughed. "Yes to the hot dogs and the raise. As for crossing the creek, you'd better call first."

Inside the ranch house kitchen, Devon bolted for the phone.

Keegan watched her, suddenly so bone tired he could barely keep his eyes open, but happier than he would have believed he could be, too. Psyche was still dying. McKettrickCo was still going down the tubes. But Devon was staying, at least for a while. Good things were still possible.

Devon chattered into the phone for a minute or so, then listened, then held the receiver out to Keegan.

"Hey," Emma said when he took it and said the obligatory hello.

"Hey," he replied.

"Good news on the kid front," Emma remarked.

"The best," Keegan answered.

"Cheyenne tells me you and Jesse were at the hospital all night, up in Flag, standing guard over Psyche Ryan."

Keegan yawned. "Yeah," he said.

"Big meeting tomorrow, too," Emma said. "At McKettrickCo."

The reminder nettled Keegan, but it wasn't Emma's fault and he didn't take it out on her. "Is there a point to this conversation?" he asked warmly.

She laughed. "Yes. And here it is—Rance and I will keep Devon overnight. You'd better get some sleep."

"Emma?"

"What?"

"You are an angel."

She laughed again. "Tell that to Rance, will you? We've been arguing about what color to paint the kitchen for three days, and I think he's about ready to drown me in the creek."

"I'll tell him," Keegan promised.

"Here's your chance," Emma said. "He's crossing the bridge to your place even as we speak."

Devon, who had vanished up the rear staircase when Keegan took the phone, thundered back down with the pink bear, a pair of pajamas and her tooth-brush.

Keegan said goodbye to Emma and hung up.

Devon dashed to the back door. "He's here!" she shouted. "And he's on a *horse!*"

Keegan followed his daughter outside. Sure enough, there was Rance, in old-time McKettrick mode, mounted on one of his growing collection of geldings. This one was black, with three white stockings.

Seeing Keegan, Rance tugged at the brim of his hat. Then he slipped one foot out of the stirrup, so Devon could put her own there, leaned down and hoisted her up behind him, pink bear, pajamas and all.

Keegan should have left well enough alone, but he couldn't. "You going to vote with Jesse tomorrow?" he asked Rance.

Rance adjusted his hat, shifted in the saddle. Devon wrapped both arms around his middle, bouncing a little because she wanted to go.

"I'm going to vote the way I damn well please," Rance answered easily. "Get some shut-eye, because it could turn out to be one hell of a row, with all those McKettricks crammed into one room."

With that, he started to rein the horse around, toward home.

"Rance?" Keegan said.

He looked back. "What?"

"Let Emma paint the kitchen whatever color she wants."

Rance chuckled. Shook his head. "A pink kitchen? I'd have to shoot myself."

Keegan reconsidered. "Pink, huh?"

"Pink," Rance confirmed. "The woman's obsessed with it."

"A man has to draw the line somewhere," Keegan decided.

Rance nodded. "And that line," he drawled, "lies just this side of pink."

Devon waved. For a kid who'd wanted so much to stay, she was sure in a hurry to leave.

Keegan waved back. "Be good," he told his daughter, and something about the way he spoke made Rance take a closer look at him.

"I'm all right," Keegan insisted.

Rance was a long time looking away. Finally, though, he and Devon were headed for the bridge spanning the creek. On the far side the reflected light of the setting sun glowed crimson on the windows.

A lump rose in Keegan's throat.

Devon's voice flowed back to him, riding softly on the breeze. "Go fast, Uncle Rance!" she pleaded.

Rance gave a yee-haw and heeled the horse into a trot.

Keegan waited until they'd cleared the bridge before going inside the house. Stood just over the threshold, more aware of the history of the place than usual, soaking it in through his pores and the raw-edged holes in his heart.

It gave him solace to know old Angus McKettrick had built the heart of that house with his own hands. He'd raised his three younger sons and a daughter, too, right here in these rooms.

They'd taken meals cooked on the old wood-burning stove over in the far corner of the room. These days, it was used only to provide heat and a pleasant crackle on cold winter mornings, though it was still in good working order. Keegan's once-a-week cleaning service kept it dusted off, and the chrome gleamed.

As a kid, he'd sometimes heard the stove lids rattle in the middle of the night when he knew nobody was downstairs. Heard the clink of horseshoes striking a metal stake in the side yard, too. His dad had said it was Angus and the boys out there, trying to best each other at the game.

"You'll scare him," his mother had protested.

But Keegan had never been afraid. He'd liked the idea of sharing the sturdy old house with those who'd worked and fought to make sure it stayed in the family.

The memories just kept coming, even after Keegan went to the refrigerator in search of something remotely edible. His grocery-shopping skills needed work, and he seldom bothered.

Now, alone in the house, he gave himself up to remembering. On summer days his mother, along with Rance's and Jesse's, had put up preserves in this kitchen—peaches and pears from the orchard a little way down the creek, now neglected and overgrown. He and Jesse and Rance, and sometimes Meg, had run in and out constantly, slamming the screen door off the side porch.

"Stop slamming that door!" one of the mothers would yell.

Keegan straightened, a beer in one hand, and closed the fridge. What he wouldn't have given, right then, to hear that door slam again.

Nobody used the side porch anymore. Nobody put fruit up in gleaming jars anymore, either. Women didn't gather in the kitchen, laughing and talking and always ready to make room in their hearts for one more noisy, sunburned, skinned-kneed, mosquito-bitten kid.

He popped the top on the beer and took a guzzle.

Damn, he thought. He was getting sentimental in his old age.

Behind him one of the stove lids rattled.

Keegan almost choked on a mouthful of beer. Spun around to look.

Of course there was no one there. Most likely the house was settling, that was all, or there'd been an earth tremor, the kind that usually went unnoticed.

The light rap at the kitchen door shook him up all over again.

He hoped he didn't look too spooked when he turned and saw Rance coming in.

"Got any more beer?" Rance asked mildly, hanging his hat on a peg next to the door, the way generations of McKettrick men had done before him.

Keegan tightened inside. First Jesse, riding herd on him last night when he'd gone chasing off to town to the clinic because of Psyche, and now Rance, riding back across the creek and pretending it was a casual visit.

"Am I on the watch list or something?" Keegan asked, none too politely.

Rance went to the fridge, helped himself to a brew and pulled the tab. Took a drink before answering. "Hell," he said, "you're not half interesting enough for that."

"Then what are you doing here?"

"I just thought I'd come over and try to get under your hide a little." He paused for another gulp. "Looks like I succeeded, too."

Keegan went to the long table, swung a leg over one of the benches lining it on both sides and sat. "Mission accomplished," he said. "You can leave now."

Rance hauled back the chair that had been Angus's, back in those thrilling days of yesteryear, turned it around and sat astraddle it, Western-style. "I'll go when I'm damn good and ready," he replied—when he was damn good and ready.

"Devon'll be staying on for a while," Keegan said.

Rance nodded. "I know." His shirt pocket rang then. So much for the cowboy image. He grimaced and answered with a gruff hello, watching Keegan while he listened to whoever was on the other end.

Keegan drank more beer and waited.

"Yeah," Rance said. "He's right here."

More listening.

"Looks like hell, if you want the truth." Rance grinned at Keegan's scowl. "My guess is he's working himself right up to a three-beer binge."

Keegan snorted. "If you're going to talk about me," he said, "at least put that damn thing on speaker so I can defend myself."

Rance shrugged, thumbed the appropriate button and set his cell phone on the table. "You're talking to the whole room now," he told the caller.

"I always appreciate an audience," Jesse said.

"You two can stop babysitting me anytime now," Keegan grumbled.

Rance interlaced his fingers on the scarred old tabletop and watched Keegan solemnly. "You'd better get down here," he told Jesse. "We need to talk about the vote. In person."

"Give me twenty minutes," Jesse said. "I assume you're at the main ranch house?"

"Look," Keegan growled, "there's no point—"

"Yep," Rance answered, right over the top of Keegan.

Jesse hung up.

Keegan set his elbows on the table, splayed the fingers of both hands and jammed them into his hair.

Rance got up, went back to the fridge, returned with two more beers.

"Don't think I don't know what's going on here," Keegan said, glaring at him. "You and Jesse plan on telling me the top ten reasons for dumping McKettrickCo onto the stock market—and I don't want to hear it."

Rance straddled the chair again. "How's Psyche?" he asked.

"Still dying," Keegan said, and almost strangled on the words, same as he had earlier on the beer when he'd thought he heard the stove lid clinking.

Rance's expression didn't change. "Are they managing the pain?"

"She's hurting worse than she lets on," Keegan said.

"So are you," Rance observed.

"She doesn't deserve this."

"Nobody does, Keeg."

"Do me a favor, will you, Rance? Get Jesse on the horn and tell him not to come. I'm not up to this."

"He's left his place by now, and you know he doesn't carry a cell phone. We need to settle a few things, Keeg, and we need to do it before that meeting tomorrow."

"What's there to settle? Jesse's made up his mind, and so have you. I'm outnumbered. I'll get over it."

"Will you?"

"Yeah."

Rance left his chair again, went back to the fridge

even though he hadn't finished his beer. He rummaged around, came up with a carton of eggs, a block of cheese and a few limp salad onions.

"Make yourself at home," Keegan said with irony.

Rance chuckled, setting the grub on the counter to wash his hands at the sink. "Damn," he remarked, "you're about as companionable as an old bear with a stick up its ass."

"What are you doing?"

"Making an omelet," Rance answered, getting out a well-seasoned cast-iron skillet, another holdover from days of old, setting it on a stove burner and lobbing in a chunk of butter. Turning up the heat. "Unlike some people around here, I work every day, and I'm hungry."

Keegan gave up. Waited in stubborn silence while Rance did his cooking thing. Didn't even trouble himself to argue the obvious—that *he* worked every day, too. When Devon wasn't around, he lived at McKettrickCo.

Jesse showed up just in time to load up a plate and take a place at the table directly opposite Keegan. He salted the omelet and dug in, just as if he'd actually been invited to supper.

"That company's going to kill you, Keeg," he said. "When was the last time you rode a horse, anyway?"

Keegan bristled, but he was hungry, too, and it turned out that Rance wasn't half-bad as a cook.

He filled his mouth with the egg concoction so he wouldn't have to answer right away.

"Maybe he needs the money," Rance said to Jesse.

"Yeah," Jesse agreed. "It's tough when you're down to your last twenty or thirty million."

"Look at it this way, Keeg." Rance grinned. "Your net worth will probably double once McKettrickCo goes public. You can pay Shelley twice the alimony she's getting now. She'll be so busy shopping, it'll be as if she didn't exist."

Keegan leaned in, lowered his voice as though to breathe some great secret. "This isn't making me feel better."

"Right now," Jesse observed, "there isn't much that could do that."

"Losing McKettrickCo sure as hell isn't going to help," Keegan snapped.

Jesse sighed. Glanced at Rance.

Something silent passed between them, something Keegan wasn't privy to, and that rankled him.

"Okay," Rance said decisively.

"Okay, what?" Keegan asked.

"Okay, we'll vote with you," Jesse said.

"Against our better judgment," Rance added.

Jesse nodded thoughtfully. "And with no guarantee that we'll win."

Keegan looked from one man to the other. "You're doing this because…?"

"Because we're going soft," Rance lamented.

"Speak for yourself," Jesse told him. Then he fixed

his gaze on Keegan. "Trouble with you is," he went on, "you spend way too much time in your head. It isn't healthy."

Keegan heaved a great sigh. "Thanks," he said, and realized he wasn't thanking Rance and Jesse so much for promising to vote his way regarding McKettrickCo's fate, but for standing with him.

They stayed long enough to finish off Rance's monster omelet, set their plates and silverware in the sink and advise Keegan to get some sleep.

He was glad to comply.

CHAPTER 8

MOLLY SAT UP IN BED, blinking. Two floors below, somebody was laying on the doorbell.

Beside her, Lucas stirred, opened his eyes, looked at her in wonder. He'd been fitful in the night, she remembered, and she'd changed his diaper, settled him in with her.

She groped for the small clock on her night table, peered at the digits.

Eight thirty-five.

Not good. She was usually up by six at the latest. Today she felt rummy and wished she could go right on sleeping.

The doorbell chimed again, bonging loudly through its Westminster bit.

"We slept in, buddy," Molly told Lucas, sitting up and hastily reaching for her robe. "We slept *way* in."

Lucas giggled. Headed on all fours for the edge

of the mattress, heedless, like all small children, of the law of gravity.

Molly grabbed him before he could tumble off the side—he was soaked—and nuzzled his neck.

Whoever was downstairs could wait.

But where was Florence?

Suddenly alarmed, Molly took a tighter hold on Lucas, detoured through the nursery to snatch a fresh diaper from the box and made for the elevator.

When they got to the first floor she hurried to the front door.

A deliveryman stood on the porch, about to turn away. "We got a hospital bed on the truck," he said when Molly peered at him through the screen.

"I'll show you where to put it," Molly said, balancing Lucas on her hip, now moist from the leakage.

The man nodded.

Thoughts of rape and pillage went through Molly's mind—she was secretly addicted to TV shows like *Forensic Files* and *Body of Evidence*—and she peered past him, to make sure there really *was* a delivery truck at the curb. Psychotic killers used many ruses.

There was a truck, and it said, "Acme Hospital Supply" on the side in big letters. Despite the grave reality of the situation, she smiled, inwardly and very slightly, wondering if Wile E. Coyote and the Road Runner were around somewhere.

Molly raised the hook on the screen door. "Follow me," she said in a businesslike tone.

Once she'd blazed a path to the back of the house, where Psyche wanted to spend her last days with a view of the garden, the deliveryman left, leaving his clipboard behind on the little table where Psyche and Keegan had lunched just a few days before.

The white peonies Keegan had sent Psyche were still there, like little sentinels keeping a lonely vigil, mildly bedraggled but still bravely holding up their heads.

Molly swallowed hard, changed Lucas on the chaise longue at the other end of the glassed-in porch and carried him back to the kitchen, depositing the saturated diaper in the trash.

Florence was there, wearing her familiar chenille bathrobe. "I don't know what's wrong with me today," she lamented. "I'm usually up at the crack of dawn, but last night I slept like a dead woman." She flinched at her own choice of words.

Molly didn't make a comment. Instead, she scanned the room, found one of Lucas's several playpens and put him inside it, handing him a toy. She washed her hands at the sink, watching out of the corner of her eye as Florence fumbled with the coffeepot.

"I'd better call the hospital," Florence said. "Make sure there's an ambulance to bring Psyche back home."

The deliveryman returned with a partner, the two

of them making a resounding clatter as they rolled the rented hospital bed over priceless hardwood floors.

Lucas stood up in his playpen, watching with wide, curious eyes.

"There's a crazy guy outside," one of the deliverymen said in passing.

Molly frowned. "What?"

"An old dude. Says he's here to fire his agent. Like he's some Hollywood actor or something."

"Ask me," commented the second man, "he's three sheets to the wind."

"Damn," Molly muttered.

"I'll call Wyatt," Florence said, already reaching for the phone.

"He's harmless," Molly said. "Just keep an eye on Lucas. I'll deal with the crazy dude."

Sure enough, Denby Godridge stood on the front porch, dramatically clad in black trousers and a matching turtleneck sweater. His white hair was in wild disarray, his paunch had expanded since the last time Molly had seen him and his big nose was even redder and more purple veined than usual.

"I came to fire you," he said with ominous portent.

"Get in here before the neighbors see you," Molly muttered.

Denby's bloodshot eyes widened. "You're *fired*."

"Yes," Molly said, taking him by the arm and dragging him in off the porch. "I get it, Denby. I'm eighty-sixed. Out of here. Pink-slipped. Toast. History. Do you have anything to add?"

Denby looked baffled. Then he drew his drunken self up and said importantly, "No."

"Please tell me you didn't drive here in your condition."

"My *condition?*"

"You're obviously blotto, Denby. Schnockered—"

"Spare me the colloquial adjectives, if you don't mind," Denby said with lofty disdain, chest swelling in indignation. "I *did* win a Pulitzer Prize, you know."

"Then *act* like it," Molly whispered. "Have a little class."

Denby's tape skipped, not an unusual occurrence of late. "It just so happens that I came to this backwater burg in a private jet, and there was a *limo* waiting," he imparted. "As befits my station in life."

Molly heaved a sigh of relief. At least Denby was no threat to people on the road.

The deliverymen reappeared, gave Denby a wide berth as they made for the door. Evidently Florence had done clipboard duty and signed for the bed.

"Follow me," Molly told Denby sternly.

She led the way to the kitchen.

Florence stared at Denby.

"Haven't you ever seen a Pulitzer Prize winner before?" Denby snapped.

"Mind your manners," Molly said to him, "or I'll rip your lips off."

"Who *is* this nut?" Florence wanted to know.

Molly poured fresh coffee, set it down on the table and ordered Denby to sit. Amazingly, he did.

"Denby Godridge," she said in answer to the housekeeper's perfectly reasonable question, "meet Florence Washington."

"Charmed," Denby said.

"Whatever," Florence retorted with a sniff.

Denby bridled, but fortunately the phone rang, and Florence was constrained to answer, buying Molly a few more minutes before she would have to explain. Evidently Psyche hadn't told the august Mrs. Washington that Molly was a literary agent.

Meanwhile, Denby slurped his coffee with the air of a man beset by imbeciles on all sides but determined to remain civilized against all odds.

Molly went through a mental list of ways to get rid of him. A flame-thrower, maybe. Or some kind of bomb, preferably nuclear. Or the proverbial team of wild horses, which never seemed to be around when she needed it.

"All right, then," Florence said into the telephone receiver. "We'll expect you later, Keegan."

Molly froze. Of course Keegan was coming over. There were papers to sign and, besides, she needed another jerk orbiting her personal sphere like some junk satellite.

"He's having Psyche airlifted from Flagstaff," Florence said.

Molly was instantly chagrined. Keegan's jerkhood,

she must remember, didn't extend to Psyche. He *loved* Psyche.

For a moment a dismal cloud settled over Molly's normally resilient spirit.

"Somebody's being airlifted?" Denby inquired, his bristly white brows rising. Denby loved drama, and was probably thinking he might want to use whatever was happening in whatever long and tiresomely literary novel he happened to be writing.

"Yes," Molly said. "You see, Denby, there are people in the world with worse problems than not making a bestseller list."

"You're my agent. You should be properly sympathetic."

"I'm not your agent. You fired me at least three different times."

"I'm devastated by this setback," Denby said.

"Well, get over it," Molly replied, dumping cereal into a bowl for Lucas and adding a slosh of milk. Denby had a devoted—and sane—wife who loved him. He was rich. He owned a waterfront house outside Seattle, and that was only his *main* residence. "Go home and write."

Just then, a black man wearing a chauffeur's cap and uniform stuck his head through the dining-room doorway. He was an older version of Denzel Washington, with some Morgan Freeman mixed in.

"Excuse me," he said, removing the cap. "I don't mean to intrude—"

"Come in and have some coffee," Molly said,

bending over the playpen and spooning the first bite of cereal into Lucas's open mouth. He reminded her of a chubby little bird, her son, waiting for a worm.

The chauffeur nodded cordially, almost shyly, to Florence.

Florence patted her hair and smoothed her chenille bathrobe.

Molly treated herself to a private grin. A rare enough luxury these days.

"Wilkins," Denby said to his driver, who must have accompanied him on the private jet to take over the wheel of the waiting limo at the airport, "they do not appreciate me here."

Wilkins took off his hat, nodded his thanks to Florence for the coffee she instantly provided, and sat down at the table. "They seem pretty hospitable to me," he remarked.

Molly racked her brain, trying to remember meeting Wilkins.

"That's why you're a limo driver and I'm a best-selling novelist," Denby said.

"Denby," Molly interjected, *"shut up."*

Wilkins chuckled. "I kind of like it here," he said, but Molly noticed he was looking at Florence when he spoke, not Denby. "Maybe I'll stick around awhile."

Molly could have sworn the air crackled.

Florence excused herself and retreated into her room.

Denby finished his coffee.

Lucas finished his cereal.

Florence returned, wearing a floral print dress, and with her hair pouffed. Molly caught a whiff of perfume.

Wilkins eyed the housekeeper appreciatively. "You ever get to Seattle?" he asked.

"I'm moving there to live with my sister," Florence replied coyly.

Molly shook her head. She *hadn't* just seen Florence Washington bat her eyelashes—had she?

Wilkins flashed a Denzel smile. Produced a card. "Well, now," he said. "I happen to live in Seattle. Been chauffeuring for Mr. Godridge here, and a few other select clients, for years. You ever need a driver, you call."

Florence snatched up the card, crossed to the counter and tucked it under the cookie jar.

"What's going on here?" Denby asked.

"That ole black magic." Wilkins beamed.

Florence refilled his coffee cup, and Molly could have sworn she was blushing, though it was hard to tell, given the rich mahogany shade of the older woman's skin.

"There are still good things happening in this world," Molly whispered to Lucas.

He stood on tiptoe in his playpen. "Kiss," he said, puckering his lips.

And Molly blinked back tears as she gave him a smooch.

KEEGAN'S GUT CHURNED in the back of his throat.

It was standing room only at McKettrickCo—the conference room was barely big enough to contain the whole unruly bunch, even with the folding dividers pushed back.

There were Texas McKettricks.

New York McKettricks.

San Francisco and Chicago McKettricks.

Even a few who lived in Europe.

Old Angus would have been amazed to see what a herd had come of four sons and a daughter.

Jesse stood at Keegan's right, Rance at his left, so close their shoulders touched his. Meg, seated with Sierra, caught Keegan's eye.

"McKettrick-tough," she mouthed.

Keegan returned the favor.

Eve McKettrick, Sierra and Meg's mother, stepped to the front of the room. She was a beautiful woman, with red hair and green eyes. Keegan remembered her helping to put up preserves in the kitchen at the main house, out on the Triple M, and yelling right along with the others about the running in and out and the screen-door slamming.

Today she was all business. The CEO of a major corporation with financial interests in practically every capital city on the globe.

Eve rustled some notes, but she didn't need them. Her memory was almost as legendary as her business acumen. "We've all been arguing about this question long enough," she said. "It's time to take a vote and decide the matter, once and for all."

There was a lot of shifting, shuffling and muttering, but nobody actually spoke up.

"I'd open the floor for discussion," Eve went on, "but there's been plenty of that already. Every last one of us has a definite opinion."

The ensuing silence reminded Keegan of the uneasy weight that always preceded a high-country thunderstorm.

"Will those opposed to the agreement, as outlined in the reports all of you were given earlier, please raise their hands?" It was a backward way of doing things, asking for the dissenting vote first, but that was Eve.

Keegan was the first to respond, followed by Jesse and then Rance.

Sierra raised her hand, and so did Meg.

A half dozen other hands went up, too.

The pit of Keegan's stomach plunged.

It wasn't enough.

"Those in favor?" Eve asked, after holding Keegan's gaze for a long moment.

It was a landslide.

McKettrickCo would go public, with an IPO that would make them all ridiculously wealthy.

"It's decided, then," Eve said, lowering her own hand very slowly.

Jesse's shoulder pressed harder against Keegan's, and so did Rance's.

The floor felt soft, and the blood pounded in Keegan's ears.

The many descendants of Angus McKettrick began to file out of the room.

Meg and Sierra lingered, sitting rigid in their chairs.

Eve approached Keegan, stood square in front of him, looking directly into his eyes. "I'm sorry, Keegan," she said.

He managed a nod. There were a lot of things he wanted to say, but all of them were jammed up tight in his throat.

Eve touched his face, her fingers light and cool. When his folks were killed, during his teenage years, she'd been one of the first to step up. Offered him a home with her, in her San Antonio mansion. In the end he'd chosen to stay on the ranch, and had bounced back and forth between Jesse's parents' place and Rance's until he went away to college.

"This is for the best," she said. Then, without another word, she turned and left the conference room.

At some signal from either Jesse or Rance, Meg and Sierra got up and left, too. Meg closed the conference-room doors softly behind her.

"We lost," Keegan heard himself say in a voice he didn't recognize.

"Seems that way now," Rance said quietly.

As if it was going to change.

Jesse had Cheyenne, and poker. He was a world champion.

Rance had Emma, a couple of kids who lived under his roof instead of being dragged back and forth between two houses the way Devon was, and he'd morphed into a rancher.

And he, Keegan, was a part-time father with nothing constructive to do between visitation weekends. Without McKettrickCo, who would he be? What reason would he have to get up in the morning, once Devon went back to Shellcy?

Jesse pushed a chair behind Keegan's knees, and he sank into it.

"Think about Devon," Jesse said. "You won't be too busy to be a father to her now."

Rance pulled a silver flask from the inside pocket of a suit he hadn't worn since before he shit-canned his McKettrickCo nameplate and turned cowboy.

Keegan considered the flask, then shook his head.

Rance put it away. "We're saddling up around sunsct," he said. "Riding up to Jesse's ridge, with the women and the kids and some of these relations of ours. Devon wants to go along, and we'll take her, but she'd sure get a lot more out of it if you went, too. You in, Keeg?"

Keegan thought of Psyche, and the papers he was supposed to sign that afternoon, the ones that would make him executor of her estate and Lucas's guardian, at least unofficially. He thought of the boy and, inevitably, of Molly.

"I have some things to do," he said woodenly.

Rance laid a hand on his shoulder. "I know," he

replied. "Travis mentioned it. Matter of a couple of hours, at most." He paused, drew a breath, released it. "A trail ride would do you good, Keeg. Put you back in touch with who you are. And that's a McKettrick, born and bred."

The backs of Keegan's eyes throbbed. "Is that who I am?" he asked.

"Yeah," Jesse said. "That's who you are. You've been riding a desk chair, instead of a horse, for so long that you've forgotten. You need to saddle up, Keeg. Sit around a campfire and swap yarns. Sleep under the stars. And your daughter needs that even more than you do."

He'd do it, he decided. Go along on their dumb-ass trail ride. For Devon. And because if he spent the night knocking around alone in the ranch house, he knew he'd go crazy.

He nodded stiffly.

"Buy you a beer over at Lucky's?" Jesse asked.

Keegan shook his head. If he started drinking now, he might not stop. Ever.

Rance and Jesse left then, reluctantly.

And Keegan sat alone in the conference room and began the process of letting things go, one by one.

Psyche.

McKettrickCo, and the identity that went with it.

He still had Devon, though.

And there was Lucas, the son he'd never had.

He would dig in his heels, set his back teeth and hold on, he decided.

After all, he was a McKettrick.

Whatever the hell *that* meant.

BY THE TIME PSYCHE ARRIVED home—brought by ambulance from the airstrip just outside town, where she'd landed half an hour before—Wilkins had collared Denby, muscled him into the hired limo and driven him to Phoenix to catch the next flight back to Seattle.

Molly had showered, put on makeup, slipped into panty hose, high heels and a snazzy black suit with white lapels. After all, there were official papers to sign, and she wanted it known that she was taking the agreement seriously.

Before tending to herself, she'd bathed Lucas and wrestled his giggly, squirmy little body into a pair of blue shorts, with diaper-bulge, and a matching shirt with a duck on the pocket. Slicked his golden hair down with water, and combed it, but it still curled over his ears.

Wheeled through the front door on a gurney, Psyche looked fragile as dandelion fluff, but she brightened when she saw Lucas.

The ambulance attendants, guided by Florence, transferred her into the waiting hospital bed on the porch behind the kitchen, and left again.

There were rails on either side of Psyche's bed, so Molly set Lucas beside her and stood at a slight distance, ready to grab him if he tumbled.

"Are you hungry?" Florence asked Psyche, desperate to be doing something, anything, to help. "I've got some of that chicken soup you like, simmering in the Crock-Pot."

Psyche shook her head, caressed Lucas's hair with its curls and little comb ridges. "I just want to hold my baby," she said very softly.

Molly's eyes filled.

"We had some excitement around here this morning, I'll tell you that," Florence said, bustling. Straightening Psyche's blanket, patting her foot. "Some writer showed up on the doorstep, raving about a Pulitzer Prize." By that time, Molly had explained her vocation. "I thought I'd have to call Wyatt and have him booted out of here, but Mr. Wilkins handled him just fine."

Psyche looked questioningly at Molly, a little smile playing on her lips.

"A former client of mine," Molly explained. "He won't be back."

"Who was it?" Psyche asked, reaching for the little vial attached to her IV tube and pressing the red button on top with a practiced motion of her thumb.

"Denby Godridge," Molly said, wondering how bad Psyche's pain was, and if the stuff in the vial would be enough to ease it.

"I love his books," Psyche said.

Molly chuckled, but it came out as a sob.

Lucas began to bounce on the bed, jostling Psyche.

She closed her eyes, flinching.

Silently Florence removed the child. Carried him into the kitchen, countering his protests with the promise of a cookie.

"You're crying," Psyche said, watching Molly closely. "Don't deny it."

"It's hard," Molly sniffled. "Seeing you like—like this."

Psyche's smile was wan, and a little ironic. "It's not so great from this side, either," she said.

Molly looked at the IV bag suspended from a pole next to Psyche's rented bed. "I guess the pain must be pretty bad."

"Actually," Psyche said, "I'm stoned out of my mind."

Molly had to smile. "You're a pretty convincing actress, then. You're not even slurring your words."

Psyche sighed. "Pull up a chair, Molly. There are some things I want to say."

Molly dragged over one of the chairs pushed in around the little table where the peonies sat, nodding in their crystal vase, and sat down. Suddenly she was full of dread; she knew instinctively what Psyche was about to say. She'd decided not to let her adopt Lucas after all, but to give him to Keegan instead.

She waited, sick with tension. As desperate as she was, she wasn't about to rush Psyche for an explanation. Not at a time like this.

"I wasn't sure I'd make it back from Flagstaff,"

Psyche said. "I did some serious last-minute thinking, and called Travis Reid this morning." She stopped, watched Molly for a few moments, a mixture of reluctance and stubborn certainty visible in her eyes. "I asked if he and Sierra would be willing to adopt Lucas and raise him as their own. He was a little surprised, of course, and he had to consult Sierra, but in the end they said yes."

Molly fully expected the floor to dissolve, along with the earth beneath it, sending her and her chair plunging through airless space. *"Why?"* she squeaked.

"I want my son to have a real family, Molly. A mother, a father, siblings."

"But you—"

"I know. I promised. But I'm going back on my word."

Molly couldn't breathe. Couldn't move. Couldn't even speak.

She was aware of Lucas chattering in the next room, and of a more distant sound, deeper in the house, some sort of banging.

"Travis and Sierra already have a little boy," Psyche went on. "His name is Liam. He'll make a fine brother to Lucas."

Molly gripped the sides of her chair, honestly afraid she'd pitch forward in a faint if she didn't hold on with everything she had.

This was it, then. Psyche's revenge—she'd set Molly up to believe she was getting another chance with Lucas, and then pulled the proverbial rug out from under her.

Paybacks. *That'll teach you to sleep with another woman's husband.*

The banging got closer. And louder.

"Where is she?" Molly heard a familiar voice demand in the nearby kitchen.

"On the sunporch," Florence answered.

Keegan burst through the doorway.

"What the hell is going on?" he demanded of Psyche. "Travis just told me…"

Psyche smiled. "What did Travis just tell you?" she asked.

"That you want him and Sierra to adopt Lucas."

Psyche merely nodded.

Keegan glanced down at Molly, frowned.

"I've already explained it to Molly," Psyche said, "so I'll give you the short version. I want Lucas to have a *family,* a real home, not just a mother and an executor."

Keegan opened his mouth, closed it again.. Gripped the door frame on either side of him with such force that his knuckles turned white. His daughter peered around him, her brown eyes enormous.

"We're going on a trail ride," the little girl said. "We're going to have a campfire and sleep on the ground."

A silence fell.

Shattered, Molly concentrated on not throwing up.

Psyche's gaze found the child and focused. "Devon?" she asked.

Devon nodded and slipped past her motionless father to approach Psyche's bed. "I'm sorry you're so sick," she said. "If you weren't, you could go camping with us, up on Jesse's ridge. There's a whole bunch of us making the trip."

Psyche smiled, touched Devon's flowing hair. "I'd like that a lot," she said wistfully. Her eyes, luminous with sorrow, rose to Keegan's face. "How beautiful she is, Keegan."

Keegan cleared his throat. "Devon," he said calmly, "go into the kitchen, please. Help Mrs. Washington look after Lucas."

The child hesitated, clearly aware that she was being given the bum's rush, and then obeyed the quiet command, casting worried looks back over one shoulder as she went.

"Would you take Lucas along?" Psyche asked Keegan, her hands knotting and unknotting where she gripped the crisp sheets covering her skeletal frame. "On the trail ride, I mean?"

"Psyche," Keegan reasoned, "he's a baby."

"How old were you when you started riding horses?" Psyche challenged.

Molly watched the answer take shape in Keegan's face. He was not himself—at least, not the self Molly knew, though scantly. He looked ravaged, somehow.

Almost broken. But there was an undercurrent of strength, too, hard as bedrock.

"My dad put me in the saddle in front of him as soon as I could sit up," Keegan admitted, but only after an internal struggle of some kind, one that corded the muscles in his neck and made his jawline harden.

"Lucas has been sitting up for a long time," Psyche said. "I don't want him to be a timid little city boy, Keegan. The sooner he learns to ride and do other things like that, the better."

Keegan relaxed his jaw, and from Molly's perspective the act looked as though it called on all his inner reserves, and then some. "Psyche, this whole conversation is crazy, and it's beside the point. We're talking about—"

"About Lucas having a family. A mother. A father. A brother." She paused, looked from Keegan to Molly and back again. Devon's voice floated in from the kitchen, she was chattering to Florence about the upcoming trail ride. "Or perhaps a sister."

A jolt of realization went through Molly, belated but no less devastating for the delay.

Psyche smiled again, clearly pleased.

"Damn it, Psyche," Keegan rasped. "Travis is a good man, but you don't have the bond with him that you do with me. And Sierra's a stranger to you." He glanced at Molly, looked as though he wanted to add something, and bit it back.

"Go on your trail ride," Psyche said serenely.

"Take Lucas along, and Molly, too, of course. Think this situation over very carefully. You said you wanted to raise Lucas, Keegan. Well, here's your chance. All you have to do is marry his mother."

CHAPTER 9

THINK THIS SITUATION OVER very carefully. You said you wanted to raise Lucas, Keegan. Well, here's your chance. All you have to do is marry his mother.

Keegan loosened his tie with a hard motion of one hand. "This is *blackmail*," he told Psyche. "I don't love Molly, and she doesn't love me. Given that minor detail, what kind of home could we possibly provide for Lucas? And I thought you wanted him to grow up in this house. Travis and Sierra just built one of their own, and they won't move here."

Psyche fidgeted with the vial attached to her IV line. The veins stood out under her skin, and the lines of her skull seemed more prominent, even though only a little over twenty-four hours had passed since he'd last seen her.

She looked at Molly, who sat silently at the edge of Keegan's awareness, then met his gaze and answered, "I want Lucas to grow up in or around

Indian Rock. As for you and Molly not loving each other—well, you'd just have to work things out, wouldn't you?"

"Psyche, this is unreasonable."

"It's swan-song time for me, Keegan. I'm not *required* to be reasonable."

Molly sat with her head down, gripping the sides of her chair. Keegan felt a swift, fierce stab of compassion for her, but it passed as quickly as it had come.

"Now," Psyche went on, "leave me alone, please. I need to cry, and I want to do it in private."

Keegan didn't move immediately, and when he did, he reached out, caught hold of one of Molly's hands and pulled her to her feet. Dragged her off the sunporch with him, through the kitchen, where Lucas and Devon and Florence all marked their passage with partially open mouths, through the enormous formal dining room beyond and finally into the study just off the front entrance.

At no point in the journey did Molly resist, which was cause enough for concern, to Keegan's way of thinking, admittedly disjointed as it was. Inwardly, he was still wrestling with the implications of losing McKettrickCo—and now *this*.

He plunked Molly into a leather chair, wing-backed and ancient, and dragged its twin up square in front of it. Sat down, facing Molly, their knees almost but not quite touching.

"Don't you *dare* accuse me of putting Psyche up

to that!" Molly cried in a sudden eruption of emotion she must have been holding in before. Her face was so bloodless, the desolation in her eyes so vivid, that Keegan found himself believing her. She was as surprised and dismayed by this new development as he was.

"Do you need a glass of water or something?" he asked.

She shook her head. Dashed at her cheeks with the back of one hand.

If she was putting on an act, it was a damned good one.

Keegan rested his hands on his thighs, tried some deep breathing. It didn't help in the least.

"It's because of the affair," Molly murmured miserably. "This is Psyche's way of getting back at me."

He sighed. "No," he said. "Psyche's not that kind of person."

"Isn't she?" Molly said, her eyes welling up again. Her nostrils were red, and there was a little catch in her breathing.

Keegan repressed an urge to pull her onto his lap and hold her close until she felt better. "No," he repeated, but Molly didn't seem to hear him.

"I should have known it was some kind of trap," she fretted. "*I should have known* she'd never let me raise Lucas."

"Psyche," Keegan said again, evenly, "is not that kind of person."

Molly gripped the arms of her chair, as though

meaning to thrust herself upright but not quite able to attempt it. "I didn't know Thayer was married," she said.

"If you didn't," Keegan said, "you should have."

She nodded wretchedly. "You're right. Does that make you happy, Keegan? Are you satisfied? Or should I have a scarlet *A* printed on a T-shirt and wear it every day for the rest of my *life?*"

Keegan took a certain grim enjoyment in the image—the T-shirt was wet in his version—but in the next instant he was ashamed of himself. "We all make mistakes," he said, though not with much generosity.

"Even you?" Molly challenged, straining to pluck a handful of tissues from the box sitting on the corner of the desk that had belonged to Psyche's father.

"Even me," Keegan said.

She dabbed at her eyes—a hopeless endeavor, given that her mascara was running down her face in pitiful streaks—and then blew her nose with such unselfconscious vigor that Keegan had to fight back a smile. "What am I going to do?" she asked plaintively.

"What are *you* going to do? Seems to me this is a *we* kind of problem."

"How do you figure that?" Molly immediately demanded. "As I understand it, Psyche's lawyer and his wife live in Indian Rock. You'll be able to see Lucas

Romance Reading...

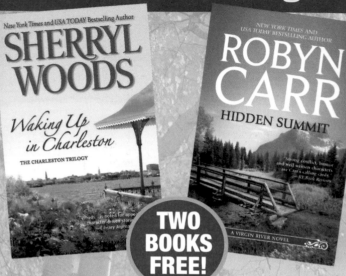

The Reader Service — Here's How it Works:

Accepting your 2 free books and 2 free gifts (gifts valued at approximately $10.00) places you under no obligation to buy anyth[ing]. You may keep the books and gifts and return the shipping statement marked "cancel". If you do not cancel, about a month later w[e'll] send you 4 additional books and bill you just $5.99 each in the U.S. or $6.49 each in Canada. That's a savings of at least 25% [off] the cover price. It's quite a bargain! Shipping and handling is just 50¢ per book in the U.S. and 75¢ per book in Canada.* You [may] cancel at any time, but if you choose to continue, every month we'll send you 4 more books, which you may either purchase at [the] discount price or return to us and cancel your subscription.

*Terms and prices subject to change without notice. Prices do not include applicable taxes. Sales tax applicable in N.Y. Canadian residents will be charged applicable taxes. Offer not valid in Quebec. All orders subject to credit approval. Credit or debit balances in a customer's account(s) may be offset by any other outstanding balance owed by or to the customer. Please allow 4 to 6 weeks for delivery. Offer available while quantities last.

any time you want. I, on the other hand, am—forgive the expression—shit out of luck."

Keegan remembered kissing Molly in the park on the Fourth of July, and wanted, incomprehensibly, to do it again. Since the timing was obviously lousy, he didn't give in to the urge—but it was there.

Oh, it was there.

"Keegan?"

He gave himself an internal shake. "I care about Lucas, too," he said. "It's almost as though—"

There was a change in her face, barely discernible but eloquent. "As though you and Psyche had him together?"

"Something like that," he admitted.

"You really love her, don't you?"

"I really love her."

"So it follows that you love Lucas."

Keegan nodded. "It follows," he said, a little distracted, important as the conversation was, by the strangely bruised look in Molly's eyes.

She nodded, sniffled, pitched the wad of tissue into a nearby wastebasket. "Of course it would be really stupid if we got married. You and me, I mean."

Keegan thought of his big house, empty except when Devon came to visit, and of the bed he hated to sleep in alone. Usually he bunked on the living-room couch, or the one in his office. Might as well have been a park bench, with newspapers for covers, for all it mattered.

Not that the office couch was going to be an option much longer.

Maybe he'd get a sleeping bag and share Spud's stall, out in the barn.

"Really stupid," he agreed, long after the fact.

She began to cry again.

Keegan was overwhelmed by the conflicting emotions the sight stirred in him. He did what he'd decided *not* to do only moments earlier—took Molly's hand and pulled her onto his lap.

She stiffened with resistance for a moment, then allowed him to hold her.

He was alarmed at how good it felt.

"What am I going to do?" she asked again, her voice muffled by his shoulder.

His shirt felt soggy from her tears, and he pondered the inevitable mascara stains. Decided he didn't give a rat's ass if the shirt was ruined—he had way too many just like it.

"You're going to pack some gear for you and Lucas and take a trail ride," he said in answer to her question.

She lifted her head, stared into his eyes. "What?"

He grinned. "What's the matter, city girl? Are you chicken? Afraid of snakes and bears and bugs?"

She smiled wetly, but with some spirit. "No," she said. "I'm *not* chicken."

"Have you ever ridden a horse?"

"Once, when I was nine," she said. "I went on a pony ride at a carnival on Santa Monica Beach."

"Oh, well, then, that makes you an expert," Keegan replied, bemused by the fact that he felt so good, while his life was collapsing around his ears.

"Which is not to say I won't be saddle sore," she said, looking worried.

"So will I," he admitted, at some cost to his pride. He was a McKettrick. He was supposed to be a hand with horses—and women.

"You don't ride? But Psyche thinks you can teach Lucas—"

"I didn't say I couldn't ride," Keegan told her. "It's just been a while, that's all." He set her on her feet. "Get your stuff together," he said. "You and Lucas can ride out to the Triple M with Devon and me."

Clearly wary, Molly thought for a while, finally nodded.

Taking a baby on a trail ride, it turned out, required a surprising amount of gear and getting ready.

Half an hour later, with all the stuff stashed in the trunk, Lucas and his car seat both securely fastened into the backseat of Keegan's Jag, Devon sitting solicitously beside the little boy and Molly riding shotgun, they were on their way.

Molly looked good in her old jeans and a T-shirt—alas, totally dry—but the sneakers weren't going to pack it once she was on the back of a horse. The floor of one of the downstairs closets at home was jammed with boots in a variety of sizes. He'd insist that she try them on until she found a pair to fit.

"Will Travis and Sierra Reid be along on this trail ride?" Molly asked when they were well out of town.

"Travis is a Reid," Keegan said. "Sierra goes by 'McKettrick.' And, yeah, they'll probably be there. Some of the out of towners, too, most likely."

"The out of towners?"

"More McKettricks," Keegan explained. "There was a megameeting at the office today, and a lot of them are probably still around." He waited for the pit of his stomach to drop open, like a trapdoor, with the reminder that his corporate career was over unless he wanted to work for strangers, which he didn't.

Curiously, the hinges held.

Molly looked solemn. "I want to meet them. Travis and Sierra, I mean."

Keegan glanced in the rearview mirror, saw Devon reflected there, bobbing one of Lucas's toys under his nose, making him giggle. He didn't want to discuss Psyche's adoption terms in front of his daughter.

When he looked briefly in Molly's direction before turning his gaze back to the road ahead, he knew she'd seen him check the mirror, and had picked up on his concern.

She shifted slightly in the seat, turned to smile back at Devon. "I'll bet you're a very accomplished rider," she said.

Something warmed inside Keegan.

"Not as good as Maeve is," Devon answered proudly. "But I can ride, all right."

"Who's Maeve?" Molly asked, as though she knew she ought to remember the name but didn't quite.

"My cousin, sort of," Devon said. "Really distant, though. Like Dad and Uncle Jesse and Uncle Rance. They call themselves cousins, but they're really just McKettricks."

"Oh," Molly said, frowning in pretty confusion. "What does that mean, to be 'just McKettricks'?"

Devon drew a deep breath. Like all the kids in the family, she was well versed in clan history. "A long time ago a man named Angus McKettrick settled a little piece of what's now the Triple M. That's our ranch...."

Keegan's throat caught at the word *our*. Someday he'd probably have to tell Devon she wasn't a blood McKettrick, and he was already dreading that.

"And anyway," Devon went on with touching confidence, "he had four sons—Holt, Rafe, Kade and Jeb. Sierra and Meg are related to Holt. Uncle Rance is de—de—"

"Descended," Keegan coached quietly.

"Descended," Devon said, "from Rafe. Uncle Jesse is—*descended* from Jeb, and Dad—well, Kade was his great-great, however many greats, grandfather. They all had houses of their own, of course—Holt and Rafe and Kade and Jeb, I mean—and the cool thing is, everybody still lives in the same one."

Keegan gave Molly a sidelong glance. "Clear as mud?"

She smiled, a little sadly, he thought. "Clear enough," she said.

They passed the road to Holt's place, and Devon pointed it out. Later, going by a tilted mailbox at the base of a hill, she said, "Uncle Jesse lives up that way. Our house is close to a creek, but you don't have to worry. I'll make sure Lucas doesn't fall in or anything."

"I'd appreciate that," Molly said.

"Maeve and Rianna live right on the other side," Devon elaborated. "Of the creek, I mean. But *our* house is the oldest one. Angus built it himself."

"There was a daughter, too," Keegan said, finding a singular comfort in talking about his family tree. "Katie McKettrick, Angus's youngest. She married a United States senator when she grew up. The women in the family keep the name when they marry, and the tradition started with her."

"Wow," Molly said. "She must have been something."

Keegan grinned. "According to family legend, she was a real firebrand. Held her own, even with four brothers, all grown men when she was born."

"What's your family like, Molly?" Devon asked, with the generous innocence of a child trying to make sure no one felt left out.

Molly sighed. "My mother died when I was fifteen," she said. "My dad is a retired police officer."

"Are you an only child?" Devon pressed.

"Dev," Keegan said.

"It's okay," Molly told him. Then, to Devon, "Yes. Just me."

"Me, too," Devon said wistfully. "So's Dad."

Keegan scraped his lower lip between his teeth.

Devon's cross-examination went on. "Do you ever wish you had brothers and sisters?" she asked Molly.

"All the time," Molly said, watching Keegan.

"Me, too," Devon repeated. "What about you, Dad? Did *you* ever want to be part of a big family?"

His gaze met Devon's in the rearview mirror. "I've got Rance and Jesse," he said. "They're like brothers to me. In fact, the whole McKettrick bunch is pretty tight."

"You're lucky," Molly told him.

"I know," he said. He'd forgotten it for a while, but he *was* lucky. He had a solid heritage, a daughter, a home. A long, long story had begun on this land, and he had a place in the tale.

They reached the last road, crossed over the wooden bridge spanning the creek, built by some industrious McKettrick back in the 1940s, and still sturdy, like the houses and the barns and the surrounding hills.

His own place, so familiar, looked strangely new to him.

"In the old days," Devon piped up, "everybody had to ride horses through a shallow place in the creek to get across."

Keegan smiled. So what if Devon wasn't his biological child? She was still a McKettrick, through and through.

"You really know your family history," Molly told Devon, with what sounded like sincere admiration. She was taking in the ranch house as she spoke, and Keegan wondered what she thought of the sprawling, two-story structure, with its many windows and its weathered log walls and its natural-rock chimneys.

He would have liked it better if her opinion hadn't mattered to him, but he couldn't deny, at least to himself, that it did.

"That's where Uncle Rance lives, over there," Devon said, ever the tour guide. "Do you want to see our donkey? His name is Spud, and he's in the barn."

As soon as the car came to a full stop, Devon was out the door and sprinting for Spud's stall.

Keegan grinned. "She'll run down in a while," he said quietly.

"I hope not," Molly replied. "She's delightful." She got out of the Jag, started unstrapping Lucas, who was bouncing with impatience, from the car seat.

Keegan stood behind her, admiring her shapely backside.

"I guess we'd better say hello to the donkey," she said, straightening and turning around with the child in her arms.

The sun struck them both just right, the woman and the boy, rimming them in a flash of radiant gold.

Keegan had to clear his throat. "I guess so," he agreed.

Devon was already astraddle the stall door when they got inside the barn. Like most ranch kids, she was more likely to scramble over than simply open it. He'd been the same way, and so had Jesse and Rance and Meg.

"There's a note from Doc Swann," she called, waving a sheet of yellow legal paper, ripped from a nail in the barn wall. "He gave Spud a shot for mange and said to get his feet trimmed." She grinned. "Spud's feet, I mean. Not Doc's."

Molly laughed, still carrying Lucas, but that fragility Keegan had glimpsed in her earlier was there again. She was about to lose a child she'd only recently found, and for all his disapproval and distrust of her motives, Keegan wasn't unsympathetic.

Devon, meanwhile, had moved on. "It's a good thing Uncle Rance and Uncle Jesse have a lot of horses," she remarked, now inside Spud's stall. "This is a piss-poor excuse for a barn, with only one donkey in it."

"Devon," Keegan said. "Language."

"You say 'piss-poor' all the time," she retorted.

Molly gave him a wobbly, let's-see-you-get-out-of-this-one kind of grin.

"I say a lot of things I'd better not hear you saying," Keegan told his daughter.

They all admired Spud for a little while, then Devon decided they ought to go into the house. She was going on a trail ride, and she had preparations to make. Keegan wondered distractedly if she'd want to lug the pink teddy bear along.

Molly, Lucas and Keegan went as far as the kitchen, while Devon pounded up the back stairs.

Molly set Lucas down on the floor and gravitated to the cookstove. Ran a hand over the black surface. Turned to Keegan.

"Do you still use it?" she asked.

"Sometimes," he said, oddly pleased that she'd asked. "When it snows, nothing beats a wood-burning stove for atmosphere."

"It's wonderful," Molly said, and she sounded as though she meant it.

Keegan's mind flashed to Shelley. When they were married she'd spent as little time as possible on the ranch. Seeing the stove the first time, she'd shaken her head and asked why it hadn't been hauled off to the nearest junkyard.

"This is quite a house," Molly said.

Suddenly Keegan wanted to show her every room in the place.

And one in particular.

"Thanks," he croaked, unnerved. "I like it."

Devon began hurling jeans, T-shirts and boots down the stairs.

Keegan shook his head.

Molly grinned. "How old is she?" she asked.

"Almost eleven, going on fifty-three," Keegan answered. He let his gaze slide down Molly's slight, toned figure to her feet. "Those shoes are never going to do," he told her. "You need boots."

"Who's going to feed Spud while we're on this pack trip, or whatever it is?" she asked, having acknowledged the boot issue with a slight nod.

Keegan, already on his way toward the long hallway where the boot-stash closet was, stopped. It wasn't the question she'd asked that gave him pause, but the undercurrent of cheerful nervousness.

Damn. She hadn't ridden a horse since she was nine.

She was probably scared.

Keegan beckoned for her to follow him.

She picked Lucas up, set him on her hip and moved toward Keegan. To watch her, he'd have thought she'd been schlepping little kids around for years.

"Rance has a couple of cowboys working for him," he said, answering her question about feeding Spud. "I'll ask them to come across the creek and make sure the donkey's got food and water."

She watched as he opened the closet door and began inspecting boots. Tossed them out, one at a time and in pairs, much as Devon had hurled her camping clothes down the back stairs.

"There's a lot to this ranching thing, I guess," she said.

"A lot to it," Keegan agreed, coming up with a pair of black boots embossed with blue stitching. He thought he remembered Meg wearing them, when she was twelve or so. She'd spent that year on the Triple M, with Keegan and his folks.

"Trouble at home," his mother had told him once when he asked why Meg wasn't going back to San Antonio to start school that fall.

Now, of course, he knew the story. For all her strength, Eve McKettrick, Meg's mother, had been dealing with a lot back in those days—recovering from an accident that had nearly killed her and had left an addiction to painkillers and alcohol in its wake. Agonizing over Sierra, who had been snatched, at around Lucas's age, by Eve's ex-husband. In fact, Eve and Meg's reunion with Sierra had happened only recently.

"Try these," he said, offering Molly the boots. "They look as though they might fit."

She took the boots with her free hand.

Keegan began chucking the discards back into the closet. The next time a greenhorn came along, he thought, dusting his hands together, he'd be ready.

Not that there was ever likely to be another greenhorn quite like Molly Shields.

She carried the boots back to the kitchen, set Lucas on the floor and sat down on the bench alongside the table. Kicked off her sneakers and gamely pulled on a boot.

Keegan crouched, pressed the toe with his thumb, like a shoe salesman with a customer.

It struck him as funny, and he laughed out loud.

"What?" Molly asked a little warily, pulling her foot free.

"I was just considering my career options," he said.

She frowned, puzzled.

He told her, to his everlasting surprise, about McKettrickCo going public, without trying to hide how he felt about it. If he'd thought about it in advance, he wouldn't have said anything, wouldn't have opened that particular can of worms. It was too private, too personal and way too sore to the touch.

"I know what you mean," she said, watching sadly as Lucas played on the floor at her feet.

Still on his haunches, he looked up into her face.

"I would have missed my work, too," she told him. "If Psyche hadn't changed her mind about the adoption, I mean. All the challenge and the excitement." She swallowed. "Of course, none of it can compare to raising Lucas myself. I was even starting to like Indian Rock."

Keegan shifted, sat beside her on the bench. Draped one arm loosely around her shoulders. Why was he sympathizing? he wondered. He should have been glad she was leaving. True, he wanted to be part of Lucas's life almost as much as Molly did, but he knew Sierra and Travis would love the child like their own. They were good people; Lucas would be safe and happy with them.

"Do yourself a favor, Molly," he said. "Don't think

about this right now. Let the trail ride occupy your mind."

She blinked. Swallowed again. "How can I not think about it?" she whispered miserably. "I just found Lucas—and now I'm going to lose him again."

"Psyche might change her mind."

"You know she won't," Molly said.

"She's trying to manipulate us into doing what she wants," Keegan said. "Once she realizes it won't work, she may give in."

Molly's eyes filled with tears. She shook her head. "She's *dying,* Keegan. People don't play games when they've practically got one foot in the grave. Especially not where their child's welfare is concerned." She paused, bit down on her lower lip. Glanced toward the back stairs, turned to look at him again. "What would you do, Keegan? If you were about to die—if you had to give Devon up?"

"She'd live with her mother," Keegan answered. "Just like she does now."

"What if that weren't an option? What if you were in exactly the same situation Psyche is? What would you do?"

He sighed. "I'd want her to have a mother and father," he said. "I do the best I can, and so does Shelley, all things considered. But it's still damn tough on Devon."

Molly nodded. "I know what it's like to grow up in a single-parent household," she said. "But my dad and I *were* a family, even with my mom gone. Millions of good people out there are raising kids alone, and they're doing a great job, too."

"I wouldn't argue with that," Keegan said. "But it isn't ideal."

Molly pondered that a while, then nodded again, but not with much conviction as far as Keegan could tell.

"I know Florence raised Psyche, for the most part," Molly said. "What were her parents like?"

Keegan set his back teeth, consciously relaxed his jaw. "Rich," he said. "Well educated. Her dad wrote books about Greek and Roman mythology—hence her name—and gave lectures all over the world. Her mother traveled with him, and mostly made sure their cocktails were always fresh."

Molly closed her eyes. "Alcoholics."

Keegan nodded grimly.

"She's trying to give Lucas what *she* never had," Molly mused.

"Bingo," Keegan said.

"My dad—" Molly began, but before she could finish the sentence, Devon was back, clattering down the stairs, bursting with excitement.

"Everybody's over at Uncle Rance's place!" she cried. "I saw all kinds of trucks and horses from my bedroom window. What are we waiting for? *Let's go!*"

CHAPTER 10

MOLLY, STANDING in her borrowed boots, did her best to take Keegan's advice and think about the trail ride instead of the imminent loss of Lucas, but it was hard going.

Keegan had exchanged his slacks and sports shirt for worn jeans and a blue cotton work shirt before feeding the donkey one last time, and that took some getting over, too.

Something Psyche had said popped into Molly's mind as they drove across the creek bridge, toward the gathering of McKettricks.

Wait till you see him on a horse.

Molly's stomach tightened at the prospect.

She tried to reason with herself. Keegan was Keegan, in a suit or in jeans and boots. Standing on the ground, or in the saddle.

He parked the Jag in an out-of-the-way place, which wasn't easy, given the collection of trucks, horse trailers and cars already taking up much of the area surrounding the barn.

Devon shot out of the car and raced to join the two little girls Molly had met at the bookshop, glimpsed later at the Fourth of July celebration in the park.

Molly got out slowly, took her time freeing a squirming Lucas from the car seat in back. Keegan, meanwhile, transferred all the stuff in the trunk to a nearby pickup truck, tacitly designated, apparently, to haul extras.

Jesse McKettrick approached, grinning and leading a beautiful paint horse behind him. Molly remembered him, too, of course—he'd been at the picnic with his new bride, and she'd seen him again at the clinic when Psyche had taken a turn for the worse.

He grinned at Molly in a way that made her feel slightly less nervous and much less an outsider, and turned his gaze on Keegan, who had just returned from the truck.

"Let's see if you remember how to ride," Jesse said to Keegan.

Thus challenged, Keegan stepped up beside the paint, gripped the saddle horn with one hand, simultaneously putting a foot in the stirrup, and swung himself up with an easy grace that shouldn't have taken Molly's breath away—but did.

He sat with the westward sun for a backdrop.

Keegan on a horse.

Imagination hadn't done it justice.

"Satisfied?" he asked Jesse.

"Maybe," Jesse allowed. "It's a fair distance up to the ridge, and we're taking the long way. Could be, by the time we get to camp you'll be whining for a hot tub."

Keegan chuckled at that. Then he eased the horse closer to Molly and leaned down, reaching for Lucas.

She gripped her son tightly for a moment or two, then gave him up.

Lucas crowed with delight as Keegan set him gently in the saddle in front of him, waving his little arms and kicking his feet.

Keegan smiled down at Molly. "He won't be sore by the end of this ride," he said. "He's got lots of padding."

Molly was busy branding the sight of Keegan and Lucas, together on the back of a horse, into her memory. When she was back in Los Angeles living her old life, it might be—though painful—of some paradoxical comfort, too.

Jesse, meanwhile, produced another horse. A bay, already saddled, and a lot smaller than the one Keegan was riding.

He waited while Molly assessed the animal, unable to hide her misgivings. She was aware, too, of Keegan watching her, one strong arm locked around Lucas.

"I don't know how to get on," Molly admitted.

"I'll help," Jesse assured her. And he did.

After she was up, he deftly adjusted the stirrups on both sides, and Keegan, his horse bumping against hers, showed her how to hold the reins.

Devon trotted over on a buckskin, and Maeve— it must have been Maeve, because Devon had said the other girl was an excellent rider—was with her, mounted on a white mare.

Devon favored Molly with an encouraging grin. "Lookin' good," she said, raising one hand for a high five.

Molly released one side of her two-fisted death grip on the reins to comply.

All around them, other people were mounting up, in a sort of organized confusion. There was a lot of laughter, the tension-relieving kind.

Keegan, meanwhile, watched Molly in silence, with something that could have been—but surely *wasn't*—admiration. Lucas remained within the easy protection of Keegan's arm, a little quieter now, but still eager. He seemed to know he was safe, and that brought a yearning ache to Molly's throat.

Within a few minutes they were off, a great horde of horses and riders, it seemed to Molly, raising a lot of dust. There were probably no more than a couple of dozen people altogether, but they all knew each other.

Molly was reminded, by the hardness of the saddle and the long distance to the ground, that she was a greenhorn. A city girl, as Keegan had said back in Psyche's house, when he'd issued a teasing challenge.

Are you chicken?

Molly tried to adjust herself to the saddle, and to the situation.

Cluck-cluck, she thought.

Keegan stayed close as they rode, at a blessedly slow pace, in the midst of the pack—maybe out of kindness, and maybe just because he wanted to keep her in Lucas's sight.

She began to relax—a little. Spotted Emma, the woman who ran the bookshop in town, riding alongside a dark-haired, powerfully built man—Rance, undoubtedly. And there was Jesse up ahead with his new bride, both of them looking as comfortable on horseback as if they'd been born there. A young man, probably around twenty, rode with them beaming, his withered legs dangling uselessly on either side of the saddle.

Keegan must have seen Molly looking—my God, had she been staring?—because he leaned closer and said, "That's Mitch. He's Cheyenne's younger brother."

Molly felt ashamed of her own trepidation. If Mitch could ride, with his wasted legs, so could she. "He looks pretty happy," she said.

Keegan nodded.

"What if he falls?"

"Jesse won't let that happen," Keegan replied. "See how he stays close to Mitch, without letting on that he's keeping an eye on him?"

Molly looked more closely. Jesse was engaged in a lively conversation with Cheyenne, but there was a readiness about him, subtle but plainly visible in the set of his shoulders and the way he kept his right arm free, the hand resting lightly on his hip.

"What happened to Mitch?" she asked, prepared to be told it was none of her business.

"He was in an accident when he was younger," Keegan said, and Molly saw his jawline tighten, almost imperceptibly. "He's been working at McKettrickCo—part of a training program Cheyenne set up. Now that the company's going public, he may be unemployed—along with a lot of other people."

Molly studied Keegan. "They'll need employees, won't they? The new board of directors?"

Keegan nodded, but he still looked grim.

"You really hate it, don't you?" Molly asked, and then wished she hadn't, because Keegan's face darkened for a moment and she saw the familiar ruthlessness in his eyes.

"Letting go of the company? Yeah, I hate it."

"You could stay on, couldn't you?" Molly said, knowing she was digging herself in deeper, but unable to stop.

His blue eyes glittered with ferocity. "No," he said flatly.

"Why not?" *Just give me another shovel,* Molly thought ruefully. *China's bound to be here somewhere.*

"It wouldn't be the same." Keegan bit the words off, one at a time.

"And that's necessarily a bad thing?" *Shut up, Molly. Shut up, shut up, shut up.*

"You sound like Jesse and Rance," Keegan said.

Up ahead, Mitch's horse spooked a little, and Jesse had a hand on the bridle strap in the next moment. Clearly, he could have been out of his own saddle and behind Mitch, reaching around him to take the reins, almost that fast.

Molly wondered what it would be like to be protected that way. To be a member of a clan like the McKettricks, with a long, colorful history and that bone-deep confidence that seemed so inherently theirs—right down to Devon and the other kids.

Right down to Lucas, if Psyche had gotten her way. He'd have grown up to be like Keegan and Jesse and Rance—competent, comfortable in his skin and probably cocky as hell.

Molly bit her lower lip, trying to stem a longing that threatened to rush out of her in a stream. "Are Sierra and Travis here?" she asked after a long time.

"Over there," Keegan said, pointing out a blond man and a tall woman with short chestnut hair. A little boy rode between their two horses, a black and a bay, on a squat pony.

Molly focused on the child. Liam, that was his name.

Would he be a good brother to Lucas?

Tears clogged her sinuses, turned the horses and their riders into a blur of color and movement.

She started a little when Keegan's hand came to rest briefly on her shoulder.

And the ride went on, the trail winding ever upward, between stands of cottonwood trees, across another creek—or maybe the same one, Molly couldn't be sure—into the pines jutting beyond, green against an achingly blue sky.

Finally they reached the ridge, and Molly saw that others had come ahead in trucks and set up a camp of sorts. She caught the scent of wood burning, and food cooking, savory in the fresh air. A few tents had been erected, too, though not nearly enough to accommodate everyone.

Molly didn't allow herself to wonder where she would sleep that night. At the same time, some part of her heart fluttered its wings, as if to separate itself and fly down to Psyche, so she could share the experience.

There was an improvised corral, made of rope, off to one side, with a thin part of the creek running through the center, and riders began to dismount, laughing and stiff, surrendering their horses to the waiting cowboys.

When her turn came, Molly got down out of the saddle on her own, as a point of pride, perhaps, and would have fallen if someone hadn't grabbed her.

She turned, looked into the smiling face of Sierra McKettrick. Liam, small and bespectacled and serious, stood beside her.

"You must be Psyche's friend Molly," Sierra said

after stealing a brief glance at Keegan. Then, at Molly's rather abrupt nod, having no way to know it wasn't necessary, she introduced herself.

This woman, Molly thought, *is going to raise my son.*

She waited, fully expecting to hate Sierra with the whole force of her being, but it didn't happen. Sierra's eyes were the same clear blue as Keegan's, and she had the same inborn confidence.

Lucas would be fine with her. And she would love him.

Keegan, down off his own horse, nudged Molly, then handed Lucas over. "He's wet," he said.

Sierra smiled, caressing Lucas with her gaze. "Men," she said.

"I'll get the diapers and the other stuff," Keegan said, and walked away.

Sierra and Liam walked with Molly as she followed Keegan. She sensed that Sierra wanted to hold Lucas, but she couldn't let him go, not yet, not a moment before she had to. Sierra would, after all, be the one to rock him to sleep, tell him stories, put bandages on his skinned knees.

Molly held her son so tightly that he squirmed in protest.

She kissed him on top of the head and loosened her grip a little.

By the time they caught up with Keegan, he'd found the box of diapers, along with a folded blanket Molly didn't recognize, some wipes and a bottle of hand sanitizer.

Molly might have laughed at the incongruity of it if little chunks of her heart hadn't been breaking off and falling away.

Keegan spread the blanket in a warm but shady place, out of the general flow of traffic, and Molly knelt to lay Lucas on his back and change his diaper. Keegan went back to the truck and returned with a baby bottle, filled with milk.

He was a miracle worker, Molly thought.

Or maybe just a father.

Gratefully she accepted the bottle, gave it to Lucas, who took it hungrily in both hands, bit down on the nipple and drank. Watching him, Molly forgot all about Sierra and Liam and even Keegan—until he sat down beside her, watching her watch Lucas.

"You really love him," he said.

"Of course I do," Molly whispered, near tears. This time with Lucas, it was so precious. So brief. "He's my son."

Sierra and Liam had gone, she realized. She and Lucas and Keegan were alone, despite the size of the gathering. The laughter, the tired horses drinking from the stream and munching hay, the campfire and the sizzling food—all of it seemed oddly removed.

Keegan got to his feet, said something about checking on Devon and walked away into that other dimension, so near and yet so far away.

Lucas let his bottle fall, fighting sleep.

Molly lay down beside him and promptly dozed off.

DEVON AND A TRIBE of other kids were wading in the creek a few hundred yards west of the camp—by nightfall, they'd be covered in mosquito bites and dog tired, sitting sleepily around the bonfire and roasting marshmallows over the flames. Keegan smiled, remembering similar episodes from his own childhood, when he and Rance and Jesse had ranged all over the Triple M, wild as any critter in the high country.

Heading back, he paused to get another blanket from the supply in the back of one of the pickups, then went to cover Molly and Lucas with it, careful not to wake them.

When he turned to leave again, he practically collided with Meg.

She put her finger to her lips, then crooked her arm through Keegan's and tugged him away.

Under the shade of a cottonwood tree Jesse had a poker game going with Rance and Travis and a few Texas McKettricks. Cheyenne, Emma and Sierra were setting out food on the long folding tables brought along for the purpose, chatting with an ease that reminded Keegan poignantly of other such occasions, long ago.

Meg finally perched on a large flat rock overlooking the valley below, and Keegan sat down beside her.

"You looked like somebody gut-punched you, at the meeting this morning," she said, drawing her booted feet up and wrapping both arms around her knees. She wore jeans and a long-sleeved blue T-shirt, and her blond hair was artfully cut to look mussed.

"I had a feeling it would turn out the way it did," Keegan said. "I guess I just hoped I was wrong."

Meg studied him. "Mom says the new board is probably going to offer you a pretty attractive package to stay on."

Keegan didn't say anything. He'd heard rumors to that effect ever since the talk about going public had begun, but he'd never been interested.

Meg grinned, elbowed him playfully. "Speaking of pretty attractive packages," she said, "the lady you just covered with that blanket certainly qualifies. What's her name?"

"Molly Shields," Keegan answered dryly. "As if you didn't already know."

Meg's eyes twinkled, but they were still filled with solemn secrets, just like always. "Rance and Jesse are taking bets," she said, "that she's the one."

"The one what?" Keegan asked, stalling.

She elbowed him again, a little harder this time. "The One."

"Well," Keegan said, "I hope you didn't put any money on it."

Meg shifted. "I was sorry to hear about Psyche, Keeg," she told him. "Seems like things are just piling up on you these days."

He nodded. "Shelley's in Paris, looking for an apartment. She wants to move there with the boyfriend and put Devon in some boarding school."

"You're not going to let her, are you? Take Devon to France, I mean?"

"I'm not sure I can stop her," Keegan said after a long time. "She's Devon's mother, after all."

"And you're her father." She paused, and an awkward pause followed as Keegan looked back over his shoulder to make sure Devon wasn't nearby.

"As far as I'm concerned, yes," he said. "I'm Devon's father. But Shelley's up to something, Meg. She's tried to tap Devon's trust fund a couple of times already, and once word is out about McKettrickCo and the IPO, she's going to want a piece of it. Even if she has to use her own daughter."

"Have you talked to Travis about this?"

Keegan shook his head. "Not specifically. We discussed suing Shelley for full custody once or twice, but you know what will happen if I do that. All hell will break loose, and Devon will take the brunt of it. And there's no assurance that I'll win."

"You could always offer Shelley what she loves best," Meg suggested, rubbing her fingers together in the age-old sign for money.

"Dad!" Devon called anxiously, and both Meg and Keegan turned to see her running toward them.

"Mr. Terp's here! He drove all the way out from town because—because—" She stopped, gasping.

Keegan bolted off the rock to intercept Devon, took her gently but firmly by the shoulders. "Because of Psyche?" he asked, sick with dread.

Devon nodded her head. "But it's not—what you—think!" Finally she caught her breath. "A man broke in to her house and it scared Mrs. Washington so much, she had to go to the clinic to get her heart checked, and he's in jail, the man, I mean, and he says he knows Molly—Mrs. Terp is there, with Psyche, but she can't stay—"

Keegan left Devon with Meg and headed back toward the center of camp. Molly was already sitting in the front seat of Wyatt Terp's personal vehicle, an old Suburban, Lucas fidgeting in her lap. Wyatt stood at a little distance, talking to Rance and Jesse.

When he saw Keegan, he came out to meet him. "I'm sorry for interrupting a family shindig," Wyatt said, "but I didn't know what else to do."

"It's all right, Wyatt," Keegan replied, turning back to look for Devon, who was practically on his heels, with Meg a little way behind. "Do you want to stay, Dev, or go to town with me?" he asked.

Devon looked torn. Of course she wanted to stay—she was a kid and this was a campout, complete with horses, cousins and marshmallows waiting to be roasted—but she was willing to throw all that over at his say-so.

"I'll watch out for Devon," Meg said.

Keegan kissed his daughter's forehead. "Give me an answer, shortstop," he said.

"I'd rather stay," she told him.

Keegan kissed her again. "No worrying," he said. And then he got into the back of Wyatt's rig.

The trip back down to lower ground was a rough one, since there was no real road, and by the time they reached Rance's place, where Keegan had left the Jag, Molly looked as though she'd been dragged behind the Suburban the whole way.

She fumbled so much trying to hook Lucas into his car seat that Keegan finally had to ease her aside and take over the job himself. Wyatt, having done his duty, was already on his way back to town.

Molly plopped into the passenger seat and sat limply, staring through the windshield.

Keegan got behind the wheel, started the engine and ate Wyatt's dust all the way to the city limits.

Molly didn't speak the whole way, and neither did Keegan—at least, not to her. He called the clinic, was told that Florence had been given some medication and one of the nurses had driven her home. She'd had a shock, though, and she was to rest. Taking care of Psyche was out of the question.

When they passed the police station, Keegan slowed.

"Don't stop," Molly said.

Wyatt had kept up a running commentary on the situation all the way from Jesse's ridge to Rance's place. She hadn't commented once, even when her name had come up in connection with the yahoo cooling his heels in jail on charges of breaking and entering.

"You want to tell me who this guy is?" Keegan finally asked. He tried to speak calmly, but inside, he was seething. For a while there he'd actually felt sorry for Molly, even thought she might be on the level.

"No," she said. "I don't. Not right now, anyway."

Keegan set his jaw. When they pulled up outside Psyche's place, he went around for Lucas again. Molly reached for the little boy, but Keegan held him away.

She followed Keegan up the walk.

He tried the door, found it locked.

Molly gave him a triumphant look, fished a key out of her jeans pocket and used it.

He stormed through the house, set Lucas in his playpen in the kitchen.

Psyche was in her hospital bed on the sunporch. Seeing Keegan, she held out her arms. "Thank God you're here," she said.

He allowed her to cling to him until she was ready to let go, and sagged back onto her pillows.

"Where's Florence?" Molly asked.

"In her room," Psyche answered, "resting. She's had a terrible turn."

"What happened?" Keegan asked. He'd heard Wyatt's version, but he wanted Psyche's.

"Florence was up on the third floor, vacuuming

the carpets," Psyche said. "She heard something and thought it came from Molly's room, so she went to investigate." Psyche stopped, laid a hand to her chest, took several shaky breaths. "There was a *man* in there, wearing a ski mask and ransacking the bureau drawers. Florence screamed and hurried down all three flights of stairs, burst through the doorway and told me what was happening—and then she collapsed. Thank God I'd been talking on the phone earlier, and I still had the receiver. I called 911, and Wyatt came, but I thought he'd never get here, and there was Florence moaning on the floor, and that awful prowler somewhere in the house—"

Keegan poured water from the carafe at Psyche's bedside and held the cup to her mouth so she could take a few sips.

"According to Wyatt's deputy," Psyche went on when she'd finished the water, "the prowler said Molly would explain everything...."

Keegan shot a glare in Molly's direction.

She blushed, squared her shoulders.

"Molly?" Psyche urged, looking confused and fearful.

"His name is Davis Jerritt," Molly said. "And he's a famous writer."

"DAVE," MOLLY SAID an hour later when she stood in front of her client's cell, "this time you've really gone over the line."

Keegan stared at the outlaw with apparent fascination.

A tall, skinny man with a thatch of red hair now standing out from his head in all directions, Dave paced the narrow space behind the bars. He was clearly mánic. "I've come up with a whole new character," he enthused. "Now that I've been in stir—"

"Dave," Molly interrupted, "you are *not* in 'stir.' You are in a municipal jail in Indian Rock, Arizona. Try to stay with me here. You've been *arrested,* and it's not a scene in one of your books. This is *real,* Dave. You broke in to someone's house and, believe me, you are in *big* trouble."

Dave rolled his unimpressive shoulders, and finally noticed Keegan looming beside Molly like a storm cloud. She'd expected him to stay with Psyche, but when Florence had rallied enough to take charge again, he'd insisted on driving her to the jail.

"Who's this?" Dave asked with interest.

"Keegan McKettrick," Molly said, resenting the distraction.

"A fan, I suppose," Dave said, pleased.

"Not really," Molly clarified. "If it weren't for these bars, he'd probably reach down your throat and grab your gizzard."

"Things like that happen in stir," Dave said knowingly.

Molly rolled her eyes. "When did you last take your medication?" she asked.

"There aren't enough drugs on the planet to pull this guy back through the ozone," Keegan said.

"Shut up," Molly told him. Then she remembered he wasn't a client.

"Tuesday," Dave answered. He turned an imploring gaze on Keegan. "It was research," he said. "For my new book. The hero is a psychotic stalker, and I had to know how he felt."

"Holy shit," Keegan marveled.

Molly turned on her heel, went out into the office, looking for Wyatt. She found him standing by the watercooler, staring into a cup.

"Dave needs to go to the hospital," she said. "Now."

"The hospital?" Wyatt asked, befuddled.

"He's bipolar to the power of ten, and he hasn't taken his medication since Tuesday. *Which* Tuesday is anybody's guess."

"You do this for a living?" Keegan wanted to know.

"It's complicated," Molly said. "Shouldn't you get back to Psyche?"

"She's all right," Keegan replied. "Florence is with her. I can't believe you do this for ten percent of *any* amount of money."

"Fifteen percent," Molly corrected. "I get *fifteen* percent, and fifteen percent of what Davis Jerritt can command is *a lot.*"

"I'll call an ambulance," Wyatt said.

"Good idea," Molly replied, checking her watch. "Tell them to strap him down."

"Will you be riding up to Flagstaff with him?" the lawman asked.

"No," Molly said. "He is *so* fired."

With that, she headed for the front door, stormed out into the night.

Keegan kept up. "I thought *my* job was crazy," he said.

Molly drew herself up. "Most of my clients," she replied coolly, "are sane professionals."

"Right," Keegan said. Damn him, he was *loving* this. "Florence told me about the old guy who came all the way to Indian Rock to fire you for about the tenth time. I think she's got a crush on his chauffeur."

Molly started to laugh. It was, she figured, an hysterical reaction.

"Come on," Keegan said, shuffling her toward his Jag, which was parked by the curb. "I'll take you home."

"Where would that be?" she asked.

Keegan eased her into the front seat of his car and even went so far as to lean in and fasten her seat belt for her. "Since Los Angeles is out of the question, I guess I'll take you back to Psyche's."

It was remarkable, Molly thought, how a person could be laughing one minute and crying the next.

Keegan thrust out a sigh. "Okay," he said.

"Okay?" Molly asked. "What's that supposed to mean?"

He went around the car, opened the door on the driver's side, got in. "It means 'okay,'" he said. "And stop trying to pretend you're not crying."

She sniffled. "I'm not crying," she said.

"Bullshit," Keegan answered charitably.

Molly expected him to head straight for Psyche's house, but he didn't. He turned the wrong way on the highway and pulled into the lot of a place called the Roadhouse.

"You're hungry," he said when Molly gave him a questioning look.

"I am not," she lied.

"Well," Keegan answered, "*I* am." He shut off the car, got out and came around to open Molly's door. "You can sit here and starve if you want to," he told her when she didn't move. "But it would be stupid and, believe me, it won't keep me from enjoying a double cheeseburger deluxe with everything."

"Lucas—"

"Lucas is fine," he said.

Molly unsnapped her seat belt and got out of the car. Keegan rested a hand on the small of her back and steered her toward the entrance of the restaurant.

"I'm sorry, Keegan," she said, without intending to say anything of the kind. She had to stop ambushing herself like this.

A hostess led them to a corner booth. Keegan

didn't take his hand off Molly's back. He didn't answer, either.

"About Dave," she clarified. "Florence got a terrible scare, and so did Psyche. And you had to leave your family up on the mountain."

Keegan opened a menu and studied it as though he hadn't already decided on a double cheeseburger deluxe with everything.

For some reason, Molly found his silence almost impossible to bear.

"Say something," she said.

"You really need to look into other career opportunities," he replied.

Suddenly her sinuses clogged up again, and her eyes burned. "I thought I had a whole new career lined up," she told him. "I was going to be my son's mother."

Keegan closed the menu.

The waitress came back and, without taking his eyes off Molly, he ordered for both of them.

"I'm staying at Psyche's place tonight," he announced when the food-service professional had gone. "Just in case another of your clients shows up to do research."

CHAPTER 11

PSYCHE, LUCAS AND FLORENCE were all sound asleep
on the sunporch when Keegan and Molly returned
to the house—Psyche in her hospital bed, Florence
in a chair pulled back from the table, and Lucas in
his playpen.

The sight had a curious effect on Keegan; they
were a brave little band of three, lost in some strange
and uncertain place and huddled together for safety.

Molly moved to approach Lucas, probably intending to carry him upstairs and put him to bed in his
crib, but Keegan reached out, stopped her. Shook his
head when she gave him a curious, somewhat wary
look.

He put a finger to his lips when she would have
spoken and stepped back into the kitchen. Molly followed, and he reached past her to pull the sliding
door shut, careful to make as little noise as possible.

"Sit down," he said when Molly began to look rebellious.

She balked, then shrugged stiffly, went to the table and sat. "What?" she asked in a testy whisper. Evidently the salutary effects of a double cheeseburger with everything were already wearing off.

Keegan sat down across from her. Hesitated. "This is going to sound crazy," he said.

Molly leaned forward a little, lowered her brows slightly, practically daring him to say anything she could possibly take issue with. And she waited.

"It's not just going to sound crazy," Keegan went on. "It *is* crazy."

Molly threw him off with a quick and totally unexpected smile. "It can't be any worse than what Davis Jerritt did," she said. "In terms of crazy, I mean."

Keegan wasn't so sure of that. He drew a deep breath and let it out slowly. "We could get married."

The smile faded. She looked wary again. "If this is some kind of joke," she said, "it's not funny."

"It's not a joke," Keegan said. "Maybe it should be, but it isn't."

"You?" Molly pointed to him. "And me?" Pointing back to herself.

"I don't see anybody else around here," he said. "*Yes,* you and me."

"But…"

He saw realization dawn in her face. As a kid, she'd

probably been cute. As a woman, she was beautiful—
even with puffy eyes from all that crying.

"It's what Psyche wants," he said. "And we could
raise Lucas. Together." He paused, suddenly very
uncomfortable, and cleared his throat. "Of course,
we wouldn't have sex or anything like that."

Molly leaned back a little way, folded her arms
across her chest in a reflexive motion, then let
them fall to her sides again. "Of course not," she
agreed, but she looked skeptical. "What's in this
for you, Keegan?"

"Lucas," he said simply.

"You and I don't get along very well," she reminded him. As if he needed reminding.

"Not a problem," he answered.

"*Not a problem?* How do you figure that? Psyche
wants Lucas to have a family. She has a fantasy, I
think, that we'll fall madly in love, you and I, and
live happily ever after, if she can just get us together.
We *both* know that isn't going to happen."

"We'll agree to live under the same roof. Most of
the time you can go your way, and I'll go mine. We
might not love each other, but we both love Lucas."

"What kind of home would that be for him?"
Molly asked. "And maybe *you* don't mind going
the rest of your natural life without sex, but I'm not
ready to give up on it yet. For one thing, I'd like to
have more children—someday."

"Okay," Keegan said generously. "If you want sex,
I'll oblige."

Molly widened her eyes at him. "Gee, thanks," she said.

He shook his head. "You are deliberately not understanding this," he said.

"I understand only too well," Molly replied. "What happens if one of us falls in love with somebody else? There'd be a divorce then, and Psyche doesn't want that for Lucas. Neither do I."

"Trust me," Keegan said. "I'm not going to fall in love with anybody. Been there, done that."

"Well, *I've* never been in love—" She fell silent suddenly, blushing.

"Not even with Thayer?" Keegan asked carefully. He was a man walking through a minefield, and he had to step lightly.

"That wasn't love," Molly said. "It wasn't even lust."

"What was it, then?"

"Stupidity," she answered with flushed certainty.

"Look, if sex is such a big thing to you, we could give it a trial run."

Molly's mouth fell open. She snapped it closed, drew a couple of breaths in through her flared nostrils and steamed them back out again. "A *trial run?* I've met some jerks in my life, Keegan McKettrick, but you take the freaking prize!"

"How do you know you wouldn't like it?" he asked. He was in so deep by then, there was nothing to do but keep wading and hope his boots didn't fill up, figuratively speaking.

She blinked. "Why, you *arrogant*—"

He put up a hand. "Molly," he said, "I'm offering you a choice between busing it back to L.A. empty-handed and staying right here in Indian Rock to raise your son. Think about it. Little League baseball games. School pictures. Trail rides. The kind of things Psyche wants for Lucas."

"If—if I agreed to this, where would we live?"

"Definitely on the Triple M. This mausoleum is no place for a kid to grow up."

"You think Psyche would agree? This is her family home, and one of the original terms was that Lucas had to grow up here." She paused, swallowed. Beneath her thin T-shirt her nipples hardened visibly. Not that Keegan was looking at her breasts. Much. "Besides, she'd surely suspect that it wasn't a real marriage."

"She's betting on both of us falling hard, sooner or later. And what she doesn't know won't hurt her."

Molly gnawed on her lower lip. "No, but it might hurt Lucas."

"Not if we act like civilized adults, it won't."

"This is a seriously mental idea. Did Dave Jerritt suggest it?"

Keegan ignored that. "That's the offer, Molly. Take it or leave it. Psyche made her terms pretty clear."

She wanted to agree, he could see that.

He could also see the nipples, pressing against the front of her shirt.

"You don't trust me," she reasoned. "Why would you want to *marry* me?"

"I don't. I want to raise Lucas. So do you. Connect the dots, Molly."

"But there's a tremendous risk—"

"There's *always* a risk," he interrupted, "tremendous or otherwise."

She got up out of her chair unexpectedly, and crossed the room to ease open the sliding door and peek in at Lucas. Apparently he was still sound asleep, because she closed it again, very quietly, and turned back to face Keegan.

"I want the trial run," she said.

Keegan was so stunned, he couldn't answer for a moment.

She smiled. "What's the matter, McKettrick?" she asked. "Are you chicken?"

"Molly, we can't just…"

"Why not? We can 'just' get married. We can 'just' agree to raise a child together. I'm not going for this until I know you can deliver, buckaroo."

Heat surged through Keegan, partly indignation, partly every cell in his body yelling *yahoo*. "Are you on the pill?" he asked.

She shook her head. "No reason," she said. "I'm not involved with anybody at the moment."

What did she mean by "at the moment"? he wondered. Was there another married man in L.A.?

"I didn't bring…"

"You can't seem to finish a sentence," she pointed out, clearly enjoying the fact that she'd turned the tables on him somewhere along the line. "If you were about to say you didn't bring a condom, no problem—I don't want you to wear one."

"Why—" He had to stop and swallow. "Why not?"

"Because I wouldn't mind getting pregnant," she said. "I know I can't replace Lucas, no matter how many babies I have, but if this whole thing blows up in our faces and Psyche decides to give Lucas to Travis and Sierra anyway, I might go back to California with something more than a broken heart."

Keegan pushed back his chair, but quietly, and got to his feet. "There's one flaw in your logic," he said fiercely. "If we make love and you get pregnant, the baby would be just as much mine as yours. There's *no possible* way I'd let you just vanish into LaLa Land with my child."

"If you knew there was a child in the first place," she said.

Oh, she was a negotiator, all right. Probably very good at her job.

But she was overlooking one important fact. He wasn't half-bad at driving a bargain, either.

"I'll know, Molly," he told her, and he could see by the expression on her face that she believed him.

She jutted her chin out a little way. "Fair enough," she said.

Then she started off through the kitchen, toward the dining room.

Keegan followed, wondering what the hell he was

getting himself into. Moreover, what was he getting *Devon* into, and Lucas?

They moved through the dining room, into the huge entryway.

Molly jabbed at the elevator button, a challenge in her eyes. And there was something else, too—she thought he was going to back down.

Breaking news: he wasn't.

The elevator came and they got in, standing as far from each other as they could without plastering themselves against the walls.

Keegan pushed the button for the third floor.

They jolted upward.

Presently the elevator stopped.

Keegan pushed back the folding grate, opened the door beyond.

Molly's eyes were huge. It was beginning to dawn on her that he was about to call her bluff, big-time. She could always change her mind—it went without saying that he wasn't going to force her into anything—but he was betting her pride wouldn't let her back down. And since she'd said she wanted a trial run, she was going to have to be the one to call a halt.

She stood still for a moment in the elevator, then pushed past him into the hallway, marched to the door of her room and pushed it open. Of course, she could still slam it in his face. He certainly wouldn't try to break it down.

He waited, fascinated and—he wouldn't have denied it—horny as hell.

Molly left the door open.

He smiled to himself and followed her as far as the threshold. Stood there, waiting for a cue from her.

She dragged the T-shirt off over her head, threw it defiantly aside. Her bra was pink and lacy, a gossamer thing with about as much substance as a breath. He couldn't be sure, with nothing but a little moonlight to go by, but he thought it had one of those catches at the front. One motion of his thumb and her breasts would spill, warm and deliciously natural, into his hands.

Keegan stepped into the room, closed the door and took off his shirt.

Molly waited a beat, then kicked off her boots.

Keegan, grinning a little in the semidarkness, did the same. Damn, but he'd been hoping the bra would go next, even though he relished the prospect of removing it personally.

She unsnapped her jeans, shimmied out of them, kicked them away. The moon gilded her slender thighs in silver. She was wearing a skimpy pair of panties, pink like the bra.

Keegan was so hard, it hurt. He unfastened his belt buckle, then his jeans. And he enjoyed the look of shock on Molly's face, visible even in that thin light, when she realized he wasn't wearing anything underneath.

He was naked.

She was still wearing panties and a bra.

She knew it was her move, and whatever else she was, she was a sport. She hooked her thumbs under the elastic in those panties and pushed them down. Stepped out of them.

He went to her then, more because he couldn't *not* go to her than because he had any specific intention. He cupped her face in his hands, bent his head and kissed her—

Keegan's lips seared Molly's, and his tongue— well, if this kiss was anything to go by, he knew how to use it. The possibilities made her knees go weak, and she might actually have lost her balance if he hadn't caught her, his hands strong on her bare hips, and held her upright.

And still the kiss went on.

She'd issued a challenge, down there in the kitchen and again when he'd paused on the threshold a few moments before. She'd expected him to back-pedal, been surprised and thrilled when he hadn't.

He broke off the kiss, stepped back a little way. Worked the front catch on her bra with an expertise that both galled her and vaporized her blood. He caught her breasts the instant they were free, and held them gently. Chafed the already-hard nipples— he'd noticed them in the kitchen, damn him—with the sides of his thumbs.

Molly, who had not been with a man since Thayer, well before Lucas was born, let her head fall back and groaned as Keegan caressed her. She might have told herself any man would have done, her need was that great, but she knew it wasn't true.

Like it or not, Keegan McKettrick was the only game in town.

He took one of her nipples into his mouth.

Molly gasped and plunged her fingers into his hair, not to push him away, but to hold him closer. She was going to regret this, she was sure of it, but in the dizzy meantime, she intended to give herself up to every sensation.

Keegan eased her down onto the rumpled bed, still unmade. Stretched out beside her, agile and graceful, his hard body warm and solid.

He moved on top of her, and she was relieved.

He was going to take her.

She would come to her senses soon.

Taking her wrists in a gentle grip, he raised them high above her head, pressed them into the pillows. Kissed her again, languidly, but with an intimacy that left her dazed.

Take me, she pleaded silently, too proud to say the words aloud.

He didn't, though. He moved down her body, still holding her wrists in his hands, nibbling at her neck, the upper rounding of her breasts and, finally, a nipple.

Molly groaned aloud.

Keegan chuckled, the sound a seduction in its own right, melting things inside her. He attended thoroughly to her other breast, and then guided her hands to the brass spokes of the headboard.

"You'd better hold on, Molly Shields," he murmured.

She would think about his arrogance later. About his audacity—

Oh, God.

He was kissing her belly, parting her legs with a motion of his knee.

He wasn't going to—he couldn't be about to—

He was.

He went down on Molly, took her clitoris into his mouth with no hesitation whatsoever.

She arched her back, strangling on a moan.

He feasted on her, tongued her, draped her knees over his shoulders and suckled, now slowly, now greedily, until Molly was pleading incoherently, her body slick with perspiration. She wanted him inside her, she wanted what he was doing to her now to go on and on, forever.

She came to the brink of climax, everything within her tensing for the eruption, but he made her wait. He teased her, brought her back to the edge, left her quivering there, withdrew again. Planted light kisses on the insides of her thighs.

"Oh, Keegan…" she whimpered.

"What?" he murmured.

"Do it. *Please* do it!"

"Do what?"

"Make—me—come…"

"Umm," he said, almost thoughtfully. And then she was full in his mouth again, and he was suckling in earnest.

She let go of the headboard and groped for his hair, buried her fingers in it, would not let him leave her.

The orgasm was shattering, like some enormous collision, fiery and ferocious. It would relent a little, then catch her up again, toss her helplessly about in some high, invisible place where she couldn't catch her breath. Keegan drove her into the core of it, again and again, and when he finally lowered her to the bed, she was all but insensible with the echoing force of her release.

She felt his enormous erection against her.

He'd satisfied her completely—or so she thought. This part would be for him—she would play along. Pretend a little, if she had to.

Then he moved inside her.

There would be no pretending, she realized, beginning the climb again with the first long thrust.

She had thought the initial orgasm was the pinnacle.

She'd been wrong.

She locked her legs around Keegan's thighs, tilted her hips up so she could receive everything he wanted to give her and *take* anything he might hold back, as well.

He raised himself onto his hands, hammered deeper into her, and then deeper still.

After several frenzied minutes they came together, with a ragged cry that might have come from either one of them but probably came from both, Keegan with his head thrown back, Molly sobbing and pressing into his back with her fingers, lest he somehow withdraw from her too soon.

But he didn't.

She descended slowly, through a series of softer, ever softer releases, so sweetly intense that she groaned at each one. And at each one, Keegan stayed with her, still hard, still plunging deep.

When it was finally over, he lay down beside her, on his back, gasping for breath. He moved her easily to lie on top of him, and tugged up the blankets, keeping her snug.

It was a very long time before either of them spoke—in fact, Molly wasn't entirely sure they didn't sleep at intervals. She'd lost all track of time.

He stroked her back, squeezed her buttocks lightly, lifted her head from his neck for a few kisses.

He was getting hard again beneath her belly.

"Keegan," she whispered, "I don't think I can…"

Keegan lifted her so she sat astraddle his hips, and entered her in one powerful thrust. By the second thrust she was moaning. By the third, she was pleading.

By the fourth, she was coming again.

After that she lost count—of the thrusts *and* the orgasms.

KEEGAN LAY ENTANGLED with Molly until he was sure she was asleep. Then, smiling a little, he got out of bed, pulled on his jeans and left the room. Dawn was breaking, and he meant to get Lucas, carry him upstairs and place him in the crib so Molly wouldn't wake up worried.

But Lucas was already awake and dressed, bouncing in his playpen in the kitchen. Florence was there, too, stirring something on the stove. She gave Keegan a sidelong glance.

"Well, now," she said. "Look at you, Mr. Keegan McKettrick. Half-decent, at this hour of the morning."

Keegan didn't bolt, though he wouldn't have set foot in that kitchen, wearing only a pair of misbuttoned jeans, if he'd known Florence was going to be there. "How's Psyche?" he asked.

"Still sleeping," Florence said.

Lucas stood on tiptoe in the playpen, his arms upraised.

Something happened in Keegan's heart as he hoisted the boy into his arms. Without saying anything to Florence, he turned and set out for the third floor again, as originally intended.

Molly was sitting up in bed, pink cheeked and sleep rumpled, when he arrived. Lucas strained in Keegan's grasp, wanting to go to her.

Keegan handed the child over, suddenly self-conscious.

He gathered up his shirt, boots and socks.

"The shower is that way," Molly told him, pointing to a door. Her expression revealed little or nothing of what she was thinking, but the soft sparkle in her eyes told the story.

The trial run had been a success.

The question was, where did they go from there?

Twenty minutes later Keegan came out of Molly's bathroom, feeling uncomfortable in yesterday's clothes. He was both relieved and disappointed to see that she was gone, and so, of course, was the boy.

He padded to the nursery door, having glimpsed a crib there earlier, but that room was empty, too. Paused to tug on his boots.

Molly was downstairs in the kitchen, chatting with Florence and sipping coffee while she spooned some kind of cereal goop into Lucas's mouth.

Keegan hesitated in the doorway, watching her.

She wore white linen shorts and a green tank top, and her honey-colored hair was caught up in some kind of clip at the back of her head. Keegan wondered if he should have warned her that Florence knew they'd slept together—she'd have had to be an idiot not to figure that out the moment he first walked into the kitchen.

Molly looked bright, rested—and she glowed with satisfaction.

As if sensing his presence, she turned and saw him standing there.

The cereal spoon froze in midair.

Damn, he thought. *She regrets it already.*

He was stuck, though, with no graceful way to retreat. "How's Psyche?" he asked Florence for the second time that morning.

Molly frowned slightly, and went back to feeding Lucas.

"Go on in there and see for yourself," Florence said.

"Shall I tell her?" Keegan asked, addressing Molly.

She turned to him again, color flaring in her cheeks.

"About the marriage thing," he clarified, annoyed. *As if* he'd been going to walk out there onto the sunporch and tell Psyche he'd spent the night in Molly's bed doing what came naturally.

Molly frowned, nodded. Left off feeding Lucas, who had lost interest anyway, and set the spoon and the bowl of cereal aside with a thump.

Keegan wondered, apropos of nothing, when she'd showered. If she'd shared a stall with him, he would have noticed. In fact, they'd probably still be there.

She followed him out after running her palms once down the front of her shorts, an anxious gesture that spoke volumes.

Sorely tempted to bait her a little, Keegan took the high road and assumed a dignified manner. No, sirree, he was not going to mention to Molly, the next time they were alone, that he could still feel her inner thighs squashing his ears.

Psyche looked as though there had been a miraculous healing—her eyes were bright and focused, there was color in her cheeks and she was sitting up, with a book lying open on her lap.

"Good morning," she said, smiling.

Molly murmured a response. Keegan said nothing.

Psyche raised her eyebrows. "You've decided," she concluded.

"Yes," Keegan said.

Molly elbowed him. "Tell her *what* we decided."

Keegan couldn't resist nettling her a little. "Last night, you mean?"

She narrowed her eyes at him. He figured she could be dangerous, under the right circumstances.

"Molly and I are getting married," he said.

Florence must have been eavesdropping. Something, probably a skillet, clattered loudly to the floor.

Lucas gave a chortling belly laugh and clapped his hands, delighted by any sort of ruckus.

"When?" Psyche asked.

"As soon as you promise to let us raise Lucas if we do," Molly answered.

Psyche smiled, triumphant. "You have to live together, of course," she said.

"Of course," Keegan agreed solemnly. If last night was any indication, all he and Molly had to do was stay in bed 24/7, practicing body slams, and they were good to go.

"It's all settled, then," Psyche said. "We'll have the wedding ceremony right here in the house. Three days from now. That's how long it takes to get a marriage license, isn't it?"

Keegan closed his eyes in a bid for patience. Reminded himself that the woman was terminally ill, and only trying to assure the best possible life for the child she would soon have to leave behind. "Psyche..."

"Well, of course I need to know for certain that you're actually married," Psyche said. "I can't just take your word for it."

"Why not?"

"Because too many things could go wrong. It's not as if I'm impugning your integrity—"

"The hell you aren't," Keegan growled.

Psyche merely smiled.

"We're going to live on the Triple M," he said. "Not here."

"Fine," Psyche said. "We're all agreed, then. Aren't we, Molly?"

Molly was the color of the underwear she'd been wearing the night before, and her green eyes looked feverish with hope and temper. "Yes," she said.

"If there are people you want to invite to the wedding," Psyche went breezily on, "you'd better get in touch with them. And don't forget to apply for the license."

"Maybe you'd like to choose my dress," Molly said.

Another beatific smile. "As long as it's not white, dear," Psyche replied. Then she picked up the book lying on her lap, found her place and began to read again.

Molly turned on one heel and stomped out.

Keegan lingered.

"Was there something else?" Psyche asked innocently.

Keegan approached the bed, gripped the side rail, leaned in and said, "Yeah. There's something else."

"What?"

"Call Travis and Sierra and tell them they're not going to be adopting Lucas after all. My guess is they're going to be pretty disappointed."

Psyche smiled again, endearingly. "Well, they might have been," she said, "if I'd ever actually made the offer in the first place. I asked Travis to play along, hoping you'd come to your senses, and he did." She paused, savoring his reaction. "Why don't you go out there in the kitchen and tell Molly the truth, Keegan? You can still get yourself off the hook."

He stared at her.

She beamed back at him, patted his cheek. "But you won't do that, will you?"

"What makes you think I won't?" Keegan asked angrily.

"I *know* you won't."

"Is that right?"

"Of course it is," Psyche said with cheerful finality. "You and Molly made love last night. I'd have to be blind not to know it. Molly's radiant—mad as a wet hen, but radiant—and you look…"

Keegan's neck warmed. "Damn it, Psyche, of all the sneaky, manipulative, underhanded—"

She stretched, kissed him lightly on the mouth. "You're keeping me from my book," she said.

"Did you put Molly through that to pay her back for—"

"For sleeping with my husband? Of course not. But there might have been the tiniest barb in that remark about her wedding dress. I like Molly, Keegan. I wouldn't give her my child if I didn't."

Keegan turned to walk away.

All he had to do was go into the kitchen and tell Molly the truth—that Psyche would let her adopt Lucas whether they got married or not. They could write the trial run off as just another memorable night and get on with their lives.

And if he did that, chances were he would not only lose Lucas, he would lose Molly, too.

CHAPTER 12

KEEGAN NEEDED to think.

He *wanted* to get Molly naked and take her against the nearest wall.

He *needed* distance, and perspective.

After they'd gone to the little courthouse adjacent to Wyatt's jail and applied for a marriage license, he and Molly parted ways.

Molly went back to Psyche's place, and to Lucas.

Keegan headed for the Triple M.

Once there, he changed clothes, wolfed down a nuked breakfast sandwich only two days past its expiration date, and went out to the barn.

Spud's feeder was full, and so was his waterer, but he still welcomed Keegan with a cheerful bray.

"Hey, buddy," Keegan said. After fetching the clippers and a hasp, he went into Spud's stall, picked up one of the donkey's feet and began trimming hooves. It wasn't hard work, but it required a certain amount of patience, and the critter bore it cheerfully.

"I'm getting married," Keegan told the donkey.

Spud nuzzled his shoulder, maybe in sympathy. More likely, he was hoping for a lump of sugar or a carrot.

"Her name is Molly," Keegan went on, clipping away, careful to avoid the tender flesh inside Spud's hoof, called the frog. "She's sexy as hell, but she's about as stubborn as—well—a mule. No offense."

Spud nickered. His brown eyes were full of trust.

Keegan set the clippers aside and took up the hasp, a metal file used to smooth the rough edges. The sound was rhythmic, and probably the reason he didn't hear an arriving vehicle.

He was taken by surprise when Devon's head popped up over the stall door. Her face was sunburned and there was a mosquito bite on her chin, but otherwise she looked as though she'd survived the campout and the ride down from Jesse's ridge.

"Cheyenne dropped me off," she said.

Keegan grinned, glad to see her. "Did you have a good time?"

"Excellent," Devon answered. "We roasted marshmallows and Uncle Jesse told ghost stories, and Maeve and Rianna and I stayed up *way late*. Liam ate too many hot dogs and hurled all over the place, and Sierra had to wash him off in the creek."

"Sounds typical," Keegan said, pleased. He'd

been doused a time or two in that creek himself as a boy.

"Can I get a pony?"

"Yeah," Keegan replied. "But not this very minute."

Devon grinned at Spud. "He's getting a manicure," she observed. "If he wasn't a boy, I'd put nail polish on him."

Keegan chuckled. "Go take a bath," he said.

Devon sighed. "I have to clean out Spud's stall first," she replied. "It's a mess. He's pooped *everywhere.*"

"Makes sense to do that before you take a bath," Keegan admitted, still smiling a little as he went back to filing Spud's hoof.

Devon darted away, came back pushing the wheelbarrow and carrying a pitchfork over one shoulder. She began scooping, but Keegan knew she'd picked up on something in his manner by the way she kept stealing glances. She was an intuitive kid.

Keegan straightened, rested one arm on Spud's back.

Devon stood still, too, leaning on the handle of the pitchfork. Waiting.

"I'm getting married in a couple of days, shortstop," Keegan said.

She was silent for what seemed like a long time, but was probably only a second or two. "To Molly?"

He nodded.

"Is she going to live here after Psyche dies? With Lucas?"

Keegan nodded again. The suspense was killing him—Devon could come down in favor of the marriage, or she could feel threatened. Her position on the matter was vitally important to him, he realized. He hadn't given that aspect much thought before—the whole idea of getting married, to Molly or anybody else, was so new that he was still trying to assimilate it himself.

"Will that mean Lucas is my brother?"

"Yes," Keegan said. "Are you okay with that?"

"I guess you've probably always wanted a son."

"Nothing beats a daughter," Keegan told her. "But I won't mind having a son, too."

"He'll be a McKettrick? Like me?"

"He'll be a McKettrick," Keegan confirmed. "Like you."

Devon's lower lip wobbled. "But he'll get to live here all the time, and I won't. You might start loving Lucas more than you love me, just because you get to see him every day."

Keegan crossed the short distance to where Devon stood, still gripping the pitchfork, and laid his hands on her shoulders. "McKettrick-true, Dev," he said quietly, his voice gruff. "I'm never going to love Lucas more than I love you."

She pondered that, her expression so heartbreakingly serious that Keegan's eyes burned. "Promise?" she asked.

"Promise."

She tilted her head back to look straight up into his face. "I guess you should try to love Lucas just as much as you love me, though. That's only fair."

He wrapped an arm around her shoulders, held her close for a moment. Kissed the top of her head. "I'll try," he said.

"What about Molly? Do you love her, too?"

He'd known that question would come, and he'd dreaded it. He was already living one lie where Devon was concerned, and he couldn't add another, even though it would have made things easier for both of them. "No," he said.

Devon pulled back from him, let the pitchfork fall, forgotten, to the floor. *"Dad!"* she protested.

"People get married every day, all over the world, for reasons that have nothing much to do with love," Keegan hastened to point out.

"You didn't love Mom," Devon argued staunchly, "and look what happened. There was a whole bunch of fighting and yelling, and then you moved out. You got divorced, and *I* got caught in the middle!"

"I know you did, Dev. And I'm sorry. I'd do anything to make it up to you."

She bent to retrieve the pitchfork. Straightened again. "Then tell Mom you want me to live here, all the time, with you and Molly and Lucas."

The plea in Devon's eyes bruised Keegan's heart, made his throat feel tight and raw. "I'll tell her," he said. "But you and I both know what she's going to say. And whatever our differences are, Shelley's and mine, she's your mother, Dev."

"She doesn't *want* to be my mother. She just wants to use me to get back at you."

It was a bare-bones, brass-knuckle truth, and to deny it would be to dishonor Devon. People underestimated kids, Keegan thought—and he was as guilty of that as anybody. Kids knew when they were being used. They knew whether they were loved or not. They sure as hell knew who wanted them and who didn't.

He did.

Shelley didn't.

It was that simple…and that complicated.

"Dev…" he said, because it was all he could get to come out of his mouth.

She straightened her shoulders, took a firmer grip on the pitchfork and started scooping poop. A tear trickled through the layer of trail grime and campfire soot on her cheek, and Keegan reached out to wipe it away with his thumb.

"She'll do it for money, Dad," Devon said. "Mom will give me to you for lots and *lots* of money."

Keegan ached inside. Another hard truth. And the fact that Devon knew her own mother would essentially sell her, had probably figured it out long ago, both shattered and enraged him. He longed to deny it but couldn't, not in good conscience, because it had cost his daughter so much to say it out loud. She'd

been working up to it for a long time, at who knew
what cost.

"You do understand, don't you, Dev, that this is
about her, not you?"

Devon nodded. "I know," she said with a sniffle,
shoveling more industriously than ever.

Keegan ruffled her hair. "Finish up and get your
bath," he said hoarsely. "There's nothing in the house
to eat, so we're going to have to head into Indian
Rock and load up on groceries."

She nodded.

Keegan went back to trimming Spud's hooves.

"You'll talk to Mom?" Devon asked, without
looking at him.

"I'll talk to her," Keegan said.

MOLLY CALLED HER DAD, once she'd bathed and dressed
Lucas. Florence had moved the playpen onto the sunporch, and he was there now, keeping Psyche company.

Molly sat on the window seat in her room, staring at the rumpled bed she'd shared with Keegan
McKettrick the night before, and trying to work up
a little shame.

It wasn't happening for her. She'd never met anybody who galled her more than Keegan did, but she'd
never been made love to like that, either. Up until
last night she'd honestly believed multiple orgasms
were just some tagline *Cosmo* used to sell maga-
zines.

Not so, she thought, listening to the phone ring—and ring—on the other end.

Her dad's voice mail picked up. He probably wasn't speaking to her, since his DMV record had been faxed to Joanie and she'd reported to Molly that his license was currently suspended. Ergo, she hadn't bought the truck he wanted, and though she hadn't talked to him directly since the last conversation, when she'd been sitting in the courtyard at the hospital in Flagstaff, she knew he was furious.

"This is Luke," snapped a recorded voice. "Leave a message."

Tears welled in Molly's eyes. Damn, but she was tired of crying so much. It wasn't like her at all; she'd always been strong, competent, in charge. Until she'd met Thayer Ryan, and he'd simultaneously screwed up her life and given her the greatest gift a man could give a woman—a child.

He'd taken Lucas away from her. Caught her in a weak moment, played on her guilt.

Now, miraculously, and at such a high price, Psyche was about to give that precious gift back to her.

"Dad, this is Molly," she told some telephone company computer. "I'm getting married in a couple of days, and I thought maybe you'd like to—fly up here for the ceremony. Call me back, okay? Please?"

She hung up, then placed a call to Joanie. Sooner, rather than later, she was going to have to go back to L.A., gather her small staff and make arrangements to either close or move the office. She needed to put her house on the market, too, and tie up a hundred other loose ends.

Say goodbye to friends, and to special places.

It was going to be very hard.

When she was going to do all this was a closely guarded secret of the universe, and Molly hadn't been let in on it.

"Shields Literary Agency," Joanie chimed. "May I help you?"

"I wish you could," Molly said.

Joanie's tone softened and took on a confidential note. "Dave was in this morning," she said. "He said he had a meltdown in Indian Rock, and got arrested by Andy of Mayberry. Did you really have him committed? Not that I'd blame you if you did. He's crazy as a tick."

Molly sighed. There were a lot of things she wouldn't miss about running her hotshot agency, and Dave was one of them. He'd certainly filled up her bank accounts, though, and for that she was grateful. "I didn't have him *committed*," she said. "Just hospitalized. They must have stabilized his medication and discharged him right away."

"He says you don't want to be his agent anymore," Joanie said.

"The Gospel according to Dave," Molly replied. "I've had it with him."

There was a long pause. "Could *I* be his agent, then?" Joanie asked tentatively. She served primarily as an office manager, but she had represented a few clients Molly hadn't been able to take on, and she'd gotten them modest contracts, too.

Dave, certifiable though he was, was a very big fish. Molly, as a fledgling working in someone else's agency, had signed just such a client, a romance novelist whose first book had been a runaway bestseller. After considerable negotiation, she'd gone out on her own and rapidly made a place for herself.

"Joanie," she said, "if you can deal with the stalking and the drama and everything else that goes with the Davis Jerritt package, be my guest. You might call Denby, too. He's definitely looking for an agent."

"You mean it?" Joanie asked, almost breathless. She was a divorced mother with two teenage boys, and even though Molly paid her an excellent wage, she had trouble making ends meet. Representing Davis Jerritt would be no picnic, but Joanie was up to the challenge. And the commission checks would change her life.

Molly smiled. "I mean it," she said. "But I called for another reason." She paused, searching for words, and finally just took the plunge. "I'm getting married in two days, Joanie. I'd like you to be here, if you can. It's a personal invitation—nothing to do with business."

"You're *getting married?*"

"Yeah."

"To whom, may I ask?"

"His name is Keegan McKettrick."

"McKettrick. I know that name."

"I might have mentioned it. And you've probably heard of his company. McKettrickCo."

"McKettrickCo? Holy doo-doo, Molly. He's got to be rich!"

"Beside the point, Joanie. So am I."

"You fell in love, and you didn't tell me?" Joanie sounded stunned, as well as hurt.

"I *didn't* fall in love," Molly said. "I have to marry him if I want to adopt Lucas."

"Molly, that's insane. You can't—"

"I completely agree. It's insane. But if I want my son back, and I do, I have to do it."

"Oh, my God. I suppose he's some old coot, this McKettrick dude, with a paunch and a prescription for Viagra."

Molly laughed, remembering the lovemaking. She felt it, like a visceral echo in her body, even then. "Not exactly."

"Well, that settles it. I'll be there tomorrow night. I've got to see *this* for myself."

"How do you feel about being a bridesmaid?"

"No taffeta? No ruffles? No puffed sleeves?"

"I promise," Molly said, smiling.

"What are you wearing?"

Molly remembered Psyche's remark about her wedding dress. She'd forgiven it, figuring it wasn't entirely undeserved, but it still stung. "Something not-white," she said.

"Do not shop," Joanie quipped with tender humor. "Reinforcements are on the way. That bugle you hear will be me, leading the cavalry."

"Fly in to Phoenix and rent a car. Head north on Highway 17—you'll see the signs for Indian Rock after an hour or so. And call me the instant you hit town."

"I'm on it," Joanie said, already audibly tapping at her computer keys. "One more thing, Moll. Is your dad coming?"

"Probably not," Molly answered, closing her eyes.

"That might be a good thing," Joanie replied gently. "See you tomorrow night. In the meantime, hang tough."

"I'll be listening for that bugle," Molly said.

They both said goodbye and hung up.

Molly decided to do something constructive. She made the bed, then wiped off the smudges she'd left on the rails of the otherwise shining brass headboard while holding on for dear life as Keegan McKettrick proved the credibility of *Cosmo*.

DEVON PUSHED THE CART around the supermarket, apparently greatly cheered since she and Keegan had talked in Spud's stall, or maybe just putting on an act. They loaded up on fresh vegetables, meat and a reasonable amount of junk food, and were just rounding the end of the last aisle when they practically collided with Molly.

She was pushing a cart of her own, with Lucas riding in the seat, his whole head having disappeared beneath a baseball cap with the tags still on it.

Molly's cheeks went pink at the sight of Keegan, but she instantly turned a smile on Devon.

The kid seemed to bask in that smile, lean toward it like a flower too long in the shade.

"Hello, Devon," Molly said.

Something got stuck in Keegan's throat.

"I guess you and Dad are getting married," Devon said.

Molly's gaze linked briefly with Keegan's, and there was something bruised in it, but something hopeful, too. "I guess we are," she said.

"Can I be a bridesmaid?" Devon asked. As a general rule she didn't waste a lot of time on preambles. But then, she was a McKettrick.

Molly beamed. "I'd like that," she said. "My friend Joanie is coming to town tomorrow night, and we're going shopping the next morning. Would you like to come along?" In the next instant her face changed; the smile wobbled, a little uncertain.

Devon looked up at Keegan. "Can I, Dad? Please?"

He mussed her hair, still damp from the much-needed shower she'd taken after they finished the Spud chores. "Sure," he said.

Molly looked relieved and, to her credit, delighted. She also looked delectable in those shorts and that modest little tank top. "It's settled, then."

"It's settled," Keegan said. "Call me, and I'll drop Devon off."

"Or Molly could just come out to our place right now," Devon said, as one inspired. "And bring Lucas, too. You can both get some practice living there."

Molly blushed again.

Keegan enjoyed that immensely.

"We'll be moving in soon, I suppose," Molly told Devon.

"Right after the wedding," Keegan said.

Immediately Devon remembered a favorite cereal she wanted to stock up on, and dashed off to grab a few boxes.

"Chicken?" Keegan asked Molly in an undertone.

She straightened Lucas's ball cap, perhaps to remind Keegan the child was there. "Actually," she said after a beat or two, "I think Florence is planning to serve Swiss steak for supper."

Keegan leaned in, planted a light, nibbling kiss on Molly's mouth, then nipped at her ear. "I can't wait to welcome you to the Triple M," he murmured, and loved the tremor that went through her. "I'm going to have you in my bed. I'm going to have you in my shower. And then I'm going to take you out where the grass grows deep and the ground is soft and there's nobody for miles around, and I'm *really* going to have you."

She shivered again, and blushed. Looking down,

Keegan saw her nipples jutting against the front of the tank top.

"Keegan McKettrick," she said, affronted and obviously aroused, "this is a *supermarket*. People are probably staring."

He grinned.

Devon returned with an armload of cereal boxes and dumped the works on top of the other stuff in the cart, then headed for the check-out lanes. "Let's go, Dad," she called back over one shoulder. "You said you'd make spaghetti for supper, and I'm hungry."

Keegan looked deep into Molly's eyes. "Me, too," he said.

Molly glanced fondly after Devon, then turned back to Keegan.

"Just remember one thing, Mr. McKettrick," she said. "I can give as good as I get." With that, she wheeled off down the aisle, and Keegan could have sworn there was extra sway in that saucy little backside of hers.

HE MADE THE PROMISED SPAGHETTI that night, after he and Devon had put away the groceries and fed Spud again. They were loading the dishwasher, and talking about buying horses to fill the empty stalls in the barn, when the telephone rang.

Something about the sound unnerved Keegan; it seemed unusually shrill to him. He might have braced himself for bad news about Psyche, but he knew by the double ring that it was long distance.

Shelley, he thought.

Devon seemed to have the same premonition. She went a little pale behind her sunburn, and dashed to answer.

Keegan leaned against the sink for a moment, sucked in a deep breath, listened as Devon said hello. Then she said she'd accept the charges.

He turned.

Devon met his gaze and nodded. "It's Mom," she said.

The pit of Keegan's stomach plummeted. He wanted to have a conversation with Shelley, all right, but not over the phone. And not with Devon standing there listening to every word.

"Dad's getting married," Devon announced.

Keegan rolled his eyes.

Devon frowned. "Mom wants to talk to you," she said, inevitably.

Keegan glared at Devon.

Devon grinned and held out the phone, but her eyes looked troubled.

"You're getting married?" Shelley instantly demanded.

"Yes," Keegan said.

"Do you love her?"

This was one time Keegan didn't mind stretching the truth. "Yes," he said.

Shelley was silent.

"Are you still there?" Keegan finally asked.

Devon was making a rolling, get-on-with-it motion with both hands.

Keegan glowered at her again. She subsided, but only slightly.

Unbelievably, Shelley began to sob.

"Shelley," Keegan said calmly, and with more kindness than he would be expected to feel, given all this woman had put him through and, more important, all she'd put *Devon* through. "Get a grip."

"I always…thought—maybe—"

"Shelley," Keegan interrupted. "Put Rory on the phone, okay?"

"I c-can't! We had a f-fight and he's g-gone!"

Shit, Keegan thought. He made a shooing motion at Devon, wanting her to leave the room, but he knew by the stubborn look on her face that she wasn't about to cooperate.

Shelley began to wail.

"Shelley," Keegan repeated, more forcefully this time, *"get a grip."*

"I'm—I'm stranded. He t-took my m-money and my c-credit cards—even the plane tickets…"

Keegan found a pen and a scrap of paper. "Tell me the name of your hotel. Phone number, too, of course."

"Y-you'll help me? After everything?"

"Of course I'll help you, Shelley. You're Devon's mother."

The clue train finally rolled into Keegan's station.

Shelley was drunk—or pretending to be. Most likely, this was some kind of con. Unfortunately, that didn't change the situation.

"Th-thank you, Keegan."

"Shelley, where are you?"

She gave him the name of her hotel. Posh place on a tree-lined boulevard overlooking the Seine. Keegan knew it well. "They won't even l-let me back in the room," Shelley stammered.

"Take a breath. You're in the lobby now, right?" *More likely the bar,* said a voice in his head.

Just what he needed—input from the left brain.

"R-right." She sniffled, began to sound a little more with it.

"Sit tight. I'll get you back in your room, and arrange for a ticket home. And I'll wire you some cash for cabs."

"I don't *want* to come home. I've realized that *Paris* is my true home."

Keegan unclamped his back molars. "Okay, whatever."

Suddenly Shelley was coherent. "I just need a room for the night, Keegan. And money, because I found this great little flat in the—"

So much for self-control. "Shelley, are you out of your freaking mind?"

"I just got a little—nostalgic—when Devon told me you were getting married again, that's all. I thought I'd be the first—that Rory would..." Shelley's personal roller coaster was climbing, and Keegan knew there'd be one hell of a plunge on the other side. Short of throwing himself on the tracks, he couldn't think of a way to stop it.

"Look," he said, "I'll advance you next month's alimony. I'll cover your hotel bills. Anything. But you and I need to talk, Shelley. In person, about Devon."

She was quiet again. "Then I guess you'll have to come to Paris."

"Zero chance of that."

"Two months' alimony," she wheedled. "Along with the child support, that would be enough to get me into the flat."

Keegan closed his eyes. "All right. Two months."

"And the child support."

"And the child support."

Devon, seated at the kitchen table now, laid her head down on her arms.

"Who's the lucky lady, Keeg?"

"Her name is Molly. Call me as soon as you're back in your room."

Shelley promised she would. Of course, she'd also promised to be a faithful wife, and a good mother to Devon.

He hung up, without a goodbye, and immediately dialed Shelley's hotel in Paris. Within minutes, he'd made arrangements to cover her expenses. After that he made another call, and sent Shelley double the amount she'd asked for.

He wasn't being noble. He was hoping to keep Shelley off his back for a while, that was all.

"Dad," Devon said patiently when he'd hung up, "you are *such* a sucker. Rory's probably right there with her. They just wanted more money, and Mom put on this big act."

"Maybe so," Keegan said. "But I can't take the chance that she's really stranded, shortstop."

Devon looked puzzled. "Because Mom was your wife?"

"Because she's your mom," Keegan said.

"Is that some kind of McKettrick thing?"

Keegan chuckled. "It's some kind of *Keegan* thing," he replied.

"I heard you say you wanted to talk to her, about me," Devon ventured. "Are you going to ask her to let you keep me?"

"Yes," he said. "But not over the phone."

"She didn't mind *cheating* you over the phone."

"Let it go, Dev."

The shrill ringing sounded again.

"Hello," Keegan snapped into the receiver.

"Hello," Shelley said. "We—I'm back in the room. And the concierge says I can pick up the money you sent in the morning."

"It's all good, then," Keegan said, suddenly weary.

"Keegan?"

He braced himself.

Waited.

"I know you want permanent custody of Devon."

He didn't answer, didn't need to. Shelley had his complete attention, and she knew it.

"Ten million dollars," she said lightly, "and she's all yours."

CHAPTER 13

TEN MILLION DOLLARS, and she's all yours.

"Devon," Keegan said, clenching the receiver so hard he was surprised it didn't shatter in his hand, "go upstairs. *Now.*"

"Here it comes," Shelley crooned.

Devon wanted to rebel, that was obvious, but she was a decorated veteran of the divorce wars, and evidently knew the look that must have been on his face. She pounded up the back stairs, and Keegan didn't say a word until he heard her bedroom door slam in the distance.

"You bitch," he said.

Shelley laughed. He thought he heard the clinking of wineglasses over the phone. But no, it would be champagne. She and Rory had just scored.

Again.

"Come on, Keeg," she purred. "You're a very rich man, and with McKettrickCo going public, you're about to be even richer. You can spare ten million dollars."

"It isn't the money," Keegan rasped, keeping his voice down and very afraid that Devon might have shut her bedroom door hard from the outside and crept back to listen from the top of the stairs, or simply picked up an extension. "Damn it, Shelley, you *know* it isn't the money. How can you—"

"I can always bring Devon to Paris, if you'd rather," Shelley said mildly. "Put her in boarding school. Soak you for alimony and child support until they lower you into the grave, and even after that. *Or* we can settle the matter right now. After all, Devon isn't—"

"Shelley," Keegan broke in. "Don't." *Don't say Devon isn't my child.*

"I guess I'll be hearing from Travis Reid soon?"

"You'll be hearing from Travis," Keegan said bleakly. There was a weird, hollow sound on the phone. Devon was definitely listening in.

"Good," Shelley said. More glass clinked, and Keegan heard her swallow. "Oh, and congratulations, Keeg. On your marriage, I mean. I hope you're happier with this—Molly, wasn't it?—woman than you were with me."

"It would be impossible," Keegan said evenly, "not to be happier with *any* woman than I was with you."

"Have Travis express the documents, will you? I really *want* this apartment."

Keegan couldn't take any more. He thumbed the button, shut Shelley off. And then he just stood there, sick to the center of his soul.

Devon crept back down the stairs, looking defiantly guilty. "I told you she'd sell me for the right price," she said. "Sign over my trust fund. That's all you have to do."

Keegan set the phone on the counter. Faced his daughter. "I'm not about to sign over your trust fund. And if you ever listen in on one of my private conversations again, cookie, the no-spanking rule goes right out the window."

"You're bluffing," Devon said.

"Try me," Keegan replied.

"Chill, Dad," Devon counseled. "You're just mad at Mom. I'm okay with all of it. Remember—I told you this would happen."

Keegan sighed. Her reasoning was irrefutable—but how could a kid be "okay" with being *sold,* like some racehorse? No, she'd need professional help to square all this away, and he probably would, too. "If you're going to live with me," he said, "there are rules you'll have to abide by. One of them is you don't listen in on my phone calls. Got that?"

Devon flushed. "Got it."

"Good."

"But nobody's been *spanked* on this ranch for something like a hundred trillion years."

"There's always a first time, kiddo."

"Uncle Jesse and Uncle Rance would have your hide."

"I can handle Jesse and Rance," Keegan said. "Quit while you're ahead."

She plunked down on the one of the steps, drew up her knees, wrapped her arms around her skinny legs. DNA aside, the look in her eyes was pure, undiluted McKettrick.

"Am I worth ten million dollars to you?" she asked after a long silence.

Keegan poured himself a cup of lukewarm coffee, went over to the stairs and sat down beside her. "I'd die for you, Dev. What's that worth?"

"Like, if the place was on fire, you'd come through the flames to get me out, no matter what?"

"No matter what."

"If an ax murderer got in—"

"Dev? Another rule. No more horror movies on TV."

She grinned. "Can we go up to Flagstaff tomorrow and get my clothes and books and stuff?"

"After the wedding," Keegan said, wishing Molly were there so he wouldn't have to face another night alone in his bed. Devon seemed relatively unscathed by the transaction with Shelley, but *he* wasn't. He'd *married* the woman, for God's sake. What did that say about him?

That he was a damn fool, that's what.

And there was no reason to think he'd changed.

KEEGAN SPENT the next morning tying up loose ends in his office at McKettrickCo, while the rest of the company went about its business as if nothing had happened. As far as everyone on the payroll was concerned, nothing *had* happened. Word was already out that the acting CEO wasn't planning on staff reductions, nor did he intend to eliminate Cheyenne's work/study program.

It surprised Keegan how little there was to do, given how the job had consumed him for so long.

He was filling the last cardboard box when Travis appeared in the open doorway, with a file folder tucked under one arm.

"Just the man I wanted to see," Keegan said.

Travis nodded, stepped into the office and shut the door. "Are you sure you want to go through with this thing?" he asked.

Though he had another agenda in mind, Keegan knew Travis was referring to the agreement with Psyche. His conscience jabbed him a little—he still hadn't told Molly that they didn't have to go through with the wedding in order for her to adopt Lucas.

"Yes," he heard himself say. "I'm sure. Sit down, Trav."

Travis drew up a chair, laid the file on Keegan's desk with a slight slapping sound. "You're crazy," he said. "You've been through one bad marriage—why the hell would you want to do it all over again?"

"Molly isn't like Shelley," he answered, surprised at how defensive he sounded.

Travis raised one eyebrow. "And you're so sure of that because…?"

Keegan set his jaw, relaxed it again. Sat back in his desk chair and cupped his hands behind his head. "I know what I'm doing, Trav," he said. "Let's leave it at that, at least for now. I want to talk about Shelley."

"Shelley," Travis repeated.

"She wants ten million dollars," Keegan said.

Travis let out a long breath. "Of course she does," he said. "She's Shelley."

"I want you to draw up an agreement. I get full custody of Devon. Shelley gets ten million dollars. No visitation, unless Devon specifically asks for it. No alimony, once the settlement has been paid, and no child support."

"You're serious?" Travis marveled.

"Dead serious. Draw up the papers, Trav. I don't want to give Shelley time to change her mind."

"Ten *million* dollars." Travis shoved a hand through his hair. Whistled, low, through his teeth. "And I thought *Jesse* got screwed."

Keegan knew all about the settlement Jesse had paid his first wife, Brandi. It was a different situation, because they'd been married for a grand total of a week, and there hadn't been children.

"I want to raise my daughter," he said.

Travis looked back over one shoulder, probably to make sure the door was closed, and spoke quietly. "One hitch, Keeg. Devon *isn't* your daughter, not biologically. Suppose Shelley banks the ten million, then pulls *that* rabbit out of the hat? She could use it as grounds to break the agreement. Hell, so could the father, for that matter."

"Devon's father is dead," Keegan replied.

Travis sat up a little straighter in his chair. "I thought you didn't know who he was."

"I figured it out," Keegan said. He'd figured a *lot* of things out, lying awake in a cold and empty bed the night before. And nobody needed to tell him there was a distinct possibility that Shelley was pulling another fast one. "It was Thayer Ryan."

"Thayer—*Psyche's* Thayer? Keeg, that's quite a leap. I know you've been under a lot of stress lately, but—"

"Frame it as an adoption," Keegan said.

"Shelley could still change her mind."

"She won't. She gets a million when she signs the papers, and the rest after the adoption is final. She's jonesing to buy some apartment in Paris, so she'll deal."

"You'll have to tell Devon the truth," Travis said. "Shelley's likely to do it anyway, out of spite."

Keegan sighed. "Yeah," he said as the weight of the world settled squarely on his shoulders. "I know."

"You'd better make damn sure your theory about Thayer Ryan is right. If some guy comes out of the woodwork and says Devon is his, you'll be back in court."

"I've already called Devon's pediatrician in Flagstaff. They don't even have to take blood to do the tests—saliva will do it. If Devon and Lucas are half brother and sister, the results will be all the confirmation any judge would need."

Travis went pale. "You'll need Psyche's permission for that," he said.

"Not after Molly and I are married and I become Lucas's legal father, I won't," Keegan replied.

"This is pretty ruthless, Keeg. Step back from it a little—"

"I've done all the 'stepping back' I'm going to do," Keegan said flatly. "You're one of the best friends I've ever had, but you're not the only lawyer in the world."

"Keegan. This is me, Travis. *Listen* to me."

Keegan reached for the file folder, opened it and began to read the terms of his and Molly's agreement with Psyche.

Marriage.

Living under the same roof for a period of no less than one year.

In the event of a divorce, Keegan was to retain full custody of Lucas.

He reached for a pen, found the appropriate dotted line and signed his name with a hard flourish. Then he shoved the folder across the desk to Travis.

"Conversation's over," he said.

Travis swore under his breath, grabbed the file and stood. "Where's Devon?" he asked.

"With Emma, at the bookstore," Keegan answered. "Why?"

"Oh, I thought maybe you'd already shipped her off to some lab," Travis snapped. With that, he left, slamming the office door behind him.

Keegan knew better than to think the argument was over.

Half an hour later Jesse crashed in, and Rance was right on his heels.

"Ten million dollars?" Rance yelled.

"Have you lost your fucking *mind?*" Jesse demanded at the same time.

"So much for attorney-client privilege," Keegan said.

"Keegan," Jesse bit out, "this is *bullshit.*"

"Why? You gave Brandi a million dollars to get out of your life. With Shelley, it's cheap at ten times the price."

"She's going to nail you," Rance seethed. "She'll take the ten million *and* Devon, and break the kid's heart in the process!"

"And what's this crap about running DNA tests on Devon and Lucas?" Jesse wanted to know.

Keegan explained his theory about Devon's paternity.

"You've really gone around the bend," Jesse said when he'd finished. "Wait until Shelley comes home. Talk to her then. My God, Keeg, give yourself a chance to think."

"You're either with me on this or you're not,"

Keegan said calmly. His guts were churning, but Jesse and Rance didn't need to know that. "Take your choice."

Jesse pounded a fist down on Keegan's desk, hard enough to make the cardboard box jump slightly. "Think. About. Devon."

"Believe me, I am."

"Shelley will tell her she's not yours," Rance said, very slowly and very quietly.

"Not if I tell her first," Keegan said. He'd rather eat broken glass, but he'd do it. "The truth is always best, right?"

"Keegan," Jesse said, "it will *tear her apart.*"

His eyes burned. His throat closed. "I know," he said.

Rance's jaw looked rock hard. "At least wait until Psyche's..."

"Dead?" Keegan finished for him.

Jesse and Rance exchanged glances.

"Look," Jesse said more reasonably. "I know you're in a lot of pain right now. You're not thinking straight, Keeg. *Please.* Just let the dust settle a little before you stir up another hornet's nest."

"I can't," Keegan said.

"We could hog-tie him," Rance suggested to Jesse—only half kidding, judging by the expression on his face. "Lock him up in a shed someplace until he comes to his senses."

"Not a bad idea," Jesse replied.

"Give it your best shot," Keegan said. "Right

about now I'd *love* to take somebody apart, limb by limb, and one or both of you would do just fine."

"Fine," Jesse said through his teeth. He plucked Keegan's desk clock out of the cardboard box, since he didn't wear a watch, and checked the time. "Behind the barn. One hour. Rance and I will flip a coin to see who gets to kick the crap out of you first."

"You're on," Keegan said.

Jesse banged out of the office.

Rance followed.

Keegan grinned and rolled up his sleeves.

MOLLY WAS SPOONING LUNCH into Lucas's mouth when the kitchen telephone rang. Florence, busy dropping dumpling dough into a pot of simmering chicken soup, grabbed the receiver and grumbled a hello.

Her eyes widened as she listened.

Instinctively alarmed, Molly set aside the bowl and spoon. Wiped Lucas's mouth with a napkin.

"I'll tell her," Florence said, watching Molly. "But I don't know what she can do about it. Yes. Thank you, Myrna." She hung up.

"What?" Molly asked, her voice trembling a little.

"Your future husband is about to tangle with his cousins behind the barn," Florence said. "Myrna—she's Wyatt's mama, and she works at McKettrickCo, so she knows everything that goes on there—says she called her son right away, and

he said it was McKettrick business, and he means
to stay out of it."

"You don't mean they're actually going to *fight?*"
Molly asked, but she was remembering the night
she'd rushed Psyche to the clinic. Remembering the
way Jesse and Keegan had been shoving each other.
If the receptionist hadn't stepped in, they would
surely have come to blows.

Florence gave a grim nod. "If you want that man
of yours to look halfway decent in the wedding pictures," she said sagely, "you'd better get out there to
the ranch, and waste no time doing it."

Molly got to her feet. Sat down again. "Do they
do this kind of thing often? The McKettricks, I
mean?"

"When the mood strikes them," Florence said.
"They're a rowdy bunch, all things considered."

Molly looked at Lucas. Back to Florence.

Florence tossed her the keys to her station wagon.
"Go," she said. "I'll look after the baby."

"I've never stopped a fight before," Molly fretted, but she was already on the move, kissing Lucas
on the forehead, grabbing her purse. "What do I
do when I get there? And which barn? There are at
least four on the Triple M—"

"Step between them," Florence told her. "No
McKettrick's ever laid a hand on a woman in anger
as far as I know. And it'll be old Angus's barn, the
one at Keegan's place."

"How can I be sure that's the right barn?" Molly

asked anxiously, wrenching open the inside door to the garage.

"It's a family tradition," Florence said. "They've been settling their differences behind that barn for generations."

"Call Emma and Cheyenne," Molly said as she pushed the button to roll up the outside door.

"I reckon Myrna's already done that," Florence replied.

Molly rolled her eyes, scrambled into the station wagon, stuck the key in the ignition, started the motor and eased out onto the street, headed for the Triple M.

She was crazy to be doing this.

If the McKettricks wanted to bloody each other's noses and blacken each other's eyes, it was their own affair.

But despite this conviction, she kept driving, and once she passed the city limits, she put the pedal to the metal.

Did she even know the way to Keegan's place? She'd been there only once, before the trail ride.

Rounding a bend, she spotted a pink Volkswagen up ahead, barreling over that dusty road with its wheels barely touching the ground.

As they passed the turnoff to Jesse's place—Molly recognized the tilted blue mailbox—an Escalade shot out behind Molly and stayed right on her bumper.

The Volkswagen took a turn Molly probably would have missed, fairly flying over the ruts and potholes. Praying she was right about who was driving, Molly followed.

They rattled over the old bridge spanning the creek, the three vehicles like a convoy rushing into battle.

Keegan's house was up ahead, and there were two trucks parked at crazy angles in the yard, with Keegan's black Jag jammed between them.

The Volkswagen screeched to a stop, and Emma bolted out of it and ran toward the barn, kicking off her high-heeled shoes as she went. The Escalade almost rear-ended Molly, and then Cheyenne streaked past her on foot, dark hair flying.

Molly got out of the station wagon and dashed after them.

Jesse was just flipping a coin when Molly rounded the corner of the barn. Rance and Keegan were there, too, and none of them was wearing a shirt.

"Heads," Rance said.

"Sorry," Jesse replied, immediately tucking the coin into the pocket of his jeans. "It was tails."

"Wait a second," Rance protested. "How do I know you're telling the truth?"

Cheyenne rushed to Jesse before he could answer Rance's question, and threw herself hard against his chest. "Stop it, right now!" she cried.

Gently Jesse gripped her shoulders and moved her aside.

Rance did the same when Emma approached him.

Molly looked at Keegan, and her heart sank. His

face was hard, his feet were set wide and his fists were clenched. He'd made up his mind to fight, and no power on earth was going to stop him.

She turned to Jesse and Rance, desperate.

Were they going to gang up on Keegan, two against one? Didn't they know this was all about Psyche, all because she was dying and he couldn't do anything to help her?

Florence's voice played in her mind. *Step between them. No McKettrick's ever laid a hand on a woman in anger, as far as I know.*

Molly gulped and moved in.

Keegan didn't even look at her. But he did stretch out an arm and move her aside, much as Jesse had done with Cheyenne, and Rance with Emma.

"Keegan," she said. "Please…"

He didn't so much as glance her way. "Not now, Molly."

Someone took her arm; she looked around, saw that it was Cheyenne. She was glaring at Jesse as she spoke.

"If they want to act like idiots," Cheyenne said, "let them."

Molly was terrified. She'd never seen a fight, and she didn't want to start now.

Keegan beckoned to Jesse with both hands. "Come on, hotshot," he said. "Throw a punch."

Rance gave Jesse a light push. "Yeah," he said. "Throw a punch."

Jesse's face contorted; he whirled on Rance with a fist raised.

Rance ducked at the last second, and the fist landed squarely in the middle of Keegan's face.

Molly cried out and took a step forward; Cheyenne and Emma pulled her back.

Keegan reeled slightly, lowered his head and dived straight into Jesse's solar plexus, sending him into Rance.

The three of them landed on the ground in an angry blur.

Molly put a hand over her mouth. "They'll kill each other," she murmured between her fingers.

"No such luck," Cheyenne said, but there were tears standing in her eyes.

"What we need," Emma put in, "is the riot squad."

Meanwhile, someone grunted in fury and pain somewhere in the snarl of pigheaded men rolling around on the ground.

Molly moved in again, nudged Keegan with the toe of her shoe. "You stop it!" she cried. "Right *now!*"

Keegan looked at her in confusion, and promptly took another punch, this time in the jaw.

"You're going to look *terrible* in the wedding pictures!" Molly warned.

And suddenly Keegan started to laugh. Kneeling in the dirt, with his lower lip split open and bleeding, the man sat back on his haunches and actually *laughed*.

Rance, who'd evidently been at the bottom of the dog pile, raised himself onto his elbows, looking baffled and a little suspicious, as though he suspected a trick. Jesse, rolling onto his knees as Keegan had done, threw back his head and guffawed.

He started to rise to his feet, but Cheyenne strode over, planted a foot in the middle of his chest and sent him flying backward. He caught himself on both hands and stared at his wife with an expression of such startled consternation that Keegan and Rance howled with delight.

Cheyenne was clearly not amused. "Sit there, you damn fool!" she told Jesse. "Sit there until hell freezes over!"

With that, she pivoted on one heel and stormed away.

Jesse scrambled to his feet. "Cheyenne, wait..."

"Now he's in trouble," Rance said with a smirk.

"Like *you're* not," Emma said huffily. "I'm going back to the shop, Rance McKettrick, where *your daughters* are. If you have a brain in that thick head of yours, you'll steer clear of me until you come up with a *very* convincing apology!"

The smirk dissolved. "Emma..."

But Emma turned away without another word and followed the trail Cheyenne had just blazed.

A car door crashed shut. An engine roared to life.

Molly moved around the barn to see what was happening.

Cheyenne was speeding away in the Escalade. Jesse was standing in her wake, staring after her.

Emma shrugged off Rance's attempt to stop her

from leaving, too, got into her pink Volkswagen and nearly ran over him making a U-turn.

Rance yelled a swearword. He and Jess conferred briefly, then each of them got into a truck and drove off.

Molly went back to Keegan.

He was still catching his breath. He touched the back of one hand to his split lip, lowered it again and frowned when he saw a smear of blood on his knuckles. One of his eyes was starting to swell shut, and a small cut on his forehead oozed crimson.

"You really *are* going to look awful in the wedding pictures," Molly said. "Let's go inside and get you cleaned up."

"I can take care of myself."

"Oh, yeah, that's obvious." She hooked her arm through his and ushered him toward the ranch house. "You should be ashamed of yourself. You're a grown man, for heaven's sake. What if Devon had seen this—this brawl?"

Keegan gave her a lopsided and entirely too fetching grin. "That wasn't a brawl," he said. "It was just a tussle. We got into a dustup outside the Roadhouse once that went on for an hour. Took a fire hose to break it up."

"An *hour.* Well, how very macho of you. You should be ever so proud of yourself!"

He balked, stopped right in his tracks.

Molly gave him a tug to get him moving again.

"You need some ice on that lip." She peered up at him. "No stitches, probably."

Inside the house she pressed him into a chair at the end of the table. Then she bunched up some paper towels, wet them down at the sink and shoved the wad into his hands.

"Put this against your mouth, stupid," she said. "I'll get the ice."

"Did you just call me stupid?"

Molly wrenched open drawers until she found a box of plastic storage bags. "Oh, *grow up.*"

Keegan opened his mouth, closed it again.

Molly plucked a bag out of the box, went to the refrigerator and filled it with little round cubes from the icemaker. After zipping the top of the bag closed, she crossed the room again and pressed it against Keegan's mouth.

He winced.

"Does it hurt?" Molly asked sweetly.

"Yes," he mumbled from behind the ice bag.

"Good," Molly said briskly. Then she got some more wet paper towels and began cleaning up the rest of Keegan's face, none too gently.

"There's something I need to tell you," Keegan said.

"I'm in no mood to listen to your reasons for rolling around on the ground behind the barn, if that's what you have in mind."

He flinched again as she examined the cut on his forehead. Nope, he didn't need stitches, which was kind of a shame. A scar would have served him right.

"It's about our getting married."

She stopped, took half a step back. Her heart wriggled its way up into her throat and expanded there. "Are you backing out?"

"No," he said. "But you might want to, once you hear what I have to say."

"I want to raise Lucas. I have to marry you to do that. You could confess to robbing banks, and it wouldn't change my mind."

Keegan smiled, but his eyes were sad. "Psyche was jerking us around, Molly," he said. "She never offered Lucas to Sierra and Travis."

Molly blinked, laid a hand to her stomach, which was pitching as wildly as it had during the brawl— Keegan could call it whatever he chose—behind the barn.

"She'd still let me have Lucas?"

Keegan studied her. The skin around his eye was slowly turning a greenish-purple. "Yes," he said. "I'll be Psyche's executor either way, so you'll still have to deal with me."

"But you'd lose out on adopting Lucas. Making him a McKettrick."

Keegan merely nodded. Waited.

Molly sat down hard on the bench, all the starch gone out of her. "When did you find this out?"

"Yesterday."

"And you're just now telling me?"

"I almost didn't," Keegan said. "I want to raise Lucas almost as much as you do."

She absorbed that.

Keegan reached out, took a tentative hold on her hand. "What's your choice, Molly? Will you back out? Or will you let Lucas have a father?"

CHAPTER 14

WILL YOU BACK OUT? Or will you let Lucas have a father?

Until she and Keegan had gone to bed together, Molly could have answered those questions readily. Was he kidding? *Yes,* she'd back out. And no, she definitely wouldn't have chosen Keegan McKettrick as her son's father.

So easy.

So simple.

Except that the truth had just hit her full force, maximum impact.

She *loved* this impossible, complex and strangely honorable man.

She sucked in a horrified breath and waited to see if she was going to throw up all over the place.

"Molly?" Keegan asked, tracing a light circle on the palm of her hand with the pad of his thumb. She felt the reverberations of his touch in every part of her, body and soul. "Are you all right?"

"No," she said bitterly. *"I am not* all right."

"Is there anything I can do?"

She stood, tremulously, not trusting her legs to support her. Tears, those damn *tears,* were dangerously close to the surface. Again. She'd been holding on to her sanity for dear life ever since Psyche had summoned her to Indian Rock. And meeting Keegan had only made it worse. Much, much worse. "Oh, you've done quite *enough,* thank you very much."

He looked confused—and wary. "Are you going to marry me or not?"

Molly bit down hard on her lower lip. "Yes," she said, at considerable length. "But only because of Lucas."

One side of Keegan's rapidly swelling mouth tilted up—out of relief, Molly supposed—but there was still a look of confusion lurking in his eyes. "What other reason could there be, besides Lucas?"

"None," Molly said briskly. "None at all." Then she snatched the wad of wet paper towels out of his hand, now stained with stubborn McKettrick blood, marched over to the trash and disposed of it.

She'd left her purse and car keys in the station wagon, but it was a moment or so before she remembered that, frazzled as she was, and interrupted her own automatic search.

"Are you leaving?" Keegan asked, sounding amazed.

The lunkhead. Of *course* she was leaving. Joanie's plane had already landed in Phoenix, and she was probably on her way to Indian Rock in a rental car at that very second. If Molly stayed on the Triple M, she wouldn't be on hand to greet her friend.

No, she'd be in Keegan's bed in another few minutes, in the throes of passion. And she might say something stupid at the height of one of the inevitable orgasms—like *I love you.*

"Yes, I'm leaving," she said tersely. "I have things to do in town."

Keegan sighed. "So do I," he said. "Devon's at the bookshop, and I have to pick her up."

Molly already had the outside door open. Her hand tightened on the knob. "She's going to be upset when she sees you," she said, worried. "Honestly, Keegan, your face—"

"It'll be all right," he said. "Are you still taking her shopping tomorrow? Devon, I mean?"

"Yes," Molly said, suddenly wishing she could stay. And not just because of the sex, either. Something else was going on—something concerning Devon—and little unidentified flying objects were blipping across Molly's inner radar screen. "Keegan, is—is everything all right? With Devon?"

He shook his head. Molly felt compelled to cross

the room again and take him into her arms, but she refused to let herself do it.

"No," he said. "But it's a long, involved story. And I need to talk to her about it first."

Molly stood still in the doorway, unable to leave, unwilling to stay. "Sounds big," she said.

"It is big," Keegan confirmed miserably.

"You're sure you don't want to tell me about it?"

"I want to tell you about it," Keegan said with grim certainty. "But I can't. Not yet. It wouldn't be fair to Devon."

"Okay," Molly said with equally grim *un*certainty. "But if this is something that might affect Lucas—"

"It won't," Keegan interrupted.

Still Molly hesitated. "Look, maybe *I* should pick Devon up at the bookstore. Let her spend the night at Psyche's, with Lucas and Joanie and me. That way, we could leave for Flagstaff early tomorrow morning. And it would give us a chance to get to know each other a little better."

Keegan considered the offer in silence, finally nodded. "I'll talk to her after you get back," he said. "Maybe even after the wedding."

At last Molly was able to move.

But she didn't go out the door, as she had consciously planned to do.

She went back to where Keegan sat, leaned down and kissed him very gently on the mouth.

She knew he wanted to reach for her, and that if he did, she'd be lost. In the end, he kept his hands to himself. Grinned up at her, endearing even with his face all messed up. "You'd better go," he said, "before I give you a good old-fashioned McKettrick welcome."

She laughed, even though there were tears in her eyes. Kissed him again, this time on the forehead, and stepped back out of welcoming distance.

Her practical side, long on standby, finally booted up and installed itself. "Devon will need clothes—pajamas, a toothbrush."

Keegan nodded.

Molly waited while he went upstairs.

She looked around that big, time-worn kitchen and imagined herself there, making breakfast. Going over homework with Devon, and later—when he was older and ready for school—Lucas. Doing all sorts of homey things that never would have occurred to her in her last incarnation, back in L.A.

Molly Shields, superagent, was about to morph into Molly *McKettrick,* ranch wife. And nobody could have been more amazed about *that* little twist in her life story than she was.

Presently Keegan returned with a small overnight case. It looked so incongruously feminine in his hand that she had to swallow an unexpected and slightly hysterical giggle.

He walked her out to the hastily parked station wagon, carrying Devon's overnight case. Tossed it into the backseat and waited while Molly got behind the wheel and turned the key.

"Molly?"

The way he said her name, all gravelly and low, made her squirm a little on the car seat and wish, yet again, that she could stay. Go inside with him, let him strip away her clothes, lie down with him in the bed they would soon be sharing.

He'd opened a whole new landscape inside her, one she'd never dreamed existed.

But—why? Why did it have to be Keegan Mc-Kettrick, of all people?

"What?" she asked, jolted again.

"Thanks. Thanks for coming out here to break up the fight. Thanks for being willing to pick Devon up when you get back to town. And thanks for marrying me."

Molly swallowed. To him, it was only a bargain, their getting married. A way to be part of Lucas's life. To her, it was that and so much more.

"You're welcome," she said weakly.

I love you, Keegan McKettrick.

God help me, I love you.

He backed away from the car.

Molly drove off.

Keegan was still watching her, she saw in the rearview mirror, when she crossed the bridge over the creek. Two miles up the road she pulled over onto the shoulder and sobbed.

JOANIE LOOKED TRAVEL WORN in her rumpled red linen jumpsuit, which was probably a size too small, and her tinted hair jutted around her round face in brown spikes. "Oh, Molly," she said, taking Lucas from Molly's arms, "he's *beautiful*."

"Ride," Lucas said.

Joanie laughed moistly, her eyes bright with tears. She spotted Devon, standing just behind Molly in the entryway to Psyche's house, and smiled. "And who's this?"

"Devon McKettrick," Molly said, "meet Joanie Barnes."

Devon stepped forward and put out a hand, and Joanie maneuvered Lucas to her other hip to shake it.

"Molly's going to be my stepmom," the child said formally.

"Lucky for her," Joanie replied. "And lucky for you, too."

Devon's formality gave way to a smile. "She said she has lots of shoes," she confided to Joanie. With Devon, apparently, a good supply of footwear was a prerequisite for joining the family.

Molly remembered Keegan's cryptic remarks back at the Triple M earlier that day, and felt a rush of tension. She barely knew this child, and yet she already had a fierce desire to protect her.

Joanie grinned. "Believe me," she said, "Molly has closetfuls. I should know. I just shipped something like fifteen boxes of them—along with clothes and cosmetics, of course—before I left."

Devon looked thrilled.

Molly felt a surge of gratitude. "Bless you," she said to Joanie. She'd packed hastily before leaving L.A., and there were certain outfits she really missed. Casual things, mostly, but a few suits. She was going to be a ranch wife now, but she still had almost a dozen clients, the loyal ones who hadn't jumped ship.

She needed to be that other Molly, at least some of the time. The powerful one, with the don't-mess-with-me clothes.

"We have to talk about your dad," Joanie said after graciously accepting Molly's gratitude for taking time to drive out to her house, box up and send her belongings, all before jumping on a plane to attend an impromptu wedding.

"Great," Molly replied with a tight little smile.

Devon picked up Joanie's one small suitcase. She'd be heading back to L.A. right after the ceremony.

"I'll put this in your room," Devon said, as comfortably as if she'd lived her whole life in Psyche's mansion. "It's next door to mine, and we have to share a bathroom."

"Thanks," Joanie said, handing Lucas back to Molly with what might have been relief. Joanie's boys were in their teens, and it had been a long time since she'd dealt with toddler energy.

Devon took the elevator. She'd been up and down in it at least a dozen times since Molly had brought her here from the bookstore.

"Very cute kids," Joanie observed.

Molly nodded in agreement and led the way toward the back of the house. Florence was in the kitchen, murmuring into the telephone, and Psyche was, of course, propped up in her hospital bed on the sunporch.

Molly paused to put Lucas in his playpen in the kitchen, then proceeded to the porch.

Psyche had been gazing out at the flowers in her garden, but when Molly and Joanie entered, she immediately turned her head.

Molly made the introductions.

Psyche was polite, even warm, but distant, too. It seemed to Molly that she'd been withdrawing from life more rapidly since she'd played the marriage card. She'd even pulled back from Lucas, and, no matter that Florence was constantly offering her some favorite food, she barely ate.

She's waiting, Molly thought sadly. *She's waiting for the wedding to take place. And then...*

"Will you do me a favor, Molly?" Psyche asked, startling Molly out of her reflections. "Throw out Keegan's peonies, please."

At first Molly was confused. Then her gaze fell on the flowers Keegan had brought Psyche, now faded, sagging forlornly in the vase. "Sure," she said, grateful for something to do and some reason to leave the sunporch.

"Nice meeting you," Joanie said to Psyche.

Psyche merely nodded, then turned her attention back to the garden beyond the windows.

Once she'd reached the kitchen, Molly disposed of the peonies and rinsed out the vase. By that time

Devon was back from delivering Joanie's suitcase to the third-floor guest room designated for her.

Florence served iced tea, complete with sprigs of mint, and spoke to Devon. "I'm going out back and cut Miss Psyche some fresh flowers. Would you and Lucas like to help me?"

Devon nodded eagerly.

Florence hoisted Lucas from the playpen.

And the three of them vanished, by way of the sunporch, Florence closing the sliding door eloquently behind them all.

"I guess she knew we needed to talk," Joanie said, sitting down at the table.

Molly joined her, reached for a glass of tea. Mashed the mint leaf in the bottom with the tip of her long-handled spoon. Nodded.

"Your dad's back in treatment, Molly," Joanie said quietly, after a period during which there was no sound in the room save the clinking of ice cubes. "He checked himself in yesterday. He can't make or receive any phone calls for twenty-eight days."

Molly couldn't speak. She was relieved, of course, but she was stricken, too. In some secret, little-girl part of herself, she'd been hoping her daddy would show up for the wedding, sober and wishing her well.

"Someone at the center called me with the particulars," Joanie went on. "It's a private place, and pretty pricey."

Molly nodded. Cleared her throat. "Cut them a check when you get back to L.A.," she said.

"I'm sorry, Moll," Joanie said. "I mean, I know it's a good thing, Luke going into treatment. God knows, he needs the help, and maybe this time will be the charm. But you're getting married, even if it isn't really a love match, and it would have been nice..."

Molly was crying again. Silently. Helplessly.

"Oh, Molly," Joanie whispered, squeezing her hand.

Molly sniffled. Sloshed down some iced tea. *Get a grip, for pity's sake,* she scolded herself.

Joanie glanced toward the closed door leading onto the sunporch. "How about showing me where my room is?" she asked. "You could help me unpack."

Molly was on her feet in a moment. Heading for the elevator.

Once she and Joanie were well away from the kitchen, beyond any possibility of being overheard by Psyche or anyone else in the household, Joanie said, "You really don't want to marry this guy, do you? Molly, there must be some other way to get custody of Lucas."

Molly shook her head, jabbed at the elevator button, realized it was already there and opened the door. Pushed back the metal grate and stepped inside.

"Keegan is in love with somebody else," Molly

confided when she and Joanie were bumping and jostling their way up from the main floor.

"What?"

"Psyche," Molly said. "He's in love with Psyche."

"But she's—"

"Dying," Molly finished for her.

Joanie had known Psyche was terminally ill. Keegan's love for the other woman evidently came as a surprise to her, though. "Oh, my God," she said.

"It gets worse," Molly said.

"How could it possibly be worse?"

They reached the third floor, and Molly opened the grate and the outside door. "I'm in love with Keegan," Molly whispered urgently, even though she knew the two of them had the entire upper section of the house to themselves.

"You can't be," Joanie protested. "You haven't known him long enough."

Molly located the guest room Florence had allocated for Joanie and pushed open the door. It was cool inside, and a little dark, so she went to the window and opened the blinds.

Below, in the backyard, Lucas toddled happily around in a big circle, playing tag with Devon, who allowed him to catch up to her and toppled into the grass, laughing, at a push of his hand.

Florence, cutting yellow roses nearby, watched them with a smile on her face.

Molly's heart ached.

"Molly," Joanie said. "Talk to me."

Molly turned from the window, drew a deep breath and straightened her shoulders. "I'm in love with Keegan McKettrick," she said again.

Joanie sat down on the edge of the bed, probably testing it for softness, and bounced a little. "Maybe that's good," she answered. "It's certainly going to make it easier to live with him."

"Is it?" Molly asked. "Psyche's going to die soon, Joanie. Very soon. And Keegan knows that's inevitable, but he'll still be devastated. My God, you have no idea how much he cares for that woman...."

Joanie pointed to the rocking chair across from the bed. "Sit," she said.

Molly sat, but she couldn't remain still. She rocked, harder and harder, until the back of the chair thumped into the wall and she had to pull it away.

"Molly," Joanie said firmly.

Molly stopped rocking. "And Devon," she fretted. "There's something going on with Devon—and Keegan won't tell me what it is because he wants to talk to her first."

"That's reasonable, Molly."

"I'm marrying into a situation I might not be able to handle," Molly confessed, to herself as much as Joanie. "I've always been so confident. Crazy writers? No problem. I could handle it. Tough editors? Bring them on. Right up to the day I signed Lucas away..."

"Hush," Joanie said. "You're Molly Shields. You raised yourself, and your dad. You built a business anyone could be proud of. And when you let Lucas go, you really thought you were doing the best thing you could for him. You wanted him to have two parents."

"I *knew* Thayer was a liar and a cheat, Joanie. How could I have convinced myself that he'd make a good father, when he was such a lousy husband?"

"Simple. You weren't thinking straight. The breakup with Thayer was rough, and then you went through your pregnancy alone. Give yourself some credit."

"I deserve to be in this mess," Molly lamented. "But Psyche doesn't, Joanie. *Psyche doesn't.*"

"You *deserve* a second chance with your son," Joanie said. "And it isn't your fault that Psyche is dying." She paused. "You do understand that, don't you?"

"Yes," Molly said fitfully, "but I hurt her."

"*Thayer* hurt her," Joanie insisted. "You broke it off with him the moment he admitted he was married, didn't you?"

Molly nodded, remembering that day. She'd filled her house with flowers, put on soft music, worn a vintage silk caftan. And told Thayer Ryan she was going to have his baby.

He'd told her so many times how much he wanted children.

She'd expected joy.

She'd even expected a proposal.

Instead, she'd gotten an angry confession. Thayer

told her he was married, adding the usual stuff. Psyche didn't understand him. Psyche didn't like sex. Psyche didn't this, Psyche didn't that.

Oh, yes, it was all Psyche's fault.

And he'd asked Molly to get an abortion.

Stunned—although even then she'd known she shouldn't have been—Molly had ordered Thayer out of her house. Told him she'd never, *ever* in a million years get rid of her baby.

He'd called her incessantly after that.

He and Psyche were in counseling, he said. They were gathering the broken pieces of their relationship, fitting them back together.

Molly had thrown herself into her work, kept up the pace throughout her pregnancy. In the daytime she was the high-powered agent, the wunderkind, the mover and shaker, the maker of megadeals. At night she was depressed, weak and frightened. She paced. She couldn't sleep. She sat on her terrace and waited for the sun to rise so she'd have an excuse to leave for the office.

She'd fooled almost everyone back then.

But not her dad.

And not Joanie.

The birth was easy—Molly's ob-gyn had said she was built to have babies—but the aftermath was not. Postpartum depression had taken hold before she'd even left the delivery room.

"Keep the baby," her dad had begged.

"I'll help you," Joanie had promised.

She'd heard what they said, her father and her best friend, but she hadn't been able to take it in.

And then Thayer had visited her hospital room, only hours after the birth. He'd shown her pictures of him and Psyche on a cruise, smiling together. Everything was good between them, he'd said. They'd had counseling. They were back on track.

She'd risen out of her despair just long enough to name the baby Lucas, for her wonderful, imperfect father.

And she'd signed the papers to surrender him, her own child, woven within *her* body, to the Ryans.

She hadn't even had the strength to regret it for a long time.

She'd endured the long depression—that had taken all she had, just the enduring. By the time she was herself again, it was too late.

"Molly," Joanie said, bringing her back to the present by shoving a cool washcloth into her hands, "put this on the back of your neck. You're pale as a ghost, and I really think you might faint."

Molly accepted the cloth, pressed it to her nape.

Joanie returned to her perch on the edge of the mattress. "You need a really strong drink," she said. "Brandy or something."

Molly shook her head.

"Why not?" Joanie asked.

"Number one, because my dad is an alcoholic and I don't want to follow in his footsteps. Number two, I had sex with Keegan, and I might be pregnant."

"You'll never be an alcoholic," Joanie said confidently, "and it's very unlikely you're pregnant after one night in the sack."

"I don't want to drink. Call it a show of support for my dad."

Joanie put up both hands in a gesture of concession. "Okay," she said.

"And Lucas was conceived the *one night* Thayer and I didn't take precautions. Same point in my cycle, too."

Joanie's eyes widened. "Fertile Myrtle," she said.

And Molly laughed.

It felt so good, she cried.

IT WAS MORNING.

Finally.

Sitting at his kitchen table, with a cup of badly needed coffee at his elbow, Keegan scanned Travis's draft of the adoption agreement with his one good eye.

His friend, meanwhile, stood at one of the windows with his back to the room, waiting for Keegan to finish.

"Raise the initial payment to two million," he said after giving the document a second reading.

Travis turned around. With his light hair, and the sun at his back, he looked like Jesse. Keegan felt a pang at that. He didn't like being on the outs with Jesse, or with Rance.

He'd told them about the wedding, before the

fight behind the barn, but they probably wouldn't show up.

Meg would be there for sure, and so would Sierra. Maybe Cheyenne and Emma, too.

But how could he get married without Jesse and Rance?

"Two million it is," Travis said, resigned.

"It's not like this is going to break me," Keegan told him.

"That isn't the point," Travis replied. "I've been worried about you for a long time. Now I'm worried about Devon, too. This is a lot to dump on a ten-year-old kid, Keeg. DNA tests, for God's sake. And Shelley—don't even get me started on Shelley."

"She's a stone-cold bitch, Travis. She'd sell her own child. There are women in *prison* who wouldn't stoop that low. Once you accept the truth, it gets easier."

Right.

"Have you talked to Devon yet?"

Keegan sighed. Lifted his coffee mug, set it down again without touching it to his sore lips. "No," he said. "She's gone to Flagstaff with Molly and a friend to buy some kind of getup for the wedding. Which, as it happens, is tomorrow afternoon." He paused. "You'll be there, won't you?"

"Hell, yes, I'll be there. I'm Psyche's lawyer, too, remember? And I'd have come anyhow, because even though I think you're compounding one stupidity with another, we're buddies."

"Thanks," Keegan said gruffly.

Travis slapped him on the back. "I'll draw up the final papers and call Shelley's lawyer in Flag. I imagine he's waiting for the call."

Keegan merely nodded.

Travis left.

Keegan finished his coffee and went out to the barn to feed Spud.

He was brushing the donkey down when he heard the truck pull in outside, and the familiar blare of the horn.

Jesse?

Shaking his head, Keegan put the brush aside, left Spud's stall and walked the length of the breezeway. At the doorway of the barn he stopped.

Sure enough, it was Jesse, climbing down out of his truck, grinning. He had a hell of a shiner around his left eye, but other than that, he looked like his old cheerful self.

He gestured toward the trailer hitched to his truck.

"Brought you a wedding present, Keeg," he said.

Keegan's throat ached.

Jesse went around behind the trailer and opened the back. Lowered the ramp and scrambled up inside.

Keegan, standing behind the trailer now, gaped as Jesse led a palomino gelding down the ramp.

"This one's yours," Jesse said proudly, and handed a stunned Keegan the lead rope before disappearing into the gloom again.

He returned with another gelding, this one a

black-and-white pinto, smaller than the palomino. "For Molly," he said. "He's real tame."

Keegan tried to speak, but nothing came out.

Jesse let the pinto's lead rope drop and went back into the trailer for the third time. Came back with a fat little bay pony with a splash of white on his rump.

"Devon's," he said. "I figured she and Lucas could share him for a while."

Keegan was almost overcome. "Damn, Jesse," he managed.

"You can't run a ranch without horses," Jesse said, slapping him on the back. Then he squinted, examining Keegan's battered face. "Man," he marveled, "you *are* going to look bad in the wedding pictures."

CHAPTER  15

MOLLY STOOD AT JOANIE'S bedroom window, gripping the sill and staring down into the backyard, where Keegan awaited her. The man she shouldn't marry. The man she shouldn't love.

Florence was there, too, with Lucas. Psyche sat in a wheelchair, in the shade of a great oak tree, hands folded in her lap. Devon worked the small crowd, showing off her bright yellow dress and the corsage on her wrist, moving from Jesse to Rance to Cheyenne to Emma and others, too. But always back to Keegan.

The bond between Keegan and his daughter was a shining thing, visible to anyone who took the trouble to look, and Molly felt both reverence and envy. She missed her dad keenly on this day of days, wished he could have been half as committed to her as Keegan was to Devon.

"You look pretty spiffy," Joanie told her, gently interrupting her thoughts.

Molly turned from the window, looked down at her own soft yellow dress, the strappy high-heeled sandals she'd bought to match the day before in Flagstaff. Joanie had done her hair, pinned it up in a soft arrangement, set a wreath of tiny roses and baby's breath on her head and secured it with bobby pins.

"Why do I want to do this so much?" she asked softly. "When I know it's going to break my heart?"

"Because of Lucas," Joanie reminded her, squeezing both her hands. "And because you love Keegan."

Molly bit her lower lip, nodded once, fitfully.

"Don't ruin your lipstick," Joanie said.

Molly laughed, and for once it didn't come out as a sob.

Maybe she'd cried all her tears.

Maybe pigs really *could* fly.

"I guess we'd better do this thing," she said.

Joanie nodded.

They were both silent during the elevator ride down to the first floor, and the walk through the house.

"Showtime," Joanie said when they reached the sunporch.

The minister had taken his position outside, under an arbor draped with climbing roses, the intertwined vines of separate plants producing a bright tangle of pink, yellow and white. Not unlike a marriage, Molly thought, especially one that involved children.

Keegan was just in front of the minister, resplendent in a tailored gray suit, his face bruised and

swollen. Jesse and Rance stood beside him, dressed
to the nines and looking as though they'd been in
a knock-down, drag-out fight behind a barn on the
Triple M.

Which, of course, they had.

"Ready?" Joanie asked.

Molly drew a deep breath, huffed it out. "Yes," she
said.

No. Well, maybe. Oh, God, what am I doing?

A bridal bouquet, matching Molly's not-white
dress, waited on the table, where the peonies had
been. Beyond that loomed Psyche's hospital bed, a
sad and poignant reminder that this was no ordinary
wedding.

It was the fulfilling of a dying woman's last wish.

Joanie pressed the bouquet into Molly's hands,
kissed her on the cheek and headed outside.

It was an awkward processional. Devon skipped to
take her place, and Joanie followed with a determined
stride.

There was no music.

Molly waited on the back step until Joanie beckoned.

Keegan's gaze caught hers and held as she stepped
slowly toward him.

Molly kept walking, head held high. Reached
Keegan's side.

The minister cleared his throat.

"Dearly beloved," he began, "we are gathered
here, in the presence of God and these witnesses…"

Molly didn't hear another word until the minister got to the do-you-take-this-man part. Keegan elbowed her gently, grinned down at her.

"Do you take this man?" he whispered.

"Yes," Molly said, addressing him, not the minister.

There was a silence.

Molly tried again. "I mean, I do."

"Do you, Keegan, take this woman to be your lawful wedded wife?"

Lawful wedded wife, Molly thought. *Yikes.*

"I do," Keegan answered in a deep, quiet voice. For a man basically being forced into marriage, he was remarkably calm. Or was he simply resigned?

"Then by the power vested in me," the minister said, "I now pronounce you man and wife. Keegan, you may kiss your bride."

Gently Keegan turned Molly to face him. Curled the fingers of one hand under her chin, and bent to touch his mouth to hers.

Considering his swollen lips, he did an outstanding job.

"Ladies and gentlemen," the minister said, "may I present to you Mr. and Mrs. Keegan McKettrick."

Devon began to jump up and down, unable to contain her exuberance.

And Molly was fiercely grateful, in that moment, that the child was willing to make her welcome. It was no small blessing.

When Keegan reluctantly released Molly, Jesse stepped forward and kissed her cheek, and so did Rance, both of them grinning out of faces as battered as Keegan's own. Emma and Cheyenne hugged her, and finally Joanie.

Molly accepted their congratulations, then sought out Psyche, sitting small and fragile and brave in her wheelchair, under the generous, sheltering branches of the tree.

"Take good care of him," Psyche said solemnly, her eyes shining with a mixture of joy and sorrow.

"I'll be a good mother to Lucas," Molly replied.

"I know," Psyche said, looking up at her with clear, resigned eyes. "I was talking about Keegan. There's a lot he probably hasn't told you, Molly. About the way his parents died, and about Devon's mother—please, give him every chance to find his way to you."

Molly's throat tightened. Gently she laid her bridal bouquet in Psyche's lap. "Thank you, Psyche. Thank you for forgiving me, and thank you for Lucas—and for…"

"Keegan?" Psyche smiled, raised the bouquet to breathe in its fragrance. "He's not an easy man to deal with, but he's easy to love—isn't he?"

Molly swallowed, glanced back over her shoulder. Keegan was in a huddle with Jesse, Rance and Travis Reid. When she turned back to face Psyche, she whispered. "Yes. Yes, he is."

Tears stood in Psyche's eyes. "Love him, Molly. Love Keegan not just for yourself, but for me, too."

Molly couldn't speak. She could only nod.

Psyche handed back the bouquet. "This belongs to you," she said. "So does Keegan. And Lucas? He was really yours all along. I just borrowed him for a while."

Molly's vision blurred, and by the time she'd blinked the tears away, Florence had arrived, standing behind Psyche, taking hold of the wheelchair handles.

She rolled Psyche toward the house.

Molly watched, stricken by the same emotions she'd seen in Psyche's eyes moments before, as Keegan broke away from Jesse, Rance and Travis to take over for Florence. He gripped the handles of Psyche's chair in strong, competent hands, bent to whisper something in her ear.

She giggled and wiped her eyes.

"Somebody wants to congratulate you," a feminine voice said, and Molly turned to see Emma and Cheyenne standing close behind her, Emma holding Lucas. He strained toward Molly, and when she took him into her arms, he immediately reached for the floral wreath on top of her head.

She loosened the pins and let him have the circlet of flowers.

"Welcome to the family, Molly," Cheyenne said gently. "You're a McKettrick now."

Molly *had* chosen to take Keegan's name. She told herself it was because Lucas would be a McKettrick as soon as the papers were filed and recorded.

"Thanks," Molly managed, but even with Lucas safely in her arms, legally her child, she couldn't help looking toward the sunporch. Psyche's wheel-

chair stood abandoned at the bottom of the steps;
Keegan must have carried Psyche inside to her hospital bed.

Cheyenne touched her shoulder. "Molly?"

She turned back to meet Cheyenne's steady gaze.
"We'll be here for you. Emma and me. We just—we
just want you to know that we understand."

Emma nodded, her eyes bright, and sniffled.

The sound of a door shutting drew Molly's attention back to Keegan. He'd just left Psyche, and his
poor, bruised face was a bleak mask.

Cheyenne took Lucas.

Emma gave Molly a little shove in Keegan's direction. "Go to him," she whispered.

And Molly went.

Keegan barely seemed to see her, at least at first.
In fact, they nearly collided. At the last second he
caught her shoulders in his hands, steadied her.

Molly forced herself to look directly into his eyes.

Neither of them said anything.

Then Keegan kissed her forehead. "It'll be all
right," he said.

And Molly wondered if he was trying to convince
her of that—or himself.

HE WAS MARRIED.

Married.

Propping his chin on top of Molly's head, there
in the middle of Psyche's backyard, Keegan looked
up at the sky. The day had been beautiful, but now

the wind was picking up, and dark clouds were rolling in from the west, dimming the sunlight.

Instinctively he held Molly a little tighter.

Here comes the rain, he thought.

Molly pulled back a little way, offered him a tentative smile. "I guess we'd better take this party
inside," she said as the first drops of water began to
fall.

He nodded. There would be no honeymoon—there
wasn't time for that. Travis had faxed an agreement to
Shelley's lawyer earlier that day, and all hell was bound
to break loose any minute. He had to be ready to deal
with that, and to shelter Devon from the fallout as best
he could.

And Psyche was dying.

He and Molly would spend the first night of their
marriage alone, at the ranch house. Devon was going
home with Jesse and Cheyenne. Lucas would stay
with Florence and Psyche—days, hours, even minutes with the child had become a precious commod-
ity.

Keegan gazed down at his bride.

Molly deserved so much more than he could give
her.

So much more.

He took her hand, tugged her toward the house.

The wedding party swelled around them, a laughing horde, running ahead of the rain.

After that, there was cake.

Pictures were taken.

Keegan wasn't tracking very well; he just wanted it all to be over.

He wanted to be alone with Molly.

His wife.

Other guests arrived, alone and in groups, to share in the celebration. Wyatt and his mother, Myrna. Cora Tellington and Doc Swann. Rianna and Maeve.

Hadn't Rance's girls been at the wedding?

Keegan couldn't remember. The whole thing had been a blur to him, something to be navigated, gotten through, like a blinding blizzard or a sandstorm.

At a tug on his sleeve, he looked down.

Devon smiled up at him. "Molly said you fell down in the barn," she said. "That's how your face got so messed up." She paused, frowned. "Did Uncle Jesse and Uncle Rance fall down, too?"

Keegan laughed, and it helped. Released some of the tension that had plagued him since—when? Since Molly had erupted into his life? Since he'd learned that Psyche was sick, and there would be no saving her? Since he'd sensed the demise of McKettrickCo as he knew it?

Since the day Jesse's and Rance's dads had broken the news that his folks were dead.

"No, shortstop," he told her, his voice husky. "Molly was just trying to spare your delicate sensibilities. Your uncles and I got into it behind the barn, day before yesterday."

Devon's eyes widened. "Why?"

"Why did we fight?"

"Yeah."

"Because we're stupid sometimes," Keegan said. "And because we're McKettricks."

Travis, one ear to his cell phone, beckoned to Keegan.

Keegan bent to kiss the top of his daughter's head. "Get some cake," he said. And then he left her.

Travis snapped the phone shut, acknowledged Keegan with a nod that told him nothing, led the way into Psyche's father's study and closed the door behind them.

"Shelley doesn't like the adoption angle," Travis said.

The bottom of Keegan's stomach fell open.

"But for five million up front, with the rest payable after the adoption is final, she'll sign."

"She'll do it?"

"Keegan, we're talking about *five million dollars* here. And it might be a trick."

"No," Keegan said. "We're not talking about five million dollars. We're talking about *Devon*."

"All I'm trying to say is you're taking a very big chance here. Not just with your own peace of mind, but with Devon's, too."

"What would you do in my place, Travis? No lawyer bullshit. Tell me the truth."

Travis sighed. Shoved a hand through his hair.

"I'd give Shelley the money and hope to God she wants the rest enough to play ball."

Keegan swallowed. "Tell Shelley's lawyer we'll transfer the funds as soon as we have a signed, notarized document."

"You're sure?" Travis asked.

"I'm sure," Keegan said.

"When do you plan to tell Devon?"

"Tomorrow," Keegan answered. "When she gets home from Jesse and Cheyenne's."

Travis nodded. "The sooner the better, buddy," he said. Then he slapped Keegan's shoulder. "And one more thing. Congratulations." He grinned. "You got married today, remember?"

"I remember," Keegan said.

"Go get your bride," Travis urged. "Take her home."

Take her home.

Would the Triple M ever be Molly's real home? Or would she want to go back to L.A. when the obligatory year of living together was over? She had a life there, a home, friends, a business.

And she'd take Lucas with her, if she went.

Keegan felt sick at the thought. For all his big talk, there wouldn't be much he could do to stop her.

"Keeg?" Travis said.

Keegan focused on his friend's face.

Travis tapped Keegan's forehead with one finger. "Stop spending so much time up here," he said before lowering his hand to thump once at his heart, "and think from *here* once in a while."

Keegan frowned. What the hell did *that* mean?

Travis chuckled. "Think about it," he said. And then he was gone.

IT WAS RAINING HARD by the time Molly and Keegan reached the ranch house. Keegan parked the Jag as close to the back door as he could, lifted Molly into his arms and ran. And they both got drenched.

Inside, breathing hard, he set Molly on her feet. Rainwater glistened in his hair and along his eyelashes, like tears.

Molly's heart ached with happiness as she looked up at him.

I love you, she wanted to say. But she didn't dare. She wouldn't be able to bear seeing pity in his eyes, or regret.

"You'd better get into some dry clothes," he said practically.

Her suitcases were upstairs, in the bedroom they would share; Rance had delivered them earlier that day.

"Put on some jeans," Keegan added when Molly didn't speak right away.

So much for her plan to slip into the slinky negligee Joanie had given her for a wedding present.

"Jeans?" she said.

"And a flannel shirt, if you have one," Keegan said, starting for the door.

Unlike Molly, he'd changed into ordinary clothes before leaving Psyche's place. "Where are you going?" she managed, after swallowing.

"To the barn," he answered, as though surprised by the question. "I have to feed Spud and the horses."

"Okay," Molly said, mystified and profoundly disappointed.

It was her wedding day. And even though she knew Keegan didn't love her, she'd expected to come before the livestock.

Keegan went out.

Molly stood there for a few moments, then went upstairs and opened doors until she found the master bedroom. She swapped her wedding dress, panty hose and fancy shoes for a pair of jeans, heavy socks and one of Keegan's flannel shirts, since she didn't own one herself. Wedged her grateful feet into running shoes—the high heels were new, and they pinched.

Avoiding looking at the bed, she turned to the bureau. Gazed at herself in the antique mirror above it.

Who was this woman?

Molly McKettrick.

Ranch wife.

Lucas's mother, Devon's stepmother.

Owner of many, many pairs of shoes.

Tears threatened, but Molly was tired of tears. She sucked it in, turned and marched downstairs again.

When Keegan got back from the barn she had the wood cookstove going, radiating warmth, and the kitchen was only a little smoky. She stood on tiptoe to turn the knob to open the damper.

Keegan stopped, soaked, on the threshold.

"Horses all right?" Molly asked, just to break the silence.

He stepped inside. Closed the door.

Stared at her, almost as if she were a stranger, making herself at home in his kitchen.

"Keegan," Molly said.

"What?" He ground out the word.

"Come over here and stand by the stove while I get you a change of clothes. You're wet to the skin."

He paused, then dripped his way over to stand within the almost palpable heat emanating from the ancient stove. "You built a fire," he said, and he sounded flummoxed.

"Well, duh," Molly said, smiling determinedly. "It's not so hard, you know. A little crumpled newspaper, some kindling, a match and—voilà!—a lovely, crackling blaze. I've seen people do it a hundred times on the late-late show."

Something softened in Keegan's eyes.

"Stay right here," Molly told him, and dashed away.

A few minutes later she was back with towels, a pair of old jeans and a sweatshirt.

Keegan had recovered enough to start a pot of coffee brewing on the cookstove, forswearing the modern coffeemaker on the counter, perhaps getting into the spirit of the thing, and splashing mud and rainwater all over the kitchen floor in the process.

Molly set the clothes and all but one towel

down on the end of a small table next to the wall and dabbed tentatively at Keegan's face. Then she got bolder and toweled his hair so that it stood out around his head, and they both laughed.

He laid his hands on the sides of her waist, and was about to pull her close—she knew he was— when the telephone rang.

Psyche, Molly thought. Then, *Oh, please—not tonight.*

The second ring seemed more insistent than the first.

Keegan released Molly, visibly steeled himself and went to grab up the receiver. "Keegan," he said instead of "hello." His voice was ragged.

Molly watched his face and bearing change as he listened.

She took a step toward him, stopped at the stay-back look that rose instantly in his eyes.

"No," he said into the phone. "No, there's no point in that. But you shouldn't be alone right now, Florence."

Molly closed her eyes.

"All right," Keegan went on after listening again. "Okay, if you're sure. Yes. I'll be there first thing tomorrow morning. In the meantime—" He stopped, nodded. "All right," he said again. "Thanks." After a hoarse goodbye, he thumbed the button on the phone, ending the call. Set the receiver down slowly.

"Psyche?" Molly asked when she could bear it no longer.

"Yes," Keegan said, avoiding her eyes. "Half an hour ago."

Molly had expected Keegan to fall apart. Instead, she was the one who caved in. She put a hand over her mouth, but she couldn't stifle the ragged sob that came out.

Keegan looked as though he might come to her, but in the end, he didn't. He turned, opened the back door to the wind-driven rain and just stood there, neither in nor out, his broad shoulders rigidly straight.

Molly whispered his name, but if he heard her, he didn't respond.

He walked right out into the driving rain, leaving the door open.

Molly hesitated, then followed. Saw him walking, not toward the barn, where he might have had some shelter and the comfort the animals might have lent him just by their presence, but in the direction of the bridge.

Was he going to Rance's place, across the creek?

Molly moved out into the downpour herself, barely feeling the unseasonable chill as it soaked her clothes and pounded at her hair.

It was dark over at Rance's.

"Keegan!" She ran after him, splashing through puddles, slipping in mud. "Keegan!"

He stopped, turned around. There was so little light— just what came from the house and the barn—but she could see his face clearly, etched with shadows and pain.

"Keegan," she repeated, knowing she sounded desperate and not caring.

She stopped. Waited.

He stood still, as heedless of the torrent as Molly had been. She was feeling the cold more acutely now; it reached deep into her bones, and it had, she realized, little if anything to do with the weather.

She held out one hand.

Keegan hesitated. But then he clasped the hand she offered, interlaced his fingers with hers. Tightened his grip.

Molly could never remember, afterward, whether he'd led her back to the house or she'd led him.

They walked slowly inside.

Stood by the stove, both of them sodden.

Molly *did* remember that she was the one to unbutton Keegan's cotton shirt, the one he'd changed into at Psyche's, and slide it off his shoulders. She remembered trying to dry him with the towels, and how he'd clasped her wrist in one hand and stopped her.

How he'd stared down into her eyes, then pulled her hard against him and kissed her—not tenderly, but with a ferocity, a demand, that had nothing to do with her and everything to do with Psyche Ryan.

She did not recall their going upstairs, except in the dimmest way. She simply found herself with Keegan, in his room.

He undressed her—not roughly, but not gently, either.

She allowed it, craved his passion, even knowing it wasn't meant for her. He was about to use her, and she was about to let him.

She didn't expect to feel anything except overwhelming sorrow, but she did. Oh, God, *she did.*

She stood trembling as he kissed her neck, her shoulders, hoisted her up so that she had to wrap her bare legs around his waist to stay balanced. He bent his head to her breasts, first one, then the other, suckling greedily. And even the cold wetness of his jeans against the insides of her thighs did nothing to cool the primitive blaze his mouth ignited within her.

"Keegan," she pleaded.

They fell together onto the bed.

Keegan broke away from her, unfastened his jeans, peeled out of them. He looked almost savage as he stared down at her, rasped her name.

Her name. Thank God he hadn't called her Psyche.

Molly lifted her arms to him.

He flung back the covers on the bed, shoved her under them and joined her there.

There would be no foreplay this time. Molly knew that.

There would only be taking.

There would only be giving.

Keegan stretched out on top of her, balanced on his forearms, and looked down into her face. His body felt hard and icy cold, but it was beginning to warm, kindling to the answering flames within her.

She pulled the covers up over both of them, moaned with despairing pleasure as he slid down to suckle briefly at both her breasts.

He moved upward again, eased her legs apart with one knee and looked into her eyes. She felt him, ready to move inside her, hard and big. And she felt her own body expanding to receive him.

She nodded, her hands on his back.

He entered her, paused again.

Molly murmured his name.

He slammed into her then, in a single, powerful thrust of his hips, and Molly cried out, not from pain, but from passion.

He stopped. "Molly—?"

He wanted to know if he'd hurt her.

She wept, cupped her hands on either side of his beautiful, swollen, fist-battered face and kissed him with everything she felt.

When he raised his mouth from hers, both of them breathless, he looked so deeply into her eyes that she was sure he must have seen her soul, uncovered all her secrets, including the fact that, against all reason and good sense, she loved him.

The pace of their lovemaking increased after that.

It was hard.

It was fast.

It was sacred.

The first orgasm was Molly's utter undoing. She

bucked, helpless, beneath Keegan's body as it collided with hers. She tangled her fingers in his wet hair, struggled to capture his mouth with hers even as she dug her heels into the mattress and raised herself to take him deeper and deeper inside her.

Keegan came after she did, after she'd begun the sweet anguish of descent, his body flexing against hers, straining for release. She felt his warmth spill into her, held him when he fell, trembling, onto her.

She held him, and she stroked his back and his hair, until the trembling stopped. And inside her own heart, where it was safe to say the words, she spoke.

I love you, Keegan McKettrick.

CHAPTER  16

MOLLY STOOD ALONE on the front steps of the church where, in just four more weeks, Rance and Emma were to be married. It would be a traditional wedding, with all the trimmings--white lace, rose petals strewn along the aisle, guests decked out in the bright, colorful garments of celebration. A triumphant march would boom from the pipe organ under the choir loft.

Today the joy seemed far off, even though the sun was shining.

Today Psyche Ryan would be mourned in this little building and in the hearts of the townspeople, all clad in black or dark, somber blue, and buried in the grassy garden of stone angels and headstones adjoining the churchyard.

Florence sat stiffly in one of the front pews, with Lucas fidgeting on her lap, staring at Psyche's gleaming coffin, and heedless of everyone around her. The casket, closed at Psyche's own request, was draped in a blanket of white peonies; Keegan had seen to that.

Keegan.

In the three days since Psyche's death—and Molly and Keegan's backyard wedding—Keegan had been cold, remote, strangely immobile behind an impenetrable force field of grief-driven activity. He groomed the horses. He pounded nails into fences. He tore things down, out in the barn, and put them back together again. At night he'd taken Molly to his bed, satisfied her body relentlessly, ferociously—and left her heart longing for his touch.

The soft strains of "Amazing Grace" flowed out through the open doors of the church to ride a soft, cut-grass-scented breeze.

Molly steeled herself to go back in.

She couldn't use being a stranger in town as an excuse to run away. She was Molly McKettrick. She was Lucas's mother, Keegan's wife. And Psyche had been…her friend.

Tears blurred Molly's vision. Made the line of cars and the hearse parked on both sides of the tree-shaded street a hazy mingling of colors and shapes.

A hand cupped her elbow.

"It's time," Jesse told her quietly. *Keegan needs you,* his eyes said.

She nodded, allowed him to usher her back inside the stuffy, too-crowded church. Back to her seat beside Keegan, who sat so utterly still that he might have been one of the marble statues guarding the graves behind the church.

She longed to take his hand, or simply rest her palm on his shoulder, but she didn't. On his other side, Devon surveyed the proceedings solemnly, shielded somewhat by her youth and innocence. Devon had known Psyche only slightly, after all, and whatever sadness she felt was understandably directed toward Keegan.

The service began.

During the reading of the Twenty-third Psalm, Lucas freed himself from Florence's arms, scrambled down off her lap and toddled back to Molly, his little hands upraised to her, his lower lip quivering.

Molly felt such a rush of love for him, her baby, her boy, her miracle, that for a moment she could barely breathe. Then she reached for him, held him close.

Keegan, meanwhile, sat rigid, his eyes dry but red-rimmed, his profile hard. Jesse, seated with Cheyenne and Rance and Emma in the pew behind Molly and Keegan's, did what Molly had not dared to do. He rested a hand briefly on Keegan's shoulder, squeezed.

Keegan flinched under this silent reassurance. Except at night, when he buried himself in Molly's body, he couldn't bear to be touched.

There was no formal eulogy, but the minister invited anyone who wished to speak to step forward.

Molly stood in the aisle, holding Lucas, waiting for Keegan to rise.

After some hesitation, he did.

His back was straight as he moved toward the altar, stepped behind the pulpit. A tense, supportive silence filled the little church.

Molly sat down, trembling. Devon slid close to Molly and rested her head against her shoulder. Shifting, Molly draped an arm around the girl and held her briefly to her side, trying to manage an increasingly impatient Lucas at the same time.

When the little boy finally let out a wail of frustration, Jesse hoisted him off Molly's lap and took him outside.

Keegan, standing up front, swallowed visibly. "A good friend told me recently," he began, stopping in midsentence to clear his throat, "that people ought to live less from their heads and more from their hearts. Psyche did that all her life. She lived from her heart. She forgave people, and was always ready with a second chance." His gaze, bleak and unreadable, rested on Molly's face. "She died the same way she'd lived—generously. She was in a lot of pain and she was scared, but she got past all that. She made sure her son would have a home and a family." He paused again, groping for words. "Psyche was one of the bravest women I've ever known, and I'll never forget her."

With that, Keegan stepped down, stopping to

rest a hand briefly on the lid of Psyche's coffin as he passed it.

I'll never forget her.

The vow echoed, sacred and sorrowful, through Molly's heart.

She and Devon moved down so Keegan could sit on the aisle. Along with Jesse, Rance, Travis Reid, Wyatt and one of his brothers, he was a pallbearer. It would be his duty to help carry Psyche's casket out of the church when the service was over, through the dazzling summer sunlight, to the hearse.

Molly's throat constricted.

Psyche had had her revenge, albeit unwittingly. She'd given Molly an incomprehensible gift—Lucas—but she'd taken something, too. She'd taken a part of Keegan along on her journey into the mysteries of eternity, as surely as if that intangible, vital part of him had died with her.

Numbly Molly endured the rest of the service. She listened to Florence's brave, tearful tribute, but the woman might as well have been speaking another language for all the sense Molly made of it. Jesse returned, gave Lucas, now sleeping, to Cheyenne.

At last the dreaded moment of relief came. At a signal from the minister, the same one who had married Molly and Keegan, the pallbearers assembled, each taking the coffin by one of its shining brass handles.

It was over.

It was just beginning.

Psyche hadn't wanted anyone to come to the grave site, so when the doors of the hearse were closed, that was the final goodbye.

The minister's wife announced that refreshments would be served in the small community gathering place next to the church.

Molly endured that, too.

People ate cake and sipped coffee or punch, and exchanged memories of the younger Psyche, the one they'd known best.

Lucas was exhausted, caught up in the energy of something he couldn't possibly understand. He'd settled in well at the Triple M, but he had a way of moving from room to room, searching for Psyche. "Mama?" he would say in plaintive confusion. "Mama?"

Now he was scanning the crowd for the one person he would never find.

Molly approached Keegan tentatively. This was the daylight Keegan; there would be a different one later, when they were alone in their bedroom at the ranch, with Lucas sleeping in the room next to theirs, and Devon down the hall.

Molly anticipated the lovemaking on a visceral level that electrified her very cells. But she also dreaded it, dreaded giving herself up like that, all the while knowing she was a substitute for someone else—not the recent, frail Psyche, but the vibrant one Keegan obviously remembered.

"Lucas is tired," she said quietly, holding her

son, resting her chin on top of his head. Keegan's
face was healing; his fat lip was almost back to
normal, and the shiner had faded to a faint shadow.
"I'm going to take him home."

Keegan blinked, as though she were an acquain-
tance, briefly encountered somewhere, and promptly
forgotten. If she hadn't known better, she would
have sworn he was trying to place her, remember
her name.

"Home," he said.

"To the ranch," Molly clarified, then felt foolish.
Where else could she go? Psyche's big house was
effectively closed until the estate could be settled;
Florence had her belongings packed, and her sister
had come to take her to Seattle. Jesse and Rance had
brought all Lucas's things, and Molly's, too, out to
the Triple M in the backs of their trucks.

"I'll get the car," Keegan said, surprising Molly.
She didn't know what she'd expected of him
exactly—but it hadn't been this ready acquiescence.
"Where's Devon?"

"Outside, with Rianna and Maeve," Molly answered. "Keegan, you don't have to—"

"There's nothing I can do here," he said. He even
smiled a little, ruffled Lucas's hair, but when he
looked at Molly again, the distance was there in his
eyes.

He left her, spoke briefly to Florence, then went
out.

Molly had her own goodbyes to say. She approached Florence. "I'll send pictures," she said. "And you can visit Lucas any time you want."

Florence's eyes brimmed as she leaned forward to stroke the child's hair, then kiss the place where her palm had rested. "Thank you, Molly," she said.

Molly's throat closed again.

Florence smiled gently. "It was a comfort to Psyche, knowing you'd look after Lucas and love him the way she did. Gave her something to hold on to."

Still unable to speak, Molly merely nodded.

"You see that you don't forget to pass on those pictures," Florence said. "I'll send a note to the Triple M when I'm settled in Seattle, so you'll know my address." The older woman looked past Molly, to the open doorway of the community center. "You go on now, and see to that man of yours. It will be rough going for a while, but if you stick with it, I think things will turn out all right."

"Y-you'll be all right?" Molly asked after several moments spent groping for her voice.

"I'll be fine," Florence replied. "I will surely grieve for my girl, but I'll get along. Psyche saw that I'd have all I could ever need, God rest her soul. I've got my sister and plenty of good memories to see me through."

"Thank you, Florence," Molly said, in parting.

Florence nodded, and Molly turned to go.

Keegan stood beside the car, one hand resting on Devon's shoulder as he spoke to her. When he saw

Molly approaching, Keegan left his daughter to take Lucas from her arms. Placed the little boy, now half-asleep, in the special car seat. Devon sat solicitously close to Lucas.

No one spoke on the drive out to the Triple M.

Once there, Molly changed Lucas's diaper, gave him a bottle and laid him down in the playpen in the kitchen. Keegan immediately went upstairs, came back wearing jeans, boots and a work shirt.

Molly left Lucas in Devon's care for a few minutes, and went up to get out of her black dress. She put on denim shorts, a ruffly white top and slip-on sandals, and by the time she got back to the kitchen, Keegan was gone.

Devon sat in a rocking chair, watching Lucas sleep.

Molly paused beside her chair, a little worried by the child's glum expression. Yes, Devon had just attended a funeral, but Molly suspected this was something different.

Keegan had alluded to a problem concerning Devon. Maybe they'd talked.

"Want some lunch, sweetheart?" Molly asked.

Devon shook her head. "My dad's pretty upset."

"He lost a good friend," Molly said very quietly. "That's hard."

"He said we need to have a talk, him and me," Devon replied, looking up at Molly with sad, luminous eyes. "I think he's going to say Mom wants me to go live in Paris. That I can't stay here with him."

Molly was at a complete loss. She knew nothing of the situation, or of Keegan's relationship with his ex-wife, and it would be too easy to say or do the wrong thing. Still, she couldn't ignore Devon's obvious concern, either. "Is that what you want? To live here with your dad?"

"And you and Lucas," Devon said.

It struck Molly then, the full weight of all she'd done to get her son back. If she and Keegan didn't find a way to make the marriage work, there would be other casualties. Lucas, certainly, but Devon, too. "We'd like that a lot," she replied. There was so much more to say, so much more to promise, but it was too soon.

And Molly had made enough reckless promises.

Devon brightened a little. "Can I try on some of your shoes?" she asked.

Molly chuckled, relieved that the conversation had taken a turn into safer territory. "Yes," she said. "But most of them are still in boxes."

"That's okay," Devon answered. "I'll unpack them for you."

"Good idea," Molly replied.

Devon got out of the rocking chair and dashed up the back stairs.

Molly was mixing tuna, mayonnaise, onions and pickles for sandwiches when Keegan came inside. Looked around for Devon.

"Upstairs," Molly said. "Unpacking my shoes."

One corner of Keegan's mouth tilted upward in a

forlorn attempt at a smile. He raised his eyes to the ceiling at a clomping sound overhead in the master bedroom.

"I keep waiting for life to get easier," he said.

Molly longed to slide her arms around his waist, lay her cheek against his chest, but she couldn't, because the force field was still firmly in place. "It will, you know," she told him. "Get easier, I mean."

Keegan looked unconvinced, even skeptical, as without another word he turned and headed for the stairs.

"Dev?"

She'd upended one of Molly's boxes, and there were shoes all over the bedroom floor. The pair on her feet were black, with pink polka dots and fussy little bows and very high heels. "Molly said it was okay," she told him as he scanned the wreckage.

He stepped into the room, leaving the door open. "I know, honey," he said. Sat down in a rocking chair so old that Angus's second wife, Georgia, had nursed her babies, Rafe, Kade and Jeb, there. He'd been rocked in that chair himself as an infant, and so had generations of other McKettricks, from way back until now.

Devon stood absolutely still, her small shoulders straight, braced, because she knew he was about to lay some unbearable burden on them. "I have to go to Paris, don't I?" she asked.

"No," Keegan said.

"Then what?"

"Sit down, Dev."

She hesitated, then plopped down on the edge of the neatly made bed. Folded her hands in her lap.

"Your mom and I have been—negotiating the past couple of days. She's agreed to let you live here, with me, for good."

Devon's eyes lit up, then dimmed with sudden uncertainty. "That's great—isn't it? Maybe with Molly and Lucas here, it will be too crowded—"

"Dev," Keegan interrupted, "if this house was onetenth the size it is, there would still be room for you. It's not that."

"What, then?"

Keegan closed his eyes for a long moment. What if he was making a mistake? Maybe there was no need to tell Devon she wasn't his child. Shelley might be satisfied with the money, and too busy settling into her Parisian apartment with the boyfriend to stir up trouble stateside.

Maybe, hell. Shelley *lived* to stir up trouble, and she didn't give a damn who got hurt in the process. As her daughter, Devon should have been exempt, but Keegan knew she wasn't. And *Shelley* knew that the best—the only—way to get to him was to hurt Devon.

"The thing I want you to remember," Keegan began miserably, "is that I love you. And nothing is going to change that."

"You're not sick, like Psyche was, are you?"

The fear behind her words pierced Keegan's heart like a dart. "No," he said. "It's not that."

He had to say it. Get it out.

Until he did, the secret would be the emotional equivalent of live ordnance. It was a bitter irony that to protect Devon from her own mother he had to tell her something that would shake the foundations of her identity.

"I'm—I'm not your father," Keegan said. "Not biologically."

Did she understand what "biologically" meant? She wasn't even eleven years old yet.

She went white. She'd been kicking her feet back and forth, the high heels dangling from her toes, but now the motion stopped. Her voice was so small that Keegan barely heard what she said. "I'm not a McKettrick?"

"You *are* a McKettrick, Dev."

"But if you're not my dad—"

"I *am* your dad. By choice, Dev."

"Mom was with somebody else?"

Keegan swallowed a curse. He *hated* that a child as young as Devon understood the mechanics of infidelity—not to mention sex. "Yes," he said.

One of the high heels toppled to the floor with a thunk. "If you're not my dad, who is?"

"I don't know," Keegan said. He wasn't ready to tell her about Thayer Ryan, and she wasn't ready to hear it. He'd only suspected that Ryan was Devon's father—based on a gut feeling and the fact that

Thayer and Shelley had had a thing going—until he, Keegan, and Psyche had had their final conversation.

Some of Travis's papers had gotten mixed up with the copies of the documents concerning Psyche's estate and Lucas's adoption. She'd asked why he was in the process of adopting Devon, too.

And he'd told her, there on the sunporch, minutes after the backyard wedding.

In retrospect, Psyche hadn't looked all that surprised. Gazing through the window, her eyes locked on Lucas, she'd smiled a little. Wasn't fate a funny thing? she'd asked. Lucas and Devon had had the same father, and now they were going to grow up together. It was, Psyche had mused, just the way it should be.

For all that he'd suspected Thayer was Devon's father, the news had still stunned Keegan. He'd asked how Psyche knew. She'd replied that her husband had thrown it up to her once, during a fight. *You think you should have married Keegan McKettrick?* Thayer had taunted, according to Psyche. *Well, let me tell you a little secret...*

Devon was that little secret.

The joke was on Keegan—and, of course, on Psyche.

And watching Devon now, sitting on the edge of his and Molly's bed, Keegan's heart broke, right down the middle. He would not *let* her be a victim of other people's mistakes, no matter what he had to do.

"I love you, Dev," he said.

She hesitated, then crossed the room to him, crawled into his lap the way she had when she was small, the way Lucas did with Molly now, and rested her head against his chest. "It's all going to be okay, isn't it?"

Keegan rested his chin on the top of his daughter's head, and for the first time since his parents had been killed, he let tears come to his eyes. Travis had told him to spend some time in his heart, and he was doing that.

Nothing could have prepared him for the way it hurt.

"Yeah," he said hoarsely. "It's all going to be okay."

MOLLY MADE tuna sandwiches. She cut the crusts away, stacked the quarters artfully on a blue plate she found in a cupboard and waited for someone to come and eat them.

Presently Keegan came down the stairs, alone.

He paused next to the playpen to look down at Lucas, who slept, one thumb in his half-open mouth.

Molly rubbed damp palms down the legs of her jean shorts.

"My mom and dad," Keegan said, meeting her eyes, "were killed in a plane crash when I was sixteen."

She swallowed. Sensed that she shouldn't speak, or move.

"My first marriage wasn't good," he went on.

"Shelley told me she was expecting my baby, and I married her. Turned out she'd been with somebody else."

Molly's eyes filled with tears. Oh, Lord, she thought. *He'd just told Devon she was another man's child. No wonder he'd been on the ragged edge, and to have the whole thing compounded by Psyche's death—*

"Your turn," Keegan said, jolting her a little.

"My turn?"

"I don't know anything about you, Molly." He looked at Lucas again. A muscle bunched in his jaw. "Beyond the basic facts."

Molly's cheeks heated. She knew all too well what those "basic facts" were, at least in his mind. "I like chocolate ice cream with marshmallows," she said. "My secret vice."

"Not good enough," Keegan replied.

"My dad is an alcoholic," she told him. "He's in treatment—for the umpteenth time—which is why he couldn't be at our wedding."

Something moved in Keegan's eyes—sympathy, perhaps. Just so long as it wasn't pity.

Devon came down the stairs, wearing Molly's red satin flats with the crystal buckles. They'd cost the earth, but as far as Molly was concerned, the kid could wear them to the barnyard if she wanted.

"I'm starved," Devon said. Her face was streaked with tears, and her eyes were puffy, but she was smiling.

"Eat up," Molly told her, gesturing toward the plate of sandwiches waiting on the table, covered by a linen napkin.

"You actually cook?" Devon marveled, zeroing in on the food. "My mom says that's the sign of a woman with nothing better to do."

Keegan's eyes never left Molly's. "She'd know," he said. "And wash your hands first, Dev."

That was how they all sat down at the same table together for the first time, Keegan in the chair that had been Angus's. Devon took a place on the bench nearest the wall, and Molly sat with her back to the kitchen.

Molly could have sworn she heard one of the lids on the old cookstove rattle, and turned to look. When she turned back, Keegan was watching her with a faint, speculative smile on his face.

Devon gobbled down her meal, then went upstairs to change her clothes before heading for the barn to look in on Spud and clean his stall. That being, she proudly announced, her job.

When the door closed behind Devon, Molly said, "I'm sorry about your folks, Keegan."

He moved as if he might take her hand, then reached for another sandwich instead. "And I'm sorry that your dad has a drinking problem," he said.

"Me, too. He's a good guy otherwise. You'd probably like him if…" She paused, felt her cheeks go pink again.

"If what?"

"Well, if this were the kind of situation where liking my dad was pertinent."

"What kind of situation *is* this, Molly?"

"You know damn well what kind of situation it is," she said, squirming a little on the bench. Keegan could strip her naked with his eyes, and that was what he was doing right then. If he thought for one *second* she was going upstairs with him in the middle of the day, with two kids around—

"I know the sex is pretty hot," he said, well aware, damn him, of the effect he had on her. "What I keep wondering is when you're going to get bored with ranch life and jet off to Los Angeles."

Molly gaped at him. "Bored? How can I get bored? There's always something going on—you and Jesse and Rance fighting behind the barn…horses magically appearing in stalls…trail rides straight up the side of a mountain…."

He laughed. God, it was good to hear him laugh, even though he'd been baiting her a little.

Her eyes smarted.

"Are you okay?" Keegan asked.

Just perfect, Molly thought. *I'm in love with a man who loves somebody else. Oh but, hey, the sex is good.*

"Molly?"

A tear spilled over, slipped down her cheek.

Keegan wiped it away with the side of his thumb. "You're not okay," he said.

"Brilliant deduction, Sherlock," Molly said,

starting to get up. The kitchen was spotless, but she'd putter anyway.

Keegan caught hold of her wrist before she could move away, just firmly enough to make her sit down again. "What's up with all the crying?" he asked.

How could she possibly tell him the whole truth? *Because, damn it, I went and fell in love with you.* "I'm just emotional. Everything happened so fast, Keegan. We got married, then Psyche—then—"

He pulled her onto his lap and she landed facing him, astraddle his thighs. Deftly he slid his hands up under her top and beneath her bra, making her catch her breath.

"Keegan, it's broad daylight...."

He grinned, chafed her nipples to peaks. "Welcome to the Triple M, Mrs. McKettrick," he drawled.

"*Keegan.* Devon could walk in—"

"She'll be forty-five minutes cleaning up after the donkey," he said. "And Lucas is sound asleep." He uncovered one of her breasts and tongued her nipple until she moaned. "When I was listing all the places I intend to have you," he murmured, "did I mention against a wall?"

Molly hadn't *completely* lost her senses. Just mostly. "We are *not* going to do it against the kitchen wall."

"Who said anything about the kitchen?" he asked.

Then he set her on her feet, stood and led her down the corridor, past a bathroom door and around a corner, into a little out-of-the-way nook.

And sure enough, he had her against the wall.

Well, she didn't have to give him the satisfaction of making her come.

Except she did. Three times, burying her face in his shoulder so her cries of release wouldn't carry to the kitchen and wake Lucas.

When it was over, Molly nearly sagged to the floor.

Keegan grinned, righted her clothes, then his own.

Forty-five minutes later Devon came in from the barn. She was a little subdued, Molly noticed, but not visibly traumatized by the new knowledge concerning her paternity.

"You guys look happy," she said, sounding surprised.

Molly, mixing cake batter at the counter, blushed and looked away.

Keegan, reading a book at the kitchen table, with a freshly changed Lucas in the curve of his arm, balanced on his knee, caught Molly's gaze, held it effortlessly for a charged moment and grinned wickedly.

"Do we?" he asked mildly, his eyes promising another McKettrick welcome—soon.

CHAPTER 17

One month later...

MOLLY STOOD IN THE ranch house kitchen, the phone receiver pressed to one ear, squinting at the calendar.

"Hurry up, Dev," she heard Keegan call, upstairs. "The wedding starts in less than an hour!"

"Molly," Joanie said from California, "don't panic. It could be a false alarm."

"I'm *late*," she whispered, fretting over the date on the slick block of days hanging from the wall near the pantry door. "I'm *never* late!"

"You should be telling Keegan this, not me," Joanie counseled. Since returning to California after Molly and Keegan's wedding, she'd realigned the agency almost single-handedly. Molly had been amazed at her friend's business acumen, and she was content to be a mostly silent partner. It was her job to read new manuscripts, sent to the ranch in batches, and she loved weeding out the contenders from the try-again-laters.

"I can't," Molly said, casting an anxious glance toward the stairs. She and Lucas were dressed in the appropriate finery and ready to roll, and Keegan was likely to appear at any moment.

"You can sleep with the man, but you can't tell him you think you're pregnant?" Joanie asked reasonably. "What's wrong with this picture, Moll?"

"He'll think I did it on purpose."

"Didn't you?"

"Well, yes," Molly admitted, frustrated, "but not so I'd have something to hold over his head."

"May I point out that even if you *did* do this dastardly thing, he participated?"

"Participated is not the word," Molly said, smiling a little. Keegan didn't *participate* in anything. He steamrolled. He managed. And he'd met his match in Molly Shields McKettrick.

"Did it ever occur to you that Keegan might be *happy* when he finds out?" asked the sage of Los Angeles.

Just then, Keegan materialized at the top of the stairs, resplendent in a tuxedo bought and fitted especially for the occasion. His chestnut hair was a little longer than when Molly had first met him, curling at the collar, and his eyes gleamed with the lingering satisfaction of their early-morning lovemaking.

"I'll talk to you later, Dad," Molly said.

She heard Joanie laugh as she hung up.

"You look delicious," Keegan said, running his

gaze over her pink satin suit. As bridesmaids' outfits went, it wasn't too bad.

"So do you," Molly replied.

Tell him, urged the still, small voice within.

No, she answered silently. *He doesn't love me. And anyway, this isn't the time.*

Keegan turned, shouted over his shoulder. "Dev! Get a move on—we're burning daylight!"

"All *right!*" Devon yelled back.

"Ten years old," Keegan said dryly, "and she's already acting like a teenager."

Molly grinned, went to him—after just the briefest hesitation—and straightened his lapels. He smelled faintly of soap and, touching him, she couldn't help remembering the shower they'd shared. "Just you wait," she said. "You ain't seen nothin' yet."

"Well, *that's* comforting," Keegan said. He lowered his head, gave her a nibbling kiss. Under any other circumstances, things might have escalated from there— Keegan had an amazing ability to kindle instant need in Molly.

Devon clattered down the back stairs. "Well, let's *go* already," she said, "if you guys can stop kissing long enough."

Keegan rolled his eyes.

Molly laughed, shook her head. Men just didn't understand these things. Devon was rebelling a little because she felt utterly safe in Keegan's love; she knew he wasn't going anywhere and, thanks to the settlement with Shelley, now happily settled in a

Parisian apartment, Devon wasn't going anywhere, either.

Lucas jumped up and down in the playpen, arms upraised. "Go!" he cried jubilantly. "Go!"

Keegan chuckled and picked Lucas up, giving him a little swing in the process. The child loved nothing better than riding on Keegan's shoulders, and young as he was, he was already learning to sit a horse. Sometimes, when Keegan went across the creek to help Rance herd cattle from one pasture to another, Lucas and Devon went along, Lucas in the saddle with Keegan, Devon mounted on the little pony that had been part of Jesse's wedding gift to all of them.

Molly was still cautious around horses, but she knew, with Keegan's patient instruction, she'd get the hang of it.

Lucas chortled, bouncing in Keegan's arms.

Devon opened the back door and huffed out a long-suffering sigh. "Are we *going?*"

Keegan grinned down at Molly once more, and they left the house.

Spud and the three horses looked on from the corral as they all got into the Jaguar. Keegan had slipped out of bed before dawn to feed the animals, then come back to tease Molly awake. She'd been in the throes of a sweet, sleepy orgasm before she'd even opened her eyes.

Remembering, she blushed slightly, watching Keegan out of the corner of one eye.

He grinned, as if reading her mind, and reached over to stroke her thigh.

The little church was already swelling with guests when they arrived.

Rance, the bridegroom, stood nervously in the yard, enduring while Cheyenne fiddled with his tie. He looked handsome in his spiffy black tuxedo, and seemed to be taking Jesse's inevitable ribbing in stride.

Keegan parked the car, leaned across Molly to open the door, his shoulder brushing lightly across her breast. Fire shot through her system, and though she tried to hide her reaction, he knew. His chuckle was proof of that.

Devon, meanwhile, got out of the backseat and rushed off to find Rianna and Maeve. Members of the wedding, all three of them.

"Go!" Lucas fretted. "Go!"

Keegan pulled back just far enough to look into Molly's eyes. "Do you wish we'd had a big traditional shindig like this?" he asked.

He never failed to surprise her.

"No," she said. *But I wish you loved me.*

He shifted a little, opened the glove compartment. "I was going to give you this later," he said. "But now seems to be the moment."

Molly blinked, confused, and suddenly fiercely hopeful.

Keegan took out a black velvet jeweler's box, held it in the palm of his hand.

Her heartbeat sped up.

"Go!" Lucas bellowed.

Molly accepted the box, but couldn't bring herself to open it. Keegan had given her a broad, diamond-studded band the day they were married—so what could this be? And what had he meant by *Now seems to be the moment?*

He lifted the hinged lid when Molly made no move to do so.

A gold heart-shaped locket glittered inside.

Molly caught her breath.

"Go-o-o-o!" Lucas insisted.

"Hush," Keegan told him.

Amazingly, Lucas obeyed.

"Molly?" Keegan prompted.

"It's—it's beautiful," Molly whispered.

Keegan curved a finger under her chin, lifted her face to his. Smiled a little at her confusion, which must have been clearly visible in her eyes.

"What does it mean?" she heard herself ask.

Keegan opened the locket with a motion of his thumb. Inside were pictures—Devon and Lucas on one side, himself and Molly on the other. The second picture had been taken on their wedding day, and Keegan had a shiner and a swollen lip.

"It means I love you, Molly," he said simply.

Her eyes filled with tears. He was giving her his heart—his strong, stubborn McKettrick heart—and she was inside it, with Devon and Lucas.

"You're supposed to say, 'I love you, too, Keegan,'" he teased.

"I do," she said. "Oh, Keegan, I do—"

He kissed her.

"Go?" Lucas said tentatively.

Organ music sounded from inside the church.

Keegan took the locket out of the box, fastened the chain around Molly's neck. "We'd better go inside," he said.

Molly grasped his hand. "There's one thing I have to tell you first," she said. "I—I think I have something for you, too."

"What?" he asked, the slightest frown creasing his forehead.

"A baby," she answered.

A smile broke over his face, but before he could say anything, Jesse appeared beside the car.

"Hey," he said, grinning as he opened the back door of the Jag and began unhitching Lucas from his car-riding gear. "The wedding's about to start, and they're short one best man and a bridesmaid."

Inside the church Molly gave Lucas to Cora Tellington, Rance's former mother-in-law, to hold. Doc Swann, the local veterinarian and Cora's fiancé, sat beside her in the pew, grinning. They were holding hands, their fingers intertwined.

Jesse and Keegan took their places up front, next to Rance.

Molly hurried back to join Cheyenne, Rianna and Maeve, all wearing the same shade of pink. Beyond them, on the step, stood Emma, a vision in billowing white lace, beaming tearfully behind her veil. The handsome man at her side, ready to give the bride away, was Rance's father.

The wedding itself passed in a happy blur.

The reception was lively, with excited children running everywhere, high on a plentitude of sugar. There was cake, and pictures were taken, and whenever Keegan caught Molly's eye, she touched the exquisite gold heart at her throat and marveled.

He loved her.

Keegan McKettrick loved *her.*

"Molly?" The voice came from just behind her, and it was one she'd longed to hear.

She whirled, thinking she must surely be mistaken. It *couldn't* be—

But it was. There he stood, her dad, wearing his best suit—a little ill-fitting and smelling faintly of extended storage—and a cautious smile. He looked tanned, rested—and sober.

"Dad," Molly whispered, as though if she didn't say his name, he would disappear.

"I hope it was okay to crash the party," Luke Shields said.

Molly threw her arms around his neck, kissed him on both cheeks. Her eyes burned with happy tears, and her heart swelled until she really thought it would burst.

He chuckled. "Does this mean you're glad to see me?"

"Yes." Molly clasped his hand. "Come and meet the new men in my life," she said. Keegan, standing with Jesse and a few of Rance's friends, Lucas in one arm, watched as they approached.

"Dad," Molly said, "this is Keegan—my husband." *My husband.* "And here's Lucas."

Luke put out a hand. "Hello, Keegan," he said. "Thanks for the lift."

Thanks for the lift? Molly wondered.

Keegan nodded, and shook his father-in-law's hand readily. "Good to meet you," he replied, handing Lucas over to his grandfather.

Luke's eyes glittered with tears. "Well," he said to Lucas, his voice hoarse with emotion. "Hello, there."

"Go," Lucas said solemnly.

"He's a born hitchhiker," Keegan commented wryly.

Luke laughed.

Molly tried to remember the last time she'd heard her dad laugh that way, and she couldn't. After exchanging glances with Keegan, she tugged at Luke's coat sleeve, led him away, Lucas still snug in his arms.

Outside, they sat on a bench, the three of them.

"Are you happy, Molly?" Luke asked after a long time.

"I'm happy," Molly answered. "What about you?"

Luke watched fondly as Lucas played in the grass at their feet. "I think I'm going to make it this time," he said. He turned to Molly then, and his eyes searched hers. "I'm sorry I couldn't be there for *your* wedding, sweetheart."

"You're here now, Dad. That's what counts."

"I can't stay long," Luke told her. "Ninety meetings in ninety days, that's the rule."

Molly squeezed his hand. Rested her head against the curve of his shoulder for a moment. "How did you get here?" she asked softly.

"Keegan sent the company jet," Luke answered, grinning. "I traveled in style."

Thanks for the lift.

Luke's grin intensified, but his eyes were tender. "That's quite a man you married, Molly. He called me yesterday afternoon, asked if I'd like to come up for a visit. I told him about the AA meetings, how I had to attend them as part of my treatment, and he said he could have me here in a couple of hours, and back in L.A. in plenty of time. He didn't tell you?"

"He didn't tell me," Molly confirmed. "But I'm so glad you came."

"Me, too. Wasn't sure how you'd react, after all that's happened. I told Keegan straight out that I was scared, and he said not to worry, he could handle you."

Molly smiled. "Oh, he *did,* did he?"

Luke returned the smile. "And he can, can't he?"

"Yes," Molly admitted.

"That's good," Luke said. "Can you handle him?"

"I can," Molly said.

"I'd like to come back," Luke told her. "When I've got all ninety of those meetings under my belt."

"I'd like that, too," Molly answered.

Luke nodded as a car pulled up, in the crowded street in front of the church. Leaned in to kiss Molly's cheek.

"I've got one more question, Molly-girl. Do you love that man? I know he loves you."

"I love him," Molly confirmed softly.

"Good," Luke said. He looked toward the waiting

car. Turned back to Molly. "Love you this much," he said, spreading his arms, the way he had when she was a little girl.

"Love you back," Molly replied, on cue.

Luke stood, admired his grandson for a few moments, then bent to ruffle the boy's gleaming hair. He raised a hand to Molly, walked away toward the car.

The driver got out, opened the back door for him.

She watched mutely as the car pulled away.

Keegan rounded the bench from behind, sat down beside Molly.

"Thanks," she said.

He put an arm around her shoulders. "Given what little I knew of Luke's history, I wasn't sure I was doing you a favor, bringing him here."

"I love you, Keegan McKettrick," Molly said, because she could. She could say it, right out loud, any time she wanted.

He kissed her temple. "When did you know?" he asked. "How you felt about me, I mean?"

"The day you told me I wouldn't have to marry you—that Psyche was going to let me raise Lucas either way." She paused. "When did *you* know, Keegan?"

Keegan grinned. "When you tried to break up the fight behind the barn."

"Can we go home now?"

He kissed her. "An excellent idea, Mrs. McKettrick," he murmured. "Devon's spending the night at Cora's, with Maeve and Rianna."

Molly looked down at her son. *Their* son. Lucas McKettrick.

Thank you, Psyche, she thought.

"It scares me a little," she confessed quietly, "being this happy."

"Get used to it," Keegan said, gripping her hand, raising it to run his lips lightly across her knuckles.

They watched as Emma and Rance came out of the community hall, next to the church, beaming with happiness. Emma was poised to fling her bouquet into the crowd of delighted spectators gathered at the bottom of the steps.

"Want to try and catch it?" Keegan asked.

"Nope," Molly answered. "I've got my McKettrick man. No need to dive for any bridal bouquets."

They watched as the bouquet soared and landed in Meg McKettrick's hands.

Jesse and Cheyenne emerged behind Emma and Rance.

Keegan's gaze followed Molly's, warmed. "Jesse's known for his luck," he said. "Seeing those two together, it's easy to understand why."

Touched, Molly looked on as Rance and his glowing bride passed beneath a shower of birdseed and goodwill. "What's Rance known for?" she asked.

"His pride," Keegan said. "It almost ruined things for him and Emma, but he came to his senses in time, thank God."

Molly met her husband's gaze. Held it firmly. "And you? What are *you* known for, Keegan?"

He sighed. Toyed with the locket shimmering against her collarbone. "Living in my head," he said, "and keeping my heart closed up tight, like some old storage shed with a rusted padlock on the door. Until you came along, that is."

Molly laid her hand on his chest, fingers splayed. Felt his heartbeat, strong and steady, beneath her palm. "Open for business?" she asked softly.

"Open for business," Keegan said. "The party's breaking up, Mrs. McKettrick. Let's go home."

"Let's do," Molly said.

Leaving was a process—there were goodbyes to be said, congratulations to be offered. Lucas had to be buckled into his car seat, and there was something of a traffic jam in front of the church. Everybody in Indian Rock must have been invited to that wedding, and there were a lot of out of towners, too.

But finally, finally they drove back to the ranch house.

Molly changed Lucas's diaper in his room, then brought him down again to feed him his supper. Keegan, having put a pot of coffee on to brew first, passed her on the stairs. Returned minutes later, sans tuxedo, looking cowboy-handsome in his work clothes.

He bent as he passed Molly where she sat facing Lucas's high chair, kissed her on the mouth, Lucas on top of the head.

"I'll be back as soon as I get Spud and the horses in from the corral and settled for the night," he said.

Molly nodded, unable to speak because of the knot of emotion in her throat.

Keegan went out.

She finished feeding Lucas, washed his face and

hands and carried him upstairs again. He was already drifting off as she maneuvered him into his pajamas, gave him the stuffed donkey Devon had bought him as a present a few days before, after she and Keegan had driven to Flagstaff to get her things, and then tucked his blanket around him.

Molly stood over her boy, marveling, long after he'd gone to sleep.

When she heard the kitchen door close in the near distance, she shook off the spell she'd fallen under and went into Keegan's and her bedroom. Began undressing. She'd laid out jeans and a tank top, intending to go back downstairs and throw together something for supper, but then she looked up and saw Keegan framed in the doorway, watching her.

Molly stood naked, except for Keegan's locket, unable to move.

His gaze raked her bare flesh, raising goose bumps wherever it paused.

Sunset blazed at the window, and Molly knew she was framed in light. A strange sense of mystical beauty surrounded her heart and melted the last walls that held it prisoner.

Keegan moved slowly into the room, closed the door quietly behind him. Approached her and laid his hands on her breasts.

Molly caught her breath as he caressed her, unhurried, touching her almost reverently. She waited, trembling a little.

He bent his head, kissed the length of her shoulder. At the same time he slipped one of his hands boldly between her legs, parted her, played with her.

She bit down hard on her lower lip, stifling a whimper of need.

Keegan straightened, looked into her eyes, grinned slightly. He knew her so well—knew when she needed a tender taking, and when she needed something else.

He lowered her onto the bed, sideways. Knelt and draped her legs over his shoulders. Burrowed through the nest of moist curls at the apex of her thighs and took her into his mouth.

She convulsed once, clutching the bedcovers, determined not to make a sound.

Keegan chuckled against her, suckled again. Idly.

Molly moaned. So much for not making a sound.

He withdrew. Teased her mercilessly with his tongue.

"Keegan," she pleaded, unable to keep his name inside her.

He slid his hands under her, raised her high off the bed and ravished her until the first orgasm seized her. As that one receded, another began to build, and then another.

When it was over, when he'd wrung the last ounce of tension from Molly's willing body, she watched, the aftershocks still echoing through her, as he stood and slowly removed his clothes.

Gathering her strength, she stretched languidly, moved to lie full length in the middle of the bed, feeling sated and sultry.

Keegan stretched out beside her, and she knew by the look smoldering in his blue eyes that he planned to let her rest for a few minutes, then take—no, possess—her. Molly craved that completion, but it just so happened that she had a few plans of her own.

She kissed him, feeling a rush of anticipation as he rolled from his side onto his back. She deepened the kiss, stroked him with her hand until his groan echoed in her mouth.

Smiling inside, Molly lifted her head. She reached for Keegan's hand, raised it slowly, fitted his fingers around one of the rails in the headboard.

His eyes widened.

Molly kissed him again.

And then she moved his other hand upward.

He could have resisted, of course—he was so much stronger than she was. Could certainly have lowered his hands. But he didn't. His fingers tightened around the rails.

Molly nuzzled his neck with her nose, nibbled at his earlobe.

"Hang on tight, cowboy," she crooned. "Wild ride ahead."

Powerful as he was, physically and in every other way, Keegan trembled. Groaned as Molly kissed her way down over his shoulder, the center of his chest, his belly.

He rasped her name.

She took him.

He tensed, sucked in a hard breath.

In the slow, lingering minutes that followed, Molly paid Keegan back for every time he'd teased her, every time he'd brought her to the brink of ecstasy and then made her wait.

And when the low, lusty cry of release finally came, it was Keegan's.

SHE LAY ASLEEP, the little vixen, a smile still curving her lips.

Watching her, Keegan marveled at all he felt.

Her hair spread across the pillows, gleaming even in the thin light of the summer moon. He laid a hand on her lower belly, lightly, not wanting to awaken her.

Not yet, anyway.

She stirred a little, sighed softly in her sleep. The heart locket caught a flash of moonlight, and Keegan's own heart caught that glimmer, and opened itself wide.

Molly had broken in, gotten past all the barriers he'd erected so carefully over the years. Opened his heart and made herself at home inside.

At first it had been a painful invasion. He'd wanted to drive her out.

He'd been raw in so many ways. Losing his folks. His first marriage, and the constant ache of being separated from Devon so much of the time. The transition from stuffed shirt to rancher.

And then there was Psyche.

All these years he'd believed he'd loved Psyche. He'd truly believed it, and he'd grieved the loss of her long before she died.

Now he realized he hadn't known what love was

until Molly had nudged him with the toe of one shoe, out there behind the barn when he and Jesse and Rance had tangled that day.

You're going to look terrible in the wedding pictures.

He grinned at the memory.

Across the hall, Lucas let out an uncertain wail.

Keegan got off the bed, pulled on his jeans, fastened them and crept out.

The boy stood in his crib, gripping the rails and sniffling.

"Hey, buddy," Keegan said, lifting Lucas into his arms. He was soaked, so Keegan grabbed up a fresh diaper as he carried him over to the changing table. "Did you have a bad dream?"

Lucas hiccuped while Keegan swapped the wet diaper for a dry one. After using a baby wipe to wash his hands, Keegan carried Lucas back into the bedroom where Molly slept.

He sat down in the old rocking chair, holding the boy, now bundled in his favorite blanket, and thought about the results of the DNA tests. Biologically, Devon was a half sister to Lucas—he and Molly had agreed to keep that knowledge to themselves, at least until both children were old enough to understand.

"Everything's going to be okay, buckaroo," he told the baby.

Lucas shivered, then settled against his chest. Stuck a thumb and half his little fist into his mouth.

Keegan rocked, thinking of all the McKettricks

that had gone before, and all that would come after. He was content with his place in that long line of lucky, proud, hard-loving men and women.

Molly stirred. Sat up partway in the tangle of covers on their bed. "Keegan?"

"Go back to sleep," he said gently.

She sighed and sank into the pillows, spent.

Keegan smiled. The house was utterly quiet, as though it, too, had been waiting, and could now let out its breath, knowing he meant to *live* within its sturdy old walls, not merely exist. He and Molly would fill the place with kids, and they had a good start on it already.

The rockers of that old chair moved silently on the well-trodden floor.

And downstairs, in the empty kitchen, a stove lid rattled.

* * * * *

*Look for Linda Lael Miller's
next original novel, BIG SKY COUNTRY,
on sale from Harlequin HQN Books
in June at your favorite retail outlet.*

Look for

Linda Lael Miller's

next original novel

BIG SKY COUNTRY

on sale from HQN Books in June at your favorite retail outlet.

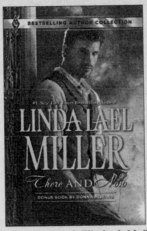

A woman's heart is dangerous territory.

A sweeping and sensual new romance from
***New York Times* bestselling author**

DIANA PALMER

The life of a paid mercenary makes sense to Special Forces officer
Grange. The jungles of South America may make his former job as a
ranch manager for his friend Jay Pendleton look like a cakewalk, but it's
nothing the former Green Beret can't handle. However, the new woman
in his life is a distraction he can't avoid. Once she breaks through his
armor, traversing the wilds of the Amazon will prove an easier task
than defending himself against her winning charms....

COURAGEOUS

Coming in July 2012!

REQUEST YOUR FREE BOOKS!

2 FREE NOVELS
FROM THE ROMANCE COLLECTION
PLUS 2 FREE GIFTS!

YES! Please send me 2 FREE novels from the Romance Collection and my 2 FREE gifts (gifts are worth about $10). After receiving them, if I don't wish to receive any more books, I can return the shipping statement marked "cancel." If I don't cancel, I will receive 4 brand-new novels every month and be billed just $5.99 per book in the U.S. or $6.49 per book in Canada. That's a saving of at least 25% off the cover price. It's quite a bargain! Shipping and handling is just 50¢ per book in the U.S. and 75¢ per book in Canada.* I understand that accepting the 2 free books and gifts places me under no obligation to buy anything. I can always return a shipment and cancel at any time. Even if I never buy another book, the two free books and gifts are mine to keep forever.

194/394 MDN FELQ

Name	(PLEASE PRINT)

Address	Apt. #

City	State/Prov.	Zip/Postal Code

Signature (if under 18, a parent or guardian must sign)

Mail to the **Reader Service:**
IN U.S.A.: P.O. Box 1867, Buffalo, NY 14240-1867
IN CANADA: P.O. Box 609, Fort Erie, Ontario L2A 5X3

Not valid for current subscribers to the Romance Collection
or the Romance/Suspense Collection.

Want to try two free books from another line?
Call 1-800-873-8635 or visit www.ReaderService.com.

* Terms and prices subject to change without notice. Prices do not include applicable taxes. Sales tax applicable in N.Y. Canadian residents will be charged applicable taxes. Offer not valid in Quebec. This offer is limited to one order per household. All orders subject to credit approval. Credit or debit balances in a customer's account(s) may be offset by any other outstanding balance owed by or to the customer. Please allow 4 to 6 weeks for delivery. Offer available while quantities last.

Your Privacy—The Reader Service is committed to protecting your privacy. Our Privacy Policy is available online at www.ReaderService.com or upon request from the Reader Service.

We make a portion of our mailing list available to reputable third parties that offer products we believe may interest you. If you prefer that we not exchange your name with third parties, or if you wish to clarify or modify your communication preferences, please visit us at www.ReaderService.com/consumerschoice or write to us at Reader Service Preference Service, P.O. Box 9062, Buffalo, NY 14269. Include your complete name and address.

LINDA LAEL MILLER

77677	McKETTRICK'S PRIDE	___ $7.99 U.S.	___ $9.99 CAN.
77642	McKETTRICK'S LUCK	___ $7.99 U.S.	___ $9.99 CAN.
77623	THE McKETTRICK LEGEND	___ $7.99 U.S.	___ $9.99 CAN.
77606	HOLIDAY IN STONE CREEK	___ $7.99 U.S.	___ $9.99 CAN.
77600	THE CREED LEGACY	___ $7.99 U.S.	___ $9.99 CAN.
77580	CREED'S HONOR	___ $7.99 U.S.	___ $9.99 CAN.
77561	MONTANA CREEDS: LOGAN	___ $7.99 U.S.	___ $9.99 CAN.
77555	A CREED IN STONE CREEK	___ $7.99 U.S.	___ $9.99 CAN.
77502	THE CHRISTMAS BRIDES	___ $7.99 U.S.	___ $9.99 CAN.
77492	McKETTRICK'S CHOICE	___ $7.99 U.S.	___ $9.99 CAN.
77446	McKETTRICKS OF TEXAS: AUSTIN	___ $7.99 U.S.	___ $9.99 CAN.
77441	McKETTRICKS OF TEXAS: GARRETT	___ $7.99 U.S.	___ $9.99 CAN.
77436	McKETTRICKS OF TEXAS: TATE	___ $7.99 U.S.	___ $9.99 CAN.
77388	THE BRIDEGROOM	___ $7.99 U.S.	___ $8.99 CAN.
77364	MONTANA CREEDS: TYLER	___ $7.99 U.S.	___ $7.99 CAN.
77358	MONTANA CREEDS: DYLAN	___ $7.99 U.S.	___ $7.99 CAN.
77330	THE RUSTLER	___ $7.99 U.S.	___ $7.99 CAN.
77296	A WANTED MAN	___ $7.99 U.S.	___ $7.99 CAN.
77200	DEADLY GAMBLE	___ $7.99 U.S.	___ $9.50 CAN.
77198	THE MAN FROM STONE CREEK	___ $7.99 U.S.	___ $9.50 CAN.

(limited quantities available)

TOTAL AMOUNT	$ _____
POSTAGE & HANDLING	$ _____
($1.00 FOR 1 BOOK, 50¢ for each additional)	
APPLICABLE TAXES*	$ _____
TOTAL PAYABLE	$ _____

(check or money order—please do not send cash)

To order, complete this form and send it, along with a check or money order for the total above, payable to HQN Books, to: **In the U.S.:** 3010 Walden Avenue, P.O. Box 9077, Buffalo, NY 14269-9077; **In Canada:** P.O. Box 636, Fort Erie, Ontario, L2A 5X3.

Name: _____
Address: _____ City: _____
State/Prov.: _____ Zip/Postal Code: _____
Account Number (if applicable): _____
075 CSAS

*New York residents remit applicable sales taxes.
*Canadian residents remit applicable GST and provincial taxes.

H HARLEQUIN®

www.Harlequin.com

ROMILI

PHLLM0512BL